Praise for the Yarn Retreat Mysteries

"If you haven't read this series yet, I highly recommend giving it a go. The mystery will delight you, and afterward you'll be itching to start a knitting or crochet project of your own."

—*Cozy Mystery Book Reviews*

"A cozy mystery that you won't want to put down. It combines cooking, knitting and murder in one great book!"

—*Fresh Fiction*

"The California seaside is the backdrop to this captivating cozy that will have readers heading for the yarn store in droves."

—Debbie's Book Bag

Praise for Betty Hechtman's National Bestselling Crochet Mysteries

"Will warm the reader like a favorite afghan."

—National bestselling author Earlene Fowler

"Get hooked on this new author . . . Who can resist a sleuth named Pink, a slew of interesting minor characters and a fun fringe-of-Hollywood setting?"

—*Crochet Today!*

"Fans . . . will enjoy unraveling the knots leading to the killer."

—*Publishers Weekly*

"Classic cozy fare . . . Crocheting pattern and recipe are just icing on the cake."

—Cozy Library

Books by Betty Hechtman

Yarn Retreat Mysteries

Yarn to Go
Silence of the Lamb's Wool
Wound up in Murder
Gone with the Wool
A Tangled Yarn
Inherit the Wool

Crochet Mysteries

Hooked on Murder
Dead Men Don't Crochet
By Hook or by Crook
A Stitch in Crime
You Better Knot Die
Behind the Seams
If Hooks Could Kill
For Better or Worsted
Knot Guilty
Seams like Murder
Hooking for Trouble
On the Hook

Inherit the Wool

BETTY HECHTMAN

BEYOND THE PAGE
PUBLISHING

Inherit the Wool
Betty Hechtman
Copyright © 2018 by Betty Hechtman

Beyond the Page Books
are published by
Beyond the Page Publishing
www.beyondthepagepub.com

ISBN: 978-1-946069-85-6

Chapter One

I looked out the window at the sunless morning with a knot in my stomach, hoping this call would help. The ringing stopped and a familiar voice answered. After barely a greeting Frank Shaw got right to the meat of the matter.

"Oh, no, Feldstein, what is it this time? Don't tell me there is another dead body," Frank said. Before I could get a word in, he continued. "I'm telling you those people in the town that sounds like a candy bar are going to start putting two and two together and notice there have been an awful lot of deaths since you came to town."

"No one is dead, at least no one that I know about," I said, finally getting a chance to speak. Frank was my ex-boss from my time doing temp work. He was a PI, and working for him was my favorite job, though it only lasted a few weeks. Since moving to Cadbury by the Sea, California, I'd gotten involved in some murder investigations and Frank had been my go-to guy for advice.

"If it's not a murder, then what is it?" he asked with a touch of impatience. "I'm a busy man." I could hear the squeak of his reclining office chair, which he tended to push to its limits, and it in turn complained. I could also hear the rustle of paper, which was no doubt wrapped around a submarine sandwich, as it was lunchtime in Chicago. Frank was closer to being the Pillsbury Doughboy than he was to James Bond, and I imagined him anxious to dig into his food.

"It's about the retreat I'm putting on this weekend," I began. "It has to be perfect and I'm worried."

"I can see your point. You've had a few snafus. More people checking into that hotel and conference center than checking out after your retreat. The way you describe that place it sounds a little sinister with all the fog and ocean crashing against the shore."

"Vista Del Mar is rustic and atmospheric, not sinister. And as for what happened to some of the guests—and about not everybody leaving who came—it wasn't my fault, and at least I did find out what happened. But that's not going to happen this time. It can't. This time I know everybody coming to the retreat. They're friends from college." I explained that we had all recently reconnected on Facebook and then someone suggested we should all get together, and someone else had seen my website advertising my yarn retreats and suggested I put on a retreat just for our group. It had all come together before I had a chance to think it through or come up with a reason not to do it.

"I get it, Feldstein," Frank said, interrupting. "What is it, a sorority?"

"Me in a sorority?" I said with a laugh. "Actually, we were sort of a team," I said. I could tell by the noise that Frank had sat upright.

"You mean like a team for a sport?" Frank said, sounding surprised. "I never thought of you as the sports sort."

"It was in a gym class," I said. "A requirement and we all hated it." I started to fumble when I got to explaining what kind of team. "It was a rhythm-ball routine team."

"Rhythm-ball routine? What's that?" There were more sounds of rustling papers and I was pretty sure Frank was working on the sandwich.

"Sort of like dancing while tossing a ball around," I said, remembering the fiasco. "And then we had to perform it for the rest of our class, only made worse by the fact that we shared the gym with a boys' class. If we'd been going for comedy, we'd have gotten an A."

"And those boys were doing the same thing?" Frank asked.

"We're getting off the subject, but no, they did weight lifting. The school was doing a remodel of their gym so we had to share ours." I could hear Frank chortling and I wanted to change the subject. "The point is they are all settled in their lives, and I'm sure they're going to be all judgy of me."

"Wow, Feldstein, I always thought of you as being someone who didn't care what people thought."

"Well, I don't most of the time. But this time I do."

"I'm surprised you called me about this. Isn't this the kind of thing you talk over with your girlfriends?"

"I would, but one of them owns the restaurant I make desserts for. She's kind of my boss and I don't want it to sound like I'm upset with my life. She could take it wrong. And the other one is one of my retreat helpers."

"And you don't want to blow your image. I get it." Frank cleared his throat. "Thanks to being a PI for a long time I've become a student of human nature. You think those friends of yours from college have such perfect lives. I doubt it. I bet they have dark secrets and messed-up pasts that you know nothing about. What's the big problem with your life anyway?"

"I'm in my mid-thirties. I'm not married. If I hadn't inherited my aunt's house along with her yarn retreat business, I wouldn't be able to get by. Even so, it only works by cobbling together the income from making desserts for the Blue Door and baking muffins for the coffee spots in town, along with the yarn retreats." I stopped myself. "Oh, no, I sound so whiny."

"My thoughts exactly, Feldstein. Get yourself together. I'm telling you, you'll find out that bunch isn't so perfect after all. Now, some of us have to get back to work. I have to go to the Drake for high tea and see who shows up with who." He seemed about to hang up when he said, "Did your group have a name?"

"Sort of. We called ourselves the Baller-rinas," I said quickly. I heard him let out a real laugh.

"If you and the girls decide to recreate that thing with the balls, send photos, or better yet, a video. I got to see that."

I held in a chuckle at the idea of him doing a surveillance at the posh hotel's very formal high tea. Frank was pretty rough around the edges and I couldn't quite see him nibbling on finger sandwiches and sipping tea. "Casey Feldstein signing off," I said, giving a mock salute before clicking off the cordless

The call had made me feel only slightly better. Frank was probably right. My former teammates only seemed to be living perfect lives. Still, I regretted agreeing to put on the retreat reunion, as we were calling it. If only I hadn't been so all over the place, I might be more settled now. I went over my past in my mind. I'd discovered after a semester of law school that it wasn't for me. I'd tried teaching and had worked as a permanent substitute at a private elementary school. But after a couple of years I was ready to move on. I'd been the dessert chef at a small bistro that unfortunately went out of business, though it had definitely helped me hone my skills at making sweets. The temp jobs had at least offered variety. I'd spritzed perfume on shoppers in a department store, handed out samples of chewing gum on downtown Chicago street corners. There had been stints at offices, but the only one I'd really liked was the time I spent working for Frank. It had only lasted a short time due to his lack of finances, but he'd said I had a real knack for getting information from people.

I had ended up in Cadbury by the Sea thanks to my aunt. I was faced with moving back in with my parents, both doctors, when she'd made the offer of her guest house. The idea of a fresh start in a town where nobody knew me was impossible to pass up. She'd also been the one to help me line up the baking jobs. Sadly, she'd died—well, had been killed—shortly after I moved in. The only consolation I had was that I had found the murderer and brought them to justice.

I'd always had a special relationship with Aunt Joan since we were both black sheep in the family. I suppose that was why she left her house and Yarn2Go to me. She'd been a master of yarn craft and I was a complete novice, but since I was pretty good at being a jack-of-all-trades, I didn't let that stop me.

Actually, putting on the retreats had turned out to be the perfect sort of career for me. I was not the kind of person who could do the same thing day after day, week after week. Each retreat was different and had a beginning with the planning, a middle when it actually went on, and an end when everybody left. The projects were different and the people different. I liked that it was always a new challenge. Even my dessert making and muffin baking were not routine. I had some standbys, but I was also always trying something new.

Even so, I wondered how long I would really stay in Cadbury.

I looked around the living room of the house that was now mine. At first, I'd left things as my aunt'd had them, but now that I'd begun to feel like it was really my place, I'd decided to redo everything, starting with the living room. It was in total disarray. The furniture was pulled into the middle of the room and the walls were half painted. I'd decided on a soft moss green with white trim. I was just considering whether to tackle finishing the wall, when I heard a knock at my kitchen door.

The sound woke Julius, who was napping on the couch in the center of the room. He stood, stretched and jumped down, running ahead of me to see who it was. The black cat had chosen me to be his human. I hadn't realized that was the way it worked, but then I'd never had a pet and knew nothing about cats. I foolishly thought I'd been the one to do the choosing when he'd shown up at my door and I'd let him in. I knew he had a past but not what it was, other than he must have belonged to somebody, and I was pretty sure they'd abandoned him. That was never going to happen to him again. He'd wormed his way into my heart, and wherever I went, he'd be coming, too.

I saw Crystal Smith through the glass at the top half of the door. There was no mistaking her. I could see the purple and orange shirt showing through her open jacket. Her short black hair naturally fell into corkscrew curls that reminded me of tiny Slinkys. She went heavy on the makeup, particularly around her eyes, but she could carry it off. I'd tried to emulate it and ended up looking like a tired raccoon. Before I'd even opened the door, I knew that her earrings wouldn't match, nor her socks. Both deliberate, I might add. She was the queen of mix instead of match.

"Hi," she said as I opened the door for her. She was pulling a plastic tote full of yarn and supplies. With the slightly wild look, it was hard to believe she was the mother of two teenage kids. She was a single parent now that her rock god ex, in a totally clichéd move, had replaced her with someone younger. I still couldn't get over the pretentiousness of his name, Rixx Smith.

Crystal and the kids were living with her mother, who owned the local yarn shop. Crystal had learned all the different yarn crafts when she was a kid and they seemed like second nature to her now. I'd hired her to do the workshops for the retreats and in the process she'd become a friend.

"I brought all the yarn and needles. Where do you want to stuff the tote bags?" she asked, indicating the bin.

"The usual spot," I said as I joined her outside. I led the way across to the converted garage that my aunt had turned into a guest house. The flat white sky and chill in the air gave no hint to the time of year. The weather in Cadbury was almost always the same, mostly cloudy skies with a temperature that required a light jacket. I had to remind myself that it was a Thursday in March. I flipped on the lights as we went inside and automatically looked around at what was basically one large room with a high counter that set off a small kitchen area. It had become retreat central for me. I kept all the supplies in there and used the open space to make up the tote bags I gave out to my retreaters. I had left six of the blood-red bags with Yarn2Go emblazoned on them out on the counter. I heard Crystal let out a sigh when she let go of the bin and flopped in a chair.

I knew what the sigh was about. It was the other reason she was here. I was grateful that Frank seemed to have forgotten about the hornet's nest I'd stirred up in the small town. Though, it was still largely a secret hornet's nest. The Delacorte sisters were the local royalty, rich, with tons of property all over town, including Vista Del Mar, the hotel and conference center where I put on the retreats. It seemed they were the end of the family line as neither had married or had any children, and their brother and his wife and child had died years before. There were rumors that their brother, Edmund, might've had a love child, but it had never gone beyond whispers. So even though the will he'd left stipulated that Vista Del Mar was to go to his children, the two sisters had gotten ownership of it.

I'd discovered that Crystal's mother, Gwen Selwyn, was the love child of the deceased Delacorte brother. It was hard to tell the story and keep it all straight. I'd held on to the information for a while, not sure of what to do with it. Frank, by the way, had told me to mind my own business and keep out of it. But you can't unknow something once you know it and I'd finally told Gwen Selwyn her true identity. The news wasn't welcome to her and she'd chosen to ignore it. She didn't like the Delacortes and it totally demolished who she thought her father was. She didn't want the change it might bring to her life, either. She owned Cadbury Yarn, and though it was a struggle now that Crystal and her two kids were living with her, Gwen was okay with things the way they were. But then she began to weaken because she thought of Crystal's kids and felt they should get their due. It was only recently that she had finally told Crystal the whole story. I'd been present when she did it.

With some reluctance they'd contacted a lawyer and looked into their options. That was when they hit the brick wall.

Crystal rocked her head back and forth. "I wish this had never started," she said, looking at me. "It was better when I didn't know. You can't regret not getting something you don't know is supposed to be yours."

I knew she was referring to Vista Del Mar. "What was it the lawyer said?" I asked.

"He said we had waited too long to come forward and the

Delacorte sisters would surely fight it. He seemed to think we might win in the end, but it would be a long and costly battle. They have deep pockets. We don't. End of story." She sighed again. "The only good thing is that we never told my kids and nobody in town knows."

"Have you ever considered talking directly to Cora and Madeleine. They might be more agreeable than you think."

Crystal looked at me and rolled her eyes. "Really? Their illegitimate niece and her family show up and want a cut of the family fortune. My mother would never do it anyway."

"Well, when you put it that way, I can see your point." I took the opportunity to change the subject. This wasn't the first time we'd gone over the hopelessness of the situation, and every time we did, I felt worse about being the hornet nest's stirrer. I pointed to the bin of yarn. "I think your idea for the retreat is perfect."

In the past I'd had two helpers, but since this retreat was so much smaller, I only needed one. I thought Crystal would mix well with the group and so had given her the job, plus I felt guilty about the mess I'd made. Since I was pretty sure none of the group knitted, Crystal had suggested teaching them how to knit and then designed an easy quick pattern for a scarf they'd be able to complete over the long weekend.

She thanked me for the compliment and looked at the six bags on the counter. "I thought you just had five people coming."

"It's six now. This last person is all very mysterious. The registration came in the mail with no return address. No name of the person was given and the payment came on a bank card."

"That does sound mysterious. I hope it doesn't mean trouble," Crystal said.

"Ditto on that." She showed me the three skeins of yarn each person would be getting and the large-size knitting needles. She had some pages stapled together with basic knitting instructions and the pattern for the scarf. After trying to fill one bag, I realized it wasn't going to work. "I should have realized they would be way too bulky for me to hand out when they arrive."

Crystal shrugged and emptied everything back into the bin. "Why not just give everything out at the first workshop." We settled for just putting in the packet of her sheets along with the ones I always added that had a schedule, map of the property and some information about the birds and the beasts in the area. I had emailed the schedule and some information about Vista Del Mar to the group but had no idea if they'd paid any attention.

As she got ready to leave, she gave me a hug. "I'm sorry for being difficult. I'm sure you thought you were doing a good thing when you told my mother who she is. I just keep thinking of Cory and how much he loves Vista Del Mar." Cory was her son, who had already worked part-time at Vista Del Mar and seemed to have inherited an affinity to the place from his great-grandfather.

"Maybe something will happen and it will all work out," I said.

Crystal rolled her eyes again. "When pigs fly." She knew that was one of my favorite sayings about impossible situations and we both laughed.

With Crystal gone, I went back into the main house. *Main house* sounded so grand, but it was really more like a cottage with two bedrooms and one bath. I had given up on the idea of doing any work on the living room with the retreat due to start in a few hours. It was just a diversion anyway, so I wouldn't have to think about facing my college group again.

I heard someone at the kitchen door again. When I walked into the room, there appeared to be no one at the door until I opened it and a man popped out of the bushes.

"Casey, all this sneaking around is exciting, but do we really have to drive all the way to Santa Cruz just to see a movie when there is a perfectly good theater with three screens in downtown Cadbury?" he said, slipping inside. Dane Mangano was in his police uniform, and all the equipment on his belt banged into me as he reached to hug me and then moved on to a kiss.

Dane and I were almost in a relationship. He was all for moving ahead on our obvious attraction to each other. I was the one holding back. I told myself that it was because I didn't want to start something in case I decided to repeat my history and ended up moving on. But bottom line, his directness scared me. I'd finally agreed to go out with him on the condition that nobody in town knew about it. We had gone out once in public view and we'd been the immediate subject of teasing speculation. Dane didn't seem to mind. I couldn't handle it.

"If anybody asks, I'm here because you thought there was a prowler," he said, pulling me closer to him. He had a good-natured grin on his face and I knew this was all fun to him.

"All your stuff is poking me," I said, matching his grin, looking around as if someone was going to see us.

"Really? You think somebody is going to pop out of the bushes." The grin had turned into a laugh and then he looked at me. "We could pick this up later," he said, reluctantly letting me go. "I could shut all the curtains at my place." I knew he was teasing, maybe with a little hope attached. I'd avoided being alone with him at his place. Not that he wouldn't be a gentleman. It was more me that I was worried about. To put it mildly, Dane was hot. All his jogging and karate had left him toned and overflowing with a good-spirited sort of energy. It seemed that around me anyway, his eyes were usually dancing with a smile.

"I know, one step at a time. At least can I hold your hand at the movies?" he joked.

I reminded him about my retreat and that I probably wouldn't see much of him over the weekend. "It's supposed to be a reunion retreat, so I'm going to have to be there most of the time."

"It is just a bunch of girls, right?" he said.

"Bunch of women," I corrected. "And yes, just women this time." *As far as I knew anyway.*

"This is supposed to be my lunch break." He glanced around the kitchen for signs of food. He of all people knew that while I was adept at making desserts and muffins, when it came to cooking regular food I was pretty much a washout. It was all frozen entrees, envelopes of instant oatmeal and peanut butter sandwiches. My big step had been that I'd started making brewed coffee. I couldn't take the instant stuff anymore. I offered to put on a pot and bring out the peanut butter.

"That's okay," he said, going to my refrigerator. "I'll make my own lunch." Dane was very self-sufficient. It had come from growing up fatherless with an alcoholic mother and a younger sister he had to look after. While acting like a badass at school, he'd come home and taken care of everything. Before I could offer to help, he was making scrambled eggs. I did manage the coffee.

We were sitting down at my kitchen table when the door opened. On instinct Dane jumped up, but then he relaxed when he saw the tall hulking figure was Sammy—also known as Dr. Sammy Glickner, urologist, and the Amazing Dr. Sammy, the magician. He was also my ex-boyfriend who insisted that he hadn't followed me from Chicago and that he was only staying in Cadbury because he had a chance to be a doctor by day and a magician by night.

Sammy's eyes went over the whole scene and I knew he was trying to figure out what the situation was. His face fell when he saw the eggs on the table. "You're having breakfast together?" he said.

"It's kind of late for breakfast," I said. "Dane thought he saw a prowler outside and he came in to check."

"And cook eggs?" Sammy said.

I made some excuse about my cooking ability and said Dane was trying to rescue the food. Julius had come into the kitchen and was sitting down watching it all while eyeing the refrigerator, probably hoping someone would give him some stink fish.

No matter what Sammy said, I knew he had hopes we'd somehow get back together, and I hated to make him feel bad, so I tried to get his mind off seeing Dane there by asking him what was up.

"I wanted to drop this off," Sammy said, handing me a box. I opened it and took out a romper that was covered with shiny spangles. "It's for the show on Sunday. We really should practice since it's a new illusion."

It took a moment to compute what he was talking about. I'd gotten so caught up in the arrangements for the retreat that I'd forgotten all about Sammy's gig at one of the posh Pebble Beach resorts. Along with all my other professions, I'd become a magician's assistant. It was all because I'd stepped in at the last minute for Sammy when his assistant baled. The illusion had inadvertently turned into more of a comedy routine. Instead of it being a disaster, the audience loved it and thought it was planned. Two things happened afterward—Sammy realized how to make his act unique and he begged me to stay on because we played off each other so well.

"But I have a retreat this weekend," I said.

"Case, I can't do it without you," he said, using his nickname for me. As if Casey wasn't short enough, and all he did was take off the last syllable. His expression had crumpled and he had that puppy-dog look in his dark eyes that always got to me. Dane seemed about to say something, when his radio crackled and I heard something about a problem with some kids theater-hopping at the local movie house. He got up to leave and seemed at a loss for how to say goodbye. He finally settled on a squeeze of my shoulder and muttering that he'd see me later.

Sammy seemed relieved when he was gone. "If you can't do it, I'll have to cancel," he said with some panic in his voice. I suggested he get a replacement and his eyes grew more soulful. "No one can replace you."

It was both a compliment and a burden. I couldn't let him down. "I'll figure out a way to do it, but I don't have any time to practice it before the show." The big finale of his performance was making me levitate. I knew the basics and I hoped that would be enough. He'd been hired for an anniversary party and the gig was another shot at a step up from the small-time stuff he'd been doing. He hoped it would open the door for bigger things to follow.

Sammy's face brightened and he gave me a hug before turning to go. "Case, you're the only one who gets me."

I glanced at the spangled romper and shook my head. Me in that was going to make comedy easy.

Chapter Two

It was my habit to do a last-minute check on the accommodations for my retreaters before they arrived. It wasn't really necessary for this retreat because it was so small, but I went across to Vista Del Mar anyway.

My house was on the edge of Cadbury by the Sea and the area was a lot wilder in appearance than the main part of town. There were no sidewalks or streetlights, and instead of front lawns most people let the dirt fill in with native plants. Vista Del Mar was literally across the street from my place, but once I walked through the stone pillars that marked the entrance to the Vista Del Mar driveway, it was like a different world.

Vista Del Mar took the idea of *left to grow wild* to a whole new level. Whatever grew there had decided to on its own. I glanced along the side of the driveway at the lanky Monterey pines surrounded by brush and had more second thoughts about the upcoming retreat. I hoped I'd made it clear to my group they weren't coming to a posh resort with a manicured lawn and perfectly trimmed bushes.

I saw that one of the trees had fallen and I knew it would be left to return to nature on its own. I'd heard the same was true of any wildlife that met their demise there. Because of that I always avoided examining the underbrush too carefully.

The sky was a flat white, which was pretty typical, and by now I was used to traveling without a shadow. I passed my favorite large Monterey cypress tree. The constant breeze had shaped it so that the foliage grew horizontally. It was silly but the tree always made me think of someone running away with their hair trailing behind. I followed the driveway to the area I considered the heart of Vista Del Mar. The Lodge was in the center and was a social hall and the place where people checked in. It had been there since the days when Vista Del Mar was a camp, and like the other buildings was built in the Arts and Crafts style, which meant dark wood, lots of windows and local stone. The chapel was tucked in a corner against the sand dunes. The Sea Foam dining hall was just down the way. Trees blocked the view, but I knew that Hummingbird Hall was on the other side of them at the top of a slope. It served as an event area and auditorium.

The guest rooms were in weathered, moody-looking buildings that were spread over the one hundred or so acres that made up the grounds. Sand dunes ran along the edge of the property. A street wound around the sandy border. Beyond was the white sand beach and the ocean. I still marveled that the water really was sea foam green. I glanced around me and sighed. Personally I loved the untamed beauty of the grounds, but I wasn't so sure my group would feel the same.

When I pulled open the door to the Lodge, it was deathly quiet. But then, it was that time between people checking out and leaving and the new arrivals checking in. I was surprised that there wasn't even a clerk behind the massive wooden registration counter. Most weekends there were a number of group events planned. Bird watchers loved the place, and so did yoga and meditation groups. I'd seen writers' conferences and business retreats there as well. Oddly, on this particular long weekend the only retreat scheduled was mine. It didn't mean that the place would be empty, just that instead of groups it would be filled with individuals and families.

The interior felt cavernous due to the open construction of the ceiling and the size of the main room. I glanced around for some signs of life. There was a crackling fire going in the massive stone fireplace next to the deserted seating area, which was made up of some soft leather couches and mission-style chairs. The lamps were turned on and their amber-colored glass shades gave the space at least some feeling of coziness.

I momentarily paused when I glanced at the row of vintage phone booths near the counter. I did tell my group about Vista Del Mar being unplugged, didn't I?

With no one behind the counter I couldn't check on my people's rooms. In the meantime, the smell of fresh coffee drew me into the Cora and Madeleine Delacorte Café. It was a recent and very welcomed addition to Vista Del Mar and was the closest thing there was to room service, as long as you acted as your own waiter. Stan, the new hire, was behind the counter leaning over his laptop. He was a writer along with being a barista. He looked up when I came in. "I know you want a cappuccino, short on the milk," he said with a friendly smile.

"Where is everybody?" I asked, gesturing toward the main room.

"Well, I'm here," a woman's voice said. I had mistakenly thought the tables were all empty, but now I saw that Madeleine Delacorte was sitting in a corner by the window. Stan said he'd bring me my drink and I went to her table.

I thought about my earlier conversation with Crystal. It was so strange to think that the woman in front of me had no idea she was Crystal's great-aunt. For a moment I wondered if I should say something, but a voice in the back of my mind that sounded remarkably like my ex-boss Frank's told me to stay out of it. Madeleine was definitely the more likeable of the two Delacorte sisters and we'd actually become friends. At seventy-something, she had rebelled against the restrictive way she'd been brought up and lived for years. While her sister, Cora, kept to wearing Chanel suits and too much eye shadow, Madeleine had discovered denim and was in love with jeans. She had started hanging out at my retreats and somehow credited me with the change in her life. And by the same token, I'm sure her sister Cora blamed me.

"What do you think?" Madeleine said, sticking out her leg and showing off her dark-washed skinny jeans. "These are the best, so comfortable." She wore a black tunic on top and ankle boots and carried off the look perfectly. She had changed her hairstyle from an over-sprayed helmet look to a swingy blunt cut that made her appear cute. The current color of a soft brown and her light touch with makeup shaved years off her age.

16

"When does everybody get here?" she asked in an excited voice.

I froze, realizing that when I'd told her about the retreat she had assumed it would be like the others that she'd tagged along on. Stan dropped off my foam-topped drink as I considered how to handle it. How could I tell her this time she wasn't welcome? It was simple— I couldn't. As the owners of Vista Del Mar, the sisters had given me the same wonderful deal on accommodations my aunt had gotten. It was the difference between me making a profit and being out of business, and I was most grateful. I didn't want to do anything that might make them rethink the arrangement.

"They'll be here soon," I said. "But you understand this isn't going to be like the other retreats I've put on. These are all people I knew in college."

She was undeterred. "I know. But that makes it even better. I never had a bunch of girlfriends when I was growing up. I want to see what it's like."

"They're not exactly my girlfriends," I said. "I knew them in college, though I kind of lost touch with them since. But I guess it will give you the idea of what you missed."

I took a sip of my cappuccino. Stan had gotten the perfect mix of espresso and steamed milk. I looked toward the counter, ready to give him a thumbs-up, as two women walked into the café. They were pulling roller bags and seemed a little lost. My first thought was that they were my people, but then reality set in and I realized it was too early.

"I want to check in but there's nobody there," one of them said. She wore a floppy khaki brimmed hat, khaki cargo pants and rope sandals.

"Ditto for me," the other woman said. She seemed a little younger and her headgear was a beige baseball cap with nothing written on it. She wore loose-fitting clothes that made me think she was either deeply into comfort or recently had lost weight.

"That's terrible," Madeleine said, getting up from her table. She got me to come with her and we approached the pair. Madeleine held out her hand and introduced herself as one of the owners. Then she turned to me. "We can't leave people hanging like this. Do something, Casey."

"Like what? Should I go look for Kevin St. John?" I asked. While Madeleine and Cora were the owners of Vista Del Mar, they left most of the running of it to the manager, Kevin St. John.

"You must know how to check people in," Madeleine said to me. "Take care of them and I'll search for Mr. St. John." We were standing in the doorway by then, and before I could object, she'd taken off across the main room toward the exit like a woman on a mission.

"This isn't my usual job," I said, looking at the massive wooden counter. "I just have to find a way to get to the other side of it." I assured them it would just take a minute. The counter completely closed off the business area, and the only way to get behind it was by going through a door to the side, which of course turned out to be locked.

I looked at the shiny dark wood counter and there was no other recourse. So I took a deep breath, boosted myself onto the smooth top and slid over it, landing on my feet with a thud.

I'd never been behind the counter before and it felt very strange and maybe a little fun viewing the interior of the Lodge from this new perspective. I quickly looked around to try to figure out what was what. Vista Del Mar still had actual keys for the rooms and each one was kept in a pigeonhole marked by the building and room number. There was a computer monitor on the counter but the screen was dark. I started playing with the mouse, hoping to get the screen to light up, and I waved to the women to come toward me.

The computer screen came on, but it asked for a password to continue. I gave the two women a reassuring smile as I fiddled with the keyboard, but then I let out a mental eureka—some genius had decided to keep it simple, and my first try at typing in password

1234 had worked. "Okay, I can check you in," I said brightly. "Are you traveling together?"

Both women shook their heads and said "no." After that it became a contest of who could be more courteous by letting the other woman go first. Finally I pointed at the woman in the baseball cap. "Let's start with you."

She stepped forward, still offering the other woman the opportunity to go first. I admired their manners. If only the whole world was that considerate. "My name is Barbara Henderson," she said. I hit a roadblock on the computer as I tried to call up the reservations and made small talk with her while I tried to figure it out. Barbara seemed friendly enough, and I was relieved that she wasn't impatient. It was her first visit to Vista Del Mar and she said she was hoping to get away from it all.

"You've come to the right place," I said when I finally called up her reservation. I took one of the keys from the pigeonholes behind me and handed it to her. I caught a glimpse of a mark on her wrist as she took the key. She saw me looking at it and smiled. "It's a birthmark. I keep thinking I ought to get a tat to cover it. Maybe a sunflower," she offered.

"Like this," the other woman said, showing off a tiny flower tattoo on her wrist. "I wish I'd thought of a sunflower instead of a rose." She turned to me. "My name is Rebecca Noodleman," she said. "I appreciate your efforts, but it's obvious you're just stepping in. I came here before for a retreat and everything was handled very efficiently. I hope this isn't a sign of how the weekend is going to be." I apologized to both of them and said I was sure once we got over this glitch everything would be fine.

The door opened with a *whoosh* and Kevin St. John came in. He glanced toward the registration area and his expression went from placid to horrified as his gaze fell on me. "Ms. Feldstein, what are you doing?" he sputtered. The moon-faced manager was overdressed in a dark suit that made him look more like an undertaker than the host of a rustic resort. He was not a big fan of mine, to put it mildly, so seeing me in his domain was extra upsetting.

I considered mentioning that Madeleine had been the one to insist I step in, but since she wasn't with him I had no backup. Under the circumstances it seemed like the best thing to do was to get out of there quickly.

"They're all yours," I said, climbing back over the huge wooden counter. Just then a frazzled-looking young woman came in, holding her cell phone. Her eyes widened with horror as she took in the situation. Kevin shushed her with a stare while he went to deal with the new arrivals. As he stood with the two women, he glanced back at me, and I gathered he was apologizing and trying to smooth things over. He handed them a map and seemed to be giving them directions to the building their rooms were in. He finished with a few bows of his head and probably some more apologies before coming over to us.

"I'm sorry," the clerk said. She was new and I hadn't gotten her name. "But I had to check my phone. You can't get a signal unless you walk way down the street," she said in an indignant tone. She looked at the manager for his reaction and seemed surprised when he was hardly sympathetic. She let out a sigh. "It's not my fault someone decided to take this place back to the Dark Ages and make it unplugged." She turned to me. "You're Casey Something, right?" I nodded and she continued. "There was a message for you. One of the people coming to your retreat can't make it."

"Did you get a name?" I asked and the girl got defensive.

"Technically, we're not supposed to take messages for you since you're not a guest," she said and looked to Kevin St. John for his approval, as if it would make up for what she'd just done. "So I told her she ought to send you an email or call you directly. But I'm pretty sure her name is like Clair or Blair. She started to tell me why. Something about her hair or a fair and she had a meeting or something. Maybe it'll be in the email." She stopped for a moment. "But maybe not. I'm not sure she said she would send one. I just remember she said she was in a hurry."

I'm not sure which of us Kevin St. John glared at more.

It was obvious why he was unhappy with her, and by now I'd gotten that her name was Janet. But it was not so obvious what he had against me. I doubted the glare had to do with my invading the sacred territory behind the counter. Someone else might have actually said *thank you for trying to help out.* To cut right to the chase, he simply didn't like me. It irritated him no end that the Delacorte sisters were giving me such a deal on the rooms and meeting space, and what he really wanted was for me to give up the whole retreat business and just go away.

He kept his personal life under wraps and so far all I'd been able to find out about him was that he was probably single, was a native Cadburian, and had been brought up by his grandmother, who died under suspicious circumstances.

"If there's nothing else, Ms. Feldstein," Kevin St. John said, indicating the door. I heard him drop his voice as he began to lecture Janet. I wondered if she'd still be there when I returned.

Chapter Three

The one positive about my time behind the counter was that in looking for the reservations of the two women I'd been able to check on my group and saw that everything was in order. When I went back home, I realized I'd left the dishes on the table and cleared them off. Julius did figure eights around my ankles and then went and sat down in front of the refrigerator. His message couldn't have been clearer. I'd ignored his demand before, but this time he was standing his ground. He wanted some stink fish.

Of all the cat foods in the world, he had to zero in on the smelliest of them all. I'd never looked too closely at the ingredients—I didn't want to get that close to the can. I swear you could smell it even when the can hadn't been opened.

I had given up being tough about giving in to his demands and most of the time simply gave him a tiny dab. The only problem with that plan was that it meant I was constantly having to deal with the smell. I kept the open can wrapped in several layers of plastic wrap in a plastic bag within another plastic bag. Even so, as soon as I grabbed the plastic bag I got a faint whiff of it. I automatically closed my nose for the duration as I went through all the unwrapping and put a tiny blob of it in his bowl and wrapped it all up again.

"I'm going to be tied up a lot until Sunday," I said as the black cat hovered over his bowl, daintily licking the pink blob. "I have to spend a lot of time with this group." I looked down at him. "So you are going to have to be a good cat and stay out of trouble."

At the word *trouble* he looked up at me with his arresting yellow eyes and blinked a few times. When Julius had first come to live with me, I'd tried to make him an indoor cat. Even now I laughed at my folly. In the end he'd won and I left a window open enough for him to squeeze in and out, and he came and went as he pleased. "You can't come on the Vista Del Mar grounds looking for me. You know what happened before," I said in a stern voice. Kevin St. John didn't like Julius. He had been hostile to the cat from the first time I'd seen Julius wandering on the grounds. The manager had almost run over him then and later blamed him when there was an accident with some yarn.

Julius rubbed against my ankles a few times before going back to his food. Did that mean he understood?

I pulled out a couple of rolls of butter cookie dough I always kept in the refrigerator. I liked to bring some baked goods to the workshops. While the oven preheated, I sliced the rolls and spread the disks of dough on metal sheets. They were baked and cooling on racks in no time.

It was almost showtime and I went to check my appearance. The rust-colored turtleneck and black jeans seemed a little too casual. I found an old suede blazer and slipped it on, thinking it added a professional air. It wasn't as comfortable as the loose-fitting fleece jacket I usually wore and I realized I'd probably be cold in it, but this time I was more concerned with the look than my comfort. I always added a handmade item from my aunt's stash as a finishing touch. I picked out a knitted scarf in shades of brown and rust made out of a nubby silk yarn. I checked my reflection and gave myself an okay, all the while chiding myself for being concerned with what the Baller-rinas might think of me.

I packed the cookies in a tin, grabbed my oversized red tote bag stuff with the smaller bags for the group, and headed for the door as I convinced myself to stop fussing about the upcoming retreat. There was nothing I could do about it now anyway. And with the news that Blair wasn't coming, there would be one less person to worry about pleasing.

The sun was still in hiding and a cool breeze carried the scent of the ocean mixed with the pine trees and the wood smoke from all the fireplaces as I walked back down the Vista Del Mar driveway. I veered off before I got to the Lodge and took the path that led to our meeting room. I glanced at the golden grass on either side of the walkway, amazed at how dry it looked. With all the cloudy skies here on the tip of the Monterey Peninsula, the area didn't get a lot of rain.

I passed the Sand and Sea building, where my friends would be staying. It was covered in dark brown weathered shingles. The entrance was hardly grand, just a small stoop with an overhang held up by a column made of stones. I tried to think of a positive spin on the building to offer to my friends. It was historic and an original building from the time this place was a camp. It had actually served as a dormitory for the camp counselors. I could mention the Arts and Crafts style and that it was designed by a famous woman architect. The one thing I couldn't say was that the accommodations were luxurious or even close.

The meeting room took up part of a one-story building called Cypress and was positioned in an open area between the structures that housed the guest rooms. I'd used it many times before, and when I stepped inside the only thing that seemed a little off was that the fireplace was dark and no coffee and tea service was set up on the counter. I left the tin of cookies where the refreshments would be and took a last glance around the room. The tables and chairs seemed fine. Crystal would bring everything else. Then it was out the door and on to greet the arrivals.

I took the other path back and ended up on the side of the Lodge building that had a large deck that looked toward the sand dunes. I'd passed some new arrivals pulling their suitcases up the path and we exchanged friendly hellos. I still had a smile from the exchanges with the guests as I cut through the Lodge. When I opened the door on the other side I was surprised to see that the airport shuttle had already arrived and was unloading.

Most of the group had arranged to fly together, going from Chicago to Los Angeles and changing to a smaller plane that flew into the Monterey airport. Only Blair had planned to come in separately, but that was irrelevant now. As I looked over the arrivals, I wondered if the mystery guest was among them. Along with no name, there'd been no flight details.

I felt a last-minute surge of nerves and anxiety as I realized this was it. And how little I knew about where they all were in their lives now. There had been some wedding invitations and birth announcements, but somehow I'd never done anything beyond sending a gift. We had been such a hodgepodge of personalities that when we no longer had Clayton U. in common, I'd lost touch with them.

I watched as the van emptied and the driver opened the back and started to hand out bags. I looked over the clump of people, trying to pick out any familiar faces. I laughed at myself, realizing that I was looking for the girls I'd known, but it had been fourteen years since I'd seen them and they'd probably changed.

I had only glanced over the photos and information each of them had posted about themselves on Facebook. The truth was I was sure they'd all gone on to do great things and I hated to be reminded that I was still trying to find my way.

Out of nowhere a red ball came flying toward me and bounced off my head before I managed to catch it.

"Who threw that?" I said with mock anger.

"You didn't think we'd come ball-less," a woman said. "Not on your life. The balls are what brought us together and are an important part of this reunion." She had filled out a bit since I'd last seen her, but I recognized Elizabeth Bronsky. I'd always thought there was a primness about her. Her skin had a natural pallor and her dark hair always looked as if it had just been combed. She had never been particularly into fashion, and it seemed as if that hadn't changed. The stiff-looking jeans were topped with a nondescript white top and a black sweater. She'd taken out a tube of lip gloss and spread it over her mouth several times, and I recalled that she'd had an obsession about lip gloss.

It figured that she would have brought the balls. I chuckled as I remembered my title for her—the ballatarian, since she was the one who had come up with rules and implemented them without consulting anyone.

"Speak for yourself," Vanessa Peyton said to Elizabeth before turning to me. "I thought it was a stupid idea to bring them, but she was like a terrier about it, wouldn't give up until I agreed." I was still holding the ball and was considering what to do with it. Vanessa stared at it in my hand. "Don't even think about bouncing that to me."

Vanessa had always had that polished look from facials and designer haircuts, but it seemed she'd taken it up a notch. Her hair was long and a wheat color that I knew wasn't hers, but it had been done so expertly with variations of tones that it could have passed for natural. Her makeup was flawless and understated. She was an expert at camouflaging her curvy shape. She wore washed-out jeans that no doubt had come with a huge price tag, along with an asymmetrical cream-colored long top that was probably silk. She covered it all with a long yellow kimono-style jacket splashed with showy orange poppies.

"I don't get your attitude," Elizabeth said to Vanessa. "How could we have had a Baller-rinas reunion without our balls?" Elizabeth turned back toward me and urged me to throw the red ball back to her. It felt like a basketball but was much smaller and easy to hold in one hand, and I was happy to oblige. This ball business was something I hadn't anticipated and I hoped it wasn't going to cause a problem. The dark-haired ballatarian caught it and began to bounce it up and down. Without missing a bounce, Elizabeth spoke to me as she rocked her head with frustration. "What I had to do to get her to let me look for them at her parents' house."

I laughed inside at Elizabeth calling where Vanessa's parents lived a house. How about a mansion on a primo piece of North Shore land with a view of Lake Michigan. My family was very comfortable since both of my parents were doctors, and we had a view of Lake Michigan from our Hancock building apartment, but Vanessa's family was rich rich. The money came from the slew of car dealerships they owned. There was Peyton Ford, Peyton Buick, Peyton Mercedes and Peyton Legace.

"I can't believe you still have them," I said, as it came back to me that since we wanted to be so fabulous with our routine, Vanessa had bought a set of the balls and let us practice at her place.

"Whatever floats your boat," Vanessa said with a dismissive wave of her hand, and I caught sight of a diamond the size of a rock on her finger that probably would work well as a weapon if she ever got in a real street fight. I chuckled at the thought, as if that would ever happen.

Vanessa went to retrieve her bag as another woman joined me. "Hi, Casey," she said brightly. "In case you don't remember me, I'm Lauren Fischer. Well, it's Lauren Fischer Clark now technically, but I still go by Fischer. Taking your husband's name seems so archaic."

"Of course, I know who you are," I said. She was as cute and perky as I remembered her being. She was lucky to have the kind of roundish face and features that would never age, and she looked virtually unchanged. She'd been the one of us most likely to save the world and had always been championing some cause. I recalled that Lauren had worn jeans and a lot of graphic T-shirts that had some sort of statement on them, along with one of those green army field jackets. She was still wearing utilitarian jeans, but instead of a T-shirt wore a red print peasant top with a nubbly black shawl wrapped over it. Her brown hair was still short in the kind of cut that just needed a good shake after a shower to fall into place. If she wore any makeup, I couldn't see it.

"Do you knit?" I asked, touching the shawl to feel the texture.

"Nope. It came from a women's collective in Peru." She seemed dismayed as she caught sight of Vanessa's brown and tan monogram suitcase. "Do you have any idea how much one of those cost?" I didn't need to answer because she quickly added that the Louis Vuitton bag on wheels went for more than a couple of thousand dollars. "And it doesn't do any more than my bag that I got for fifty bucks at Costco. I wish I could send the difference to those women in Peru." She continued to mutter to herself about other ways that money could be spent that would help others, and I wondered why she was so versed on the price of the bag considering how negatively she felt about it.

By the process of elimination, I knew for sure that the sleek-looking woman with glossy mink-colored hair grabbing her bag had to be Courtney Arlington. I would have recognized her anyway as soon as I saw her face. Not to be unkind, but Courtney had a prominent nose and the space between it and her mouth was not proportional. Her navy slacks with a matching pullover sweater accessorized by a light blue paisley scarf gave her a professional air. She would never be beautiful but she'd succeeded in making herself look distinctive and maybe a little intimidating. I saw her nails were perfectly manicured and painted a blood red as she pulled out her cell phone. My momentary thought that she must have gotten over her habit of biting them turned to panic. They'd know soon enough about their cell phones not working, but I wanted to stall a little longer.

"Now that you're all here, let's get you all checked in," I said, touching Courtney's arm to distract her. I took a last look around at the people getting their bags to see if the mystery guest would make their presence known, but nobody else looked my way. I waved for the group to follow as I guided Courtney toward the door to the Lodge.

"When is Blair supposed to arrive?" Vanessa asked as she grabbed the handle of her expensive bag and followed behind me.

"Bad news," I said. "I got a message this morning that she can't make it. Something about a meeting." I wanted to give them more details, but the clerk's message-taking skills had left a lot to be desired.

"I guess you can't just leave the town of Hillston when you're the boss," Elizabeth said. "It's pretty impressive that she's the mayor." She looked at the others. "Imagine one of our Baller-rinas is in charge of the whole town."

Mayor? I felt myself getting smaller right on the spot. If I'd paid more attention to what they were all doing I never would have let Vanessa talk me into this retreat. I also now understood Janet's garbled message. She'd turned *mayor* into *hair* or *fair*.

"It's more like a suburb of Chicago," Lauren corrected. "And she's just using it as a stepping-stone. She's planning to run for Congress. I suppose it shouldn't be a big surprise. Remember she was the student government treasurer and then the next year she was the president."

Vanessa seemed vexed. "I was depending on Blair being here."

"Don't worry, we can still do our ball routine. We'll just have to make a few changes," Elizabeth said.

"Who cares about ball routines now?" Courtney said. "That's who we were, not who we are."

I held the door and they filed inside the Lodge, looking around the open area as they did. "What is this place?" Vanessa asked.

I groaned to myself as I heard the distaste in her voice. When she'd come up with the idea of me putting on the retreat I had used words like *rustic* and *atmospheric* to describe Vista Del Mar. I had given her a link to check it out online, but she'd never voiced any reservations. I realized she probably hadn't paid any attention to what I said or checked out the link.

Vanessa could have afforded to go to any college, but her grades had been average at best. She just needed a degree to please her father, and Clayton University was very open about letting in everyone, or as they put it, giving everyone a chance. She was used to the luxury of her parents' estate so a commuter school suited her perfectly. From the start she'd been the one to take charge of the Baller-rinas. It was like her own little social club.

Once again it struck me what an unlikely group we were. There was no way we would have gotten to know each other if it hadn't been for that fateful gym class.

"It used to be a girls' camp," Lauren said, reading the signboard that listed events and the story of Vista Del Mar.

"Like over a hundred years ago," Elizabeth said, reading over her shoulder. "How quaint, look at the activities. Nature walks, storytelling in front of the fire, Friday night movie, a talent show, and something called a roast and toast."

I started to get defensive. "Some people like to step back in time. I've brought a lot of groups here, and by the end of the weekend they're thanking me for the simple surroundings."

"Well, we're women and we need our spa treatments and plush surroundings," Vanessa said, glancing around the interior. The space was no longer deserted and there were several people reading in the sitting area. A pair of boisterous teens were playing table tennis and a family was playing Monopoly on one of the tables spread around the lobby-like area. "Board games, really?" she said with distaste. "Where's the bar?" She looked around the big room. "I need a glass of wine."

"Isn't it a little early for that?" Lauren said.

"What's that line—it's five o'clock somewhere," Vanessa said with an uneasy smile. "But if it's going to upset you, I can wait," she said and then turned to me. "You do have wine here, I hope."

"There's a whole selection of beer and wine," I said, hoping to get a few points with her. I pointed out the Cora and Madeleine Delacorte Café, which now served wine and beer.

"Darn, what's going on? Why won't my phone work?" Courtney said rather loudly. She was holding her smart phone, frantically scrolling down the screen. More remembrances of her came back and I recalled how she'd always seemed overly aggressive and rather humorless. She'd been the most mortified that we'd had to do our routine in view of the boys and gone on about her image.

Was it just a lapse in her memory or had she missed what I'd said? I knew that I had made it clear all along that Vista Del Mar was unplugged.

"There's nothing wrong with your phone. I'm sure I told you this whole place is unplugged. There's no cell service, Internet or even TV." There, I'd said it. I took a breath waiting for their reaction. I heard a collective groan that turned into grumbling, but Courtney's voice carried above the rest.

"What?" Courtney shrieked, looking at the others for support. "I thought you meant that there weren't a lot of outlets to plug in my electronics. You didn't make it very clear then. I never would have come if I knew we were going back to ancient times. I suppose I'll have to use the landline in the room."

"About that," I began. "I'm sure I pointed out that the accommodations were camp-like and that there were no phones in the rooms, or TVs."

Courtney looked at me in shock and then around at her surroundings. "I can't stay here. I brought work with me. I have to be in contact with my team."

"Take a breath, Courtney," Vanessa said. "There must be phones somewhere here." She looked around the large space again. "It's a problem for all of us."

"Of course there are phones," I said, gritting for their reaction when they saw what I meant. I stepped aside and pointed out the row of phone booths I'd been blocking. Courtney looked skyward and I saw her make a face.

"Pay phones in an actual booth—who sees those anymore?" Lauren said. Courtney pushed the folding door open and looked inside.

"What about getting calls?" Courtney practically barked the words and it came back to me that she had always sounded as if whatever she was doing was far more important than anything anyone else was doing. Inwardly, I bristled at how demanding she sounded, but I put on a smile and walked the group over to the message board that stood outside the door to the gift shop.

Seeing it through their eyes, it did seem a little rinky-dink in the modern world of communication, but it was all that was available, so I tried to make it sound effective. "The registration people take messages and post them here. It's alphabetical," I added.

Courtney rolled her eyes in exasperation and muttered something about an unnecessary challenge.

Lauren seemed deep in thought. "Is the whole town unplugged or just Vista Del Mar?" she asked.

"Just Vista Del Mar," I said hesitantly.

"So in other words, Courtney could use her phone if she went outside the grounds," Lauren said. Now I remembered that she'd been the one who always tried to fix everything.

"In theory it would work, but I don't think she is going to want to spend the weekend hanging out in the street waiting for a call."

Undeterred, Lauren continued. "But don't you live someplace around here?" I held on to a pleasant expression, but inside I was freaking as I knew exactly where she was headed. No way was that going to happen. Let them come over once and they'd be there all the time wanting to use their phones. I needed them to stay at Vista Del Mar so I could slip away to do my dessert making for the Blue Door and muffin baking for the town's coffee spots. I wasn't up for any judgy looks by Vanessa either when she saw my place. I didn't wait for Lauren to say more and stepped in to take control.

"I'd love to let you come over," I began, "but I'm in the midst of a remodel and everything is torn up. Besides, it would take away from the whole experience of staying at Vista Del Mar." I said it in a tone that made it clear it was settled and there would be no negotiating. Then I simply moved on and brought up our mystery retreater. "It was all done anonymously and I don't even know when they're supposed to arrive."

"Who could it be?" Elizabeth said. "There aren't any more Baller-rinas."

"That's what I thought," I said. "I guess we'll just have to wait and see who shows up." I gestured toward the registration counter. "And now let's get you all checked in."

A new woman about my age was working registration, but before she had a chance to greet my group, Kevin St. John came from somewhere in the back and took over. The manager looked over the small group and smiled.

"Welcome, ladies," he said, focusing on the four women and avoiding me. "Let me know if we can do anything to make your stay more enjoyable."

Elizabeth stepped forward and looked at him squarely. "Elizabeth Bronsky," she said, reaching out her hand. The manager seemed confused by her move and reluctantly reached across the counter and shook with her. He didn't see himself as a friend to the guests, but rather their host and most of all in charge.

"One of our group is expecting some important calls this weekend. Is there any way she can get special service for any messages you take for her." She had leaned forward onto the counter and was tilting her head and fingering a strand of her hair. I almost choked as I realized she was trying to flirt with him. I wasn't sure if her motive was to try to help Courtney or if she was actually interested in him. I had to keep myself from gagging at the thought.

There was nothing for me to do but stand back and watch. And try not to gag as Elizabeth continued on. "I know we'd all really appreciate anything you could do to help her. You must be able to pull a few strings."

Elizabeth didn't seem to be good at reading body language or she would have realized her efforts were falling flat as he showed no reaction. He finally made a small concession, but it was more about ending her show than because of it.

"We can hold her messages up here at the desk," he said and then abruptly began to check them in. He dispensed the keys, and as I was about to escort them to their rooms, he wished them a nice visit. "I'm sure Ms. Feldstein has your long weekend planned out, but if there are any problems, we're here to help." He nodded in my direction with a self-satisfied smirk. I got it, he'd placed himself above me in importance to my friends.

As we went outside, I heard Courtney fussing with Elizabeth. "I don't need you to take care of things for me," Courtney said, sounding irritated.

"I was just trying to help," Elizabeth said.

"It looked to me like you were trying to help yourself with the manager. And now he probably thinks of me as being part of your man hunt."

"Tsk, tsk," Vanessa said, looking over her shoulder at Courtney. "You seem a little edgy, being off all electronics will probably do you good."

"You can't possibly understand. You've always had a cushy safety net to catch you. Not me. If I fall, I crash." There was dead silence after that. This was so different than my usual retreat. Generally the people didn't know each other when they signed up and it took all weekend for them to figure out how not to get along.

"Maybe you should tell us how far we have to go," Vanessa said as I led them up the slope covered in golden grass.

I pointed at the weathered-looking two-story building just ahead. In the dull light it appeared rather foreboding and I really wished the sun had come out. "The building is called Sand and Sea and your rooms are all in there." They all seemed a little hesitant as I took them inside.

"This is your own personal living room," I said. A fire glowed in the fireplace and there were comfortable chairs spread around the carpeted area. Only Lauren made a comment that it seemed cozy. I dreaded moving on to the rooms. I'd been absolutely honest about Vista Del Mar when I'd described it to them and sent them that link to check it out for themselves. Judging by how surprised they were about everything, I had the feeling nobody had paid attention to what I'd said.

"This place is kind of spooky," Elizabeth said as I brought them to the hall. I could see her point. It was the middle of the afternoon and the hall was like a dark tunnel with no light at the end.

"It's because the walls and ceiling are all dark wood. It's part of the Arts and Craft style," I explained. I rattled off some more facts about the Arts and Crafts style and how Vista Del Mar was a famous example of it, but none of them were listening, They'd pushed ahead and were looking at the room numbers on the doors in the dim natural light that made its way to the hall.

"That's me," Vanessa said when we reached 112. She put her key in the door and opened it, and they all looked inside as she walked in.

"You're kidding," Vanessa said, stopping at the narrow bed. They'd pushed behind her and watched as she pulled back the utilitarian bedspread and inspected the sheets, which were clean but a little rough. I was seeing it through their eyes and it wasn't looking good. Courtney scoffed at the sink in the room and the tiny bathroom with a stall shower and a toilet that flushed with a lever like you found in public restrooms.

"It's like being inside a coffin," Vanessa said with distaste as she took in the dark wood walls and ceiling. I started to say something but she spoke first. "I know it's part of the Arts and Crafts style," she mimicked. She quickly opened the curtains and unlatched the windows.

"Quit being such a princess," Lauren said. "There are lots of people in the world who would be thrilled to have this room to stay in." She turned to me. "It's not every day you get to stay in such a historic place."

Elizabeth had come up next to me and leaned in close. "You aren't married, right?" she asked in a low voice. It seemed like an absolute non sequitur, but I shook my head in answer and she seemed relieved. "I didn't want to be the only one. Being thirty-five and unmarried doesn't mean anything anymore, right?" She'd barely taken a breath before she continued. "What about that manager? Is he single?" Then she looked at me. "I'm not stepping on your toes asking about him, am I? I mean, is there something between you. I saw how he smiled at you at the end."

I was stunned. Then she was serious when she'd tried to flirt with him. And she thought there might be something between Kevin St. John and me? Didn't she see that so-called smile was a smirk? All I could think of was—ewww. He was the absolute opposite of anything remotely sexy. The idea of holding his hand made me cringe, let alone thinking of doing anything else with him. I told her what I knew about him, which was almost nothing, and assured her he was available as far as I knew.

Courtney's room was next and they all trooped in to check it out. It was almost identical to Vanessa's room. I saw Courtney's shoulders drop as she glanced around. She went to the table next to the bed and picked up the ancient clock radio, so old that installing it meant just plugging it in. "You're kidding," she said before replacing it on the table. "Whose idea was this anyway?" she asked, looking around at the group.

"I think it was mine," Vanessa said. "I thought it would be nice for us all to reconnect someplace away from it all. I'm afraid that I didn't realize quite how away from it all this place is. Now it doesn't seem like such a great idea."

"Stop being such a spoilsport," Lauren said to Vanessa. "It's too bad Blair didn't make it. She'd know how to talk some sense into you."

"Do you happen to know if she's married?" Elizabeth asked.

"What's the difference?" Vanessa said.

"Nothing," Elizabeth said. "I was just curious who's still single."

I handed out the tote bags and they all began checking out the contents.

"You'll get yarn and needles at the first workshop," I said.

"So you really meant it about the whole knitting thing," Vanessa said, looking at the knitting instructions with disdain.

I nodded. "I know this is all strange to you, but by the end of our first session this afternoon you'll know how to knit and understand what the instructions mean. And then by the end of the weekend you'll have completed a scarf."

"I think it is a stellar idea," Lauren said. "It gives a purpose to our get-together, we'll learn something useful and have a souvenir of our time together."

"Spoken like a true do-gooder," Vanessa said. "I was thinking like more of a spa weekend. You know, massages, facials, sipping wine in a hot tub. I'd be happy to buy a slew of scarves and hand them out to everyone."

Lauren looked around at the surroundings. "Do they have spa services?" she asked and then quickly added she was just asking for Vanessa.

I shook my head and tried not to appear as annoyed as I felt. Why did I ever agree to put on this retreat?

Vanessa took out her phone and then realized it was useless. "There are some wonderful places in Pebble Beach. We could move the whole thing there," she said.

"No," Lauren said, surprisingly forcefully. "Casey put this together for us and buying scarves isn't the same as making them."

"Absolutely right," Vanessa said with a laugh. "With my idea we find us a store somewhere and a few minutes later you're wearing the scarf, and with the other way we spend all weekend fiddling around with yarn and maybe don't even end up with anything we'd want to wear."

"Hold on a second," I said, stepping in. "I went to a lot of trouble to bring in someone to teach you how to knit and we found a pattern that was simple and fast enough that you could finish the scarf while you're here. I'm sure when you see what the scarf looks like you'll be impressed."

"Okay," Vanessa said, capitulating, "We'll go to your workshop. But in the meantime, let's get some lunch. Where's the restaurant?"

"It's more like a dining hall," I said. "And I'm afraid that lunch is already over. There's a café next to the registration desk." I gave them a rundown of what they served, which was really just some premade sandwiches and salads along with coffee drinks.

Vanessa's moment of good cheer ended. "There has to be some other choice. That manager said he was willing to help. I'll go talk to him," she said.

"No, no," I said. "Don't say anything to him." The last thing I wanted was for Kevin St. John to have any inkling my friends weren't happy with the arrangements. "I have an idea. All of you meet me in fifteen minutes where you were dropped off. I know you're going to like this."

Only Lauren seemed enthusiastic.

Chapter Four

"This is more like it," Vanessa said as I held the door to the Blue Door restaurant and she walked inside. Lucinda Thornkill was waiting and led us to a table in the back room. As soon as Vanessa was seated, I went back to find the others. The three of them were still standing on the sidewalk at the bottom of the stairs. They were so immersed in the screens on their phones I had to physically touch them to get their attention.

"This way," I said, taking them up the stairs. Because they'd barely looked up from their phones, it was a slow process and I had to keep turning back to make sure they were still following me and hadn't tripped. I took them through the restaurant, which was almost empty since lunchtime was over. Lauren snagged her jacket on a chair and snapped to attention long enough to free herself. Courtney kept stopping every few steps as she apparently read something upsetting. Elizabeth took up the rear and thankfully had slipped her phone in her pocket.

I hadn't planned a trip to downtown Cadbury until later in the retreat, but when Vanessa mentioned going to Kevin St. John to see what he could arrange, I freaked. I didn't want him to know that my group was unhappy about anything. Not only would he torment me with the information, but he might pass it along to the Delacorte sisters, which could affect my deal.

I'd been able to throw together this outing in just a few minutes. All it took was a call to Lucinda and one to the van service. It had never been my intention to make a profit from this retreat, and I'd only charged them the actual costs with a little padding for errors. But I also didn't want to lose money on the weekend either. This trip would just about wipe out that padding. But what else could I do? I thought getting them some time with their electronics and a good meal might calm them all down. Or at least I had my fingers crossed, hoping so.

"The food is great," I said. I introduced them to Lucinda when she came to the table with menus. I referred to her only as a friend, never letting on she was also sort of my boss since I made the desserts for the restaurant.

The Blue Door was on the main drag of Cadbury and had been a residence at one time. Most of the dining area was in the former living room, but Lucinda had taken us to a table on what had been a sunporch. I'd been a little frantic when I called her, insisting she remove the sign that said *Desserts by Casey* on the counter by the front door. It was crazy. I'd never cared what they thought about me in college and now I was so concerned they not know how pieced together my life was. As it turned out, it was laughable that I'd been worried. Vanessa had gone by the counter with the pound cake iced with buttercream frosting and the apple pie with the crumb crust, forcing herself not to look, and the rest of them had been barely aware of their surroundings.

I waited until they all ordered and then followed Lucinda back to the front. She handed the order to the cook and turned to me. "What can we get for you?"

"Nothing," I said. "Maybe a glass of ice tea. There's too much going on for me to want to eat."

The group was out of sight and out of earshot from where we stood and Lucinda gave me a knowing nod as she poured me a glass of the amber liquid. "They're not happy with Vista Del Mar, right?"

"What are you, a mind reader?" I said.

"No, I just put a few things together. First, there was the call about coming here, and your brows have looked like they were glued together since you got here, and the one wearing that gorgeous Pierre-François jacket took ten minutes to tell me exactly how she wanted her cob salad, right down to the size of the blue cheese crumbles." Lucinda laughed. "Someone wearing a designer jacket who is that fussy about her food would never be happy with one of those cots they call beds at Vista Del Mar, or the sheets, or the towels, and certainly not a dining hall where it's *this is the food, take it or leave it.*"

"That's Vanessa and you're right." I hit my forehead in consternation. "Did I forget to introduce you?"

Lucinda pulled my hand away from my head. "Relax. You introduced me. My mind is like a sieve when it comes to names."

Maybe names of people but not designers. It seemed like everything Lucinda wore had a famous fashion person's name connected with it. She favored the stark simplicity of Eileen Fisher's designs, Ralph Lauren's western look, along with clothes from some lesser-known designers. Today she was wearing a sunny yellow shift I knew was a LaLa Lafoush design. She always looked put together and I suspected she put on lipstick to get the mail.

We'd become friends right after I moved to Cadbury. She was the one to give me the job as dessert chef for the restaurant and allowed me to use their kitchen to bake my muffins. She usually came to my retreats but had decided to sit this one out.

"I don't know why you don't want them to know about your baking. I'm sure they'd be impressed to know that people are so worried about your desserts running out that they order something set aside before they've even decided on an entrée."

"Maybe," I said, "but I'd still rather let them think my business is just the retreats." I shook my head with dismay. "You should have heard them when they saw the rooms. I know I told them what Vista Del Mar was like. It's not my fault they didn't pay attention." I heard myself and realized I was doing what I'd done with Frank. I sounded whiny, which was not my style. "Never mind. We'll get through the weekend, one way or another."

"What sort of work do they do? The one with the big nose seems very self-important," Lucinda asked.

"I don't know any of their professions, but you're right about Courtney. She does seem very wrapped up in her own importance. The only thing I know for sure is that Elizabeth—she's the one with the pale complexion and prim expression—is on a man hunt, well, a husband hunt, and you'll never guess who the object of her desire seems to be." Lucinda shrugged and said she gave up. "Kevin St. John. She's worse at flirting than I am. And at least I know I'm funny. She's all serious about it and so obvious." Lucinda had started to laugh.

"Bad flirting with Kevin St. John. That has to be quite a show," my friend said. We heard the chef say the order was almost ready.

"I better get back to them," I said, giving Lucinda a thank-you hug before going to join the group.

I let out a sigh of relief when I got back to the table and no one was complaining. But then no one was talking either. Courtney had moved herself to a nearby table and had papers spread out in front of her. She was wearing earbuds, listening to something while her fingers were busy texting, and judging by the pings coming from her phone, she was getting a lot of answers. Lauren had her phone to her ear, listening to someone go on and on. Vanessa's seat was empty and Elizabeth was staring down at the menu.

"Look at this sweet story," Elizabeth said, showing off the back of the menu. Lauren glanced up with a blank look. Courtney didn't respond at all and Vanessa wasn't there.

I nodded and said I knew it by heart and began reciting my version of it. "Lucinda and Tag were high school sweethearts but had gone their separate ways until years later they reconnected at a high school reunion. He was widowed and she was divorced and it was love at second sight. They got married and fulfilled the lifelong dream they'd shared of opening a restaurant and lived happily ever after." What the story left out was that they weren't exactly the same people they'd been in high school. Tag had become fanatical about stupid details and was really borderline obsessive-compulsive. And one of the ways Lucinda dealt with it was by coming to my retreats and getting some time away.

"Where's Vanessa?" I asked and Elizabeth appeared surprised.

"Maybe the restroom," she offered. But I'd passed it on the way back to the table and it was empty.

Lucinda and the server brought the food and Lauren hung up her phone. "Maybe it's not the worst thing to be incommunicado for a while." She let out a tired sigh as she put her phone on the table. Courtney didn't notice that her sandwich had arrived until Lucinda held it in front of her face. Even then she barely ate while she continued with all the papers, texts and calls.

Lucinda hung by the table and Elizabeth wanted to hear more of the romantic story, and it became clear pretty quickly that it was really about reassuring her that even though she was single at thirty-five it didn't mean it was hopeless for her to find true love.

I was ready to pay the check when Vanessa finally returned. By then I'd figured that she'd slipped out to do some shopping and expected to see her arms laden with packages. But she wasn't carrying anything and slid into her chair without a word. "We packed up your food," I said, expecting that to get her to explain, but all she said was thank you. Finally, I asked her where she'd gone.

"Here and there," she said in a dismissive manner before taking out her phone and tapping something in. All I could do was to let it go, but it didn't sit well with me.

I took the check up to the front and thanked Lucinda for the huge discount she'd given me. "I know this wasn't a planned expense," she said, handing me the receipt.

"Why don't you come to the retreat. One of our people canceled at the last minute. You could come in her place," I said hopefully.

Lucinda smiled. "Need an ally, huh?" I nodded. "Okay, but maybe you should check with them first."

We went back to the table together and I floated the idea of Lucinda taking Blair's place. Vanessa looked at the yellow dress. "Anybody who wears a LaLa Lafoush is my kind of people."

"It's okay with me," Lauren said. "It's better than wasting the spot in the retreat."

Courtney gave me a blank look when I tried to ask her, which I took as a yes. Elizabeth was the most enthusiastic.

"Yes, you should come," the prim-looking woman said. "We need someone to take Blair's place in the ball routine."

"Don't pay any attention to her," Vanessa said to Lucinda and then turned to Elizabeth. "We're not doing that stupid ball routine."

When they'd finished lunch and we got ready to leave, Lucinda said she'd be there later in the afternoon. Courtney stopped in her tracks when we got to the sidewalk. "Just a little while longer," she pleaded. The rest of them all agreed. I couldn't fight the lure of some more time with their phones and we sat parked in the van for fifteen minutes before heading back to Vista Del Mar. They continued to stare at their screens on the ride home and only put their phones away when we drove onto the grounds and the signal disappeared.

The sun had made a brief appearance while we were in town, but it was nowhere to be seen as we pulled up to the Lodge. Vanessa looked out the window of the van with a vexed expression as she got up to get off. She'd still said nothing about where she'd disappeared to. I groaned inwardly when I saw that Kevin St. John had just come outside and stopped next to the van. He smiled at my four retreaters. "Everything still going well?" he asked. I sensed Vanessa was about to say something and Elizabeth was going into flirt mode. I stepped in front of them to block them both.

"Of course," I said as I quickly guided them inside.

Chapter Five

I'd dragged them into the Lodge as a way to get them away from the manager, but once inside I needed to give them a reason for the move. "I wanted to show you some of the grounds," I said quickly. "I thought we'd cut through here." I indicated the door on the other side and explained the boardwalk and the proximity of the beach.

But all that changed when we passed a man standing near the phone booths. He'd turned to face us and was staring. "Can it be? The Baller-rinas in person?" he said with a chuckle.

We all stopped suddenly and I looked at him intently. He appeared familiar and strange at the same time.

"Don't tell me you don't recognize me," he said. He had a deep melodious voice with a touch of a laugh in it. "I know, it's the beard. He pointed to some scruffy growth on his face. "Beard might be overstating." His lips curved into a grin. "It's more like not shaving for a couple of days. It seemed to go along with the idea of a retreat." Now I was completely confused. What did he mean *go along with the retreat*?

Elizabeth pushed forward. "Zak Stevens," she squealed. "I can't believe it's you. I saw you on WNN. I don't remember what the story was. I was just so excited to see an actual person I knew from Clayton on TV."

Now that I had a name, I couldn't believe I hadn't recognized him. His tall frame had filled out a little, but mostly he looked the same. He still had wavy black hair, though it was cut in a short style now. His dark eyes still sparkled with intelligence and his distinctive crooked smile was as adorable as ever. All together his features gave the impression of someone who cared about everything and had a sense of adventure.

"What are you doing here?" Vanessa asked before I could.

"I got a rather mysterious message that if I came to a retreat here I'd get to see all of you and would get a lead on a great story. It

45

all came in a letter—yes, a real letter—with plane tickets and everything. How could I resist that?"

I was listening to him but at the same time thinking back to when we'd all first met. Zak had been in the boys' class who got to watch our original Baller-rinas performance. He'd won us all over when he'd stopped his weight lifting and actually applauded our routine. Actually, he hadn't won all of us over. Courtney had been mortified to realize he'd been watching us. Even then she'd taken herself far too seriously and was way too concerned about her image.

Zak had ended up hanging out with us a lot and never got tired of teasing Courtney about her ball bouncing. He told us he was going to be a journalist from practically the first time we met. He wrote a column for the school paper and then had a regular program on the student TV station. Summers, he talked his way into intern jobs at local TV stations.

He had an illusive quality that was like trying to catch a moonbeam, which I found charming. I'd thought he was exciting and fun and had a huge crush on him. I'd never let on how I felt to the others, and the crush never went beyond group coffee dates and help with a speech class we were in together—well, except for once.

It was a rainy spring night and I didn't have an umbrella. Clayton University was in the South Loop and a long walk to our apartment in the Hancock building. I'd been considering my options when Zak had appeared and offered to share his umbrella.

I'd taken him up on his offer and we'd headed out into the rainy night huddled together under his umbrella. The street was a shiny black from the rain and reflected the lights of tall buildings along Michigan Avenue. We crossed the bridge over the Chicago River, splashing in the puddles and laughing as we did our rendition of "Singing in the Rain." On the other side of the river the graceful trees were decorated with tiny white lights, making it seem very magical. It had all been crazy romantic and then out of nowhere we stopped on a street corner and he kissed me. It had lived up to my fantasy and I'd hoped it was the beginning of something. But in the end it had turned out to be just that one kiss in the rain. As I looked over at him, I doubted that he even remembered.

"I got an equally mysterious message," I said. "Mine was a letter, too. No name or return address, simply instructions to register someone for our retreat. There was a gift card with cash on it in payment. I didn't know what to make of it. I booked the room but wondered if anyone was really going to show up. And now here you are," I said, hoping that my voice didn't give away any of what I'd been thinking about.

His arrival had knocked me off-kilter. It had never occurred to me that the mystery guest would be a guy, and certainly not that it would be him. I was left with all kinds of questions. Who'd invited him? Why be so secret? What was the story he was promised? I was trying to pull myself together. "So, then you will be taking part in all of our activities—including the knitting workshops."

"Of course," he said, sounding more enthused than the rest of them. "You never know where you'll find a story. And I did some research and found out that sailors used to knit, and they're certainly manly men." He struck a pose as if to show off his biceps.

"You got here just in time. We were just about to have our first workshop. I have a tote bag for you in our meeting room." He still had to check in and I offered to help him and laughed in a good-natured way.

"Thanks, but as a field reporter I've checked in all kinds of places. I doubt there's a situation I haven't encountered," he said.

"Has your reservation ever been listed under Guess Who," I said.

"That's a first," he said with a twinkle in his eye.

I was glad that somebody saw the humor in it. Kevin St. John certainly hadn't and had wanted to list the reservation under *No*

Name. We went outside and waited in the driveway while he checked in and then we all walked him to the Sand and Sea building. He was like the shiny new thing and they were all clustered around him. I was relieved to take up the rear. I stayed on the path while they went into the building. "Workshop starts in half an hour," I said in a confident voice. Far more confident than I felt.

Chapter Six

I continued on up the path to the Cypress building. Since ours was the only retreat going on, the other room in the single-story building wasn't being used and the door was shut. The door to our section of the building was wide open and Crystal was sitting at the long table knitting with some buttercup-colored yarn. Just seeing her rainbow layers of shirts and crazy combo of earrings made me smile. She looked up when I came in and did my rounds of the room. The coffee and tea service had already been set up next to my tin of cookies and a cozy fire burned in the fireplace. There were two smallish plastic bins next to the table that had the needles and yarn for the group. My large tote bag was on the chair where I'd left it earlier. I helped myself to some coffee and flopped onto one of the chairs.

"That bad?" Crystal said, eyeing my slouch.

"This is just so different than my usual retreat. They're all so difficult," I groaned. "It's crazy. One person didn't show up, someone else who is a complete surprise did show up, and they're all having a fit about their phones not working."

"Give it a little time. They're going through electronic withdrawal. You've had retreaters like that before. It'll work out, you'll see," Crystal said in a reassuring voice.

"I'm sure you're right," I said, making myself sit up straight. "I have to stop being so whiny."

"So there's a mystery retreater," Crystal said. "That's a first. Who is she?"

"How about she's a he," I said. I was just finishing explaining who Zak was when Madeleine Delacorte came in and pulled out a chair.

"Where is everybody?" she said, looking around.

I hadn't seen her since she'd convinced me to act as the registration clerk in the morning. So much had happened since then

49

that I'd completely forgotten that she said she'd be hanging out with the group. I remembered that she'd told me a reunion of college friends was another experience she'd missed thanks to her restrictive mother. Actually, I didn't even know if Madeleine had gone to college.

I wasn't sure it was the best idea. Once the group knew she was one of the owners of Vista Del Mar, they might start laying their complaints on her. But by the same token, since I'd told her she was welcome to participate in any retreats I put on, I couldn't really do anything. And Madeleine seemed so happy to be there. She turned to Crystal with a friendly expression. "I just love all the colors you wear. I wish I had the courage to try wearing unmatching earrings." She had an impish smile. "Cora would throw such a fit."

Crystal's mouth curved into an uncomfortable smile and I knew what my helper was thinking. She was still wrapping her mind around the fact that Madeleine was her great-aunt even though the older woman didn't have a clue.

"Good, I'm not late," Lucinda said, rushing into the room. She still had her bag with her and I said I'd get her set up with her room after the workshop. She stowed her bag in the corner and smiled when she saw Madeleine. "We're the two locals, so maybe we should stick together."

"What a good idea," Madeleine said, enthusiastically patting Lucinda's hand.

Lucinda thanked me again for the invitation. "You have no idea how much I need this. These retreats are what keep me sane. Between all of Tag's fussing—" She stopped herself and looked around. "Just checking to make sure that Elizabeth isn't around. She seemed so hung up on believing the fairy tale on the menu. I wouldn't want to ruin her fantasy that everything is so perfectly happy ever after with Tag. Anyway, dealing with him and everything it takes to run the restaurant leaves me burned out. But a weekend with your knitters and I'm ready to face everything again.

She took off her Burberry trench coat and the silk scarf she had on underneath and hung them on one of the chairs. "Does it matter where I sit?"

I suggested sitting in the middle of the group. "That way you can help."

"Really? My knitting skills are pretty basic." I assured Lucinda that she knew more than the group coming in.

"I'd be glad to help, too," Madeleine said. "I can certainly help anyone who needs assistance in casting on."

Before Lucinda sat, she insisted on getting drinks for Madeleine and Crystal. I laughed as I watched her make a perfect cup of tea for Madeleine and ask what shade of brown Crystal wanted her coffee as she prepared to add the cream. Lucinda never stopped playing host.

I heard the sound of voices coming up the path and put on my brightest smile as I prepared to greet them. The four women fell silent as they came inside and looked around nervously, as if they expected a giant knitting needle to come out and spear them. I got them over the awkward moment by getting up and bringing them to the table. I quickly introduced Crystal as their teacher.

"Welcome," Crystal said brightly. Her colorful mismatched appearance and manner immediately put them at ease and all four of them let down their guard.

"Zak said he'd come by a little later," Elizabeth said. "I helped him find his room." After making sure there weren't assigned seats, she picked one and actually folded her hands on the table when she sat down.

It was impossible to miss the disdain in Vanessa's expression as she looked around the room and chose a seat. She peeled the long black sweater she wore off the yellow designer jacket and hung it on the back of her chair. Lucinda eyed the sweater with an appreciative nod and I assumed it was more designer garb.

"Who's Zak?" Lucinda asked, looking at me. I realized she

hadn't been there when I told Crystal about him and explained the mystery retreater.

Elizabeth leaned into Lucinda. "Who's she?" She tried her best to indicate Madeleine without pointing.

I heard Elizabeth's comment and quickly stepped in and introduced Madeleine, casually mentioning that she and her sister owned Vista Del Mar. I avoided Crystal's eye when I said the last part because now that she knew she was actually a Delacorte descendant and the hotel and conference center was supposed to go to her grandfather's heirs, it felt awkward. "And both Lucinda and Madeleine know how to knit already and are here to help."

"I love that story about you and your husband," Elizabeth said to Lucinda. "I guess it is never too late for the right person to show up."

Lucinda smiled at her sweetly. "Yes, it's always good to have hope. But let's hear about all of you." Lucinda broadened her view to take in the whole group. "Casey introduced you when you all came in the Blue Door, but I need a little refresher course and Madeleine is starting from scratch."

"Why don't we get started," Crystal said. "Then when you're working you can introduce yourselves." I'd seen her stealing a look at her watch and understood she was coming from a different place than the rest of them. This was a job for her and she had allotted only so much time for the workshop and then she had a life of her own.

There was a slight delay as they all got drinks and cookies and got settled. Zak came in just as Crystal went to close the door to keep in the warmth of the fire. He looked at her once and then again as he found a seat. I was a pretty good student of human nature by now and I could tell that he liked what he saw.

"Before we start I thought I'd tell you a little about the history of knitting," Crystal began. She started talking about ancient Egypt and a pair of socks and I watched as everyone's eyes glazed over. Luckily, Crystal noticed it as well and skipped ahead to the present.

She mentioned that knitting had gone from being a useful craft to make articles of clothing to a pastime. While it had faded in popularity for a while, recently there'd been a resurgence of interest in it as a hobby, and men had joined in. Lately it had become known as a stress reducer, a social craft and an art form. "But really when you get right down to it, it's all about making loops." She held up a ball of red yarn in one hand and a long red scarf in the other. "It's pretty amazing how you can turn this"—she lifted the hand with the yarn—"into this," she said indicating the scarf in the other hand. "And enjoy doing it."

"Is that what we're going to make?" Courtney asked, looking at the scarf that was now on the table.

Crystal smiled. "Nope. You're going to make something more exciting." She leaned down to open the bins and pulled out the black and silver scarf she'd shown me before. "I call it the Razzle Dazzle." She tried it on and modeled it, and then passed it around. The stitches were huge and easy to see and the spaces were filled in fluttery strands. I was surprised at how interested Courtney was in it.

She was curious how it could have the mixture of color and textures. Crystal brought out three skeins of yarn. "This is basic worsted weight yarn," she said, holding up a black peanut-shaped skein. She grabbed a smaller skein of a thinner silver yarn. "This is what adds the contrasting color." Finally she held up a fuzzy ball. "This is called eyelash yarn and it's what adds the texture." She pulled out a strand from each skein and held them together. "You'll be working with all three yarns with these." She laid a pair of huge blood-red plastic knitting needles on the table and picked up one of them to show it off. They all laughed a little nervously.

"Geez, those things look like weapons," Zak said. He reached for the one on the table and knocked it against the one she was holding in a mock swordfight. She smiled at him like he was a naughty boy and took away his needle before she continued on. "The first thing we'll do is cast on."

I got up to help her and we began to pass out a set of needles to each of them and the three skeins of yarn.

She explained that casting on was the way to get the yarn on one of the needles. I was glad that she didn't go into all the different cast-on methods and just demonstrated the one called the long-tail method. I stood by ready to help, but I was also interested to see how they'd react to the lesson. Lauren smiled with satisfaction as she managed to get the loops on the big needle. Courtney was absolutely intense and kept redoing the stitches until they all looked even. Vanessa didn't seem to care and made such a mess of it that Crystal simply cast on the stitches for her.

Elizabeth watched Crystal's hands as she went through the moves, and then tried to mimic them. Zak had the least trouble and picked it up right away, and I wondered if he'd prepared for the retreat by watching a bunch of YouTube videos. Once everyone managed to do the cast on, she showed them how to knit, which was much easier and they all caught on.

"Now just keep going," Crystal said. "And feel free to talk as you knit. Didn't you want to do some introductions?"

"I'll go first," Elizabeth said. "I'm Elizabeth Bronsky and I'm an event arranger for a nonprofit."

"Isn't that a fancy way of saying you're a fund-raiser for a charity," Lauren said. Elizabeth made an unhappy face. "By the way, I'm Lauren Fischer and I'm a social worker. Actually, I work at a child services agency and I practice what I preach. We have two foster children at the moment along with two of our own. We foster pets, too." She turned back to Elizabeth. "I hope you don't put on those extravagant events that don't raise much for the actual charity."

Elizabeth rolled her eyes. "What are you, a one-woman watchdog for the world? I don't suppose you've heard the phrase *you have to spend money to make money*."

Vanessa chuckled. "You've stayed constant. You were always

standing up for everything when we were in college."

"I like to think that I was the conscience of our group. Somebody had to keep an eye on what was going on. Not everyone had the view you did from your family's mansion. You didn't need student aid so you had no idea what a racket was going on with student loans." Vanessa put up her hand to stop Lauren.

"I know you all thought I was just some rich girl who was going to school to pass the time and snag a husband. And you probably all think I spend my time now getting spa treatments and shopping." She stopped for a moment to introduce herself to Lucinda and Madeleine. Then she chuckled. "Actually, I was just some rich girl going to school to pass the time and snag a husband. The idea was my father was going to groom the husband so he could work his way up in the family business and keep me in the style I was accustomed to. But, well, my first husband turned out to be a real dunce, and I spent all my time trying to make him look good. Until I realized why not get rid of the middle man. When I told my father who was doing what, I became the one working my way up in the family business and we gave Number One his walking papers."

"You said your first husband," Elizabeth said. "Does that mean you've had more?" *Poor Elizabeth,* I thought. She was so into what was right and rules and all, I'm sure she was thinking it was somehow unfair that Vanessa might have more than one husband and she'd had none.

"Yes, there's Number Two. He went to Clayton, too. But this time the arrangement is different. I still get my spa time in, but I'm the one with the big office and he's the one with whole days to spend at the spa or shopping, along with taking care of my daughter." She shook her head. "But all good things come to an end and I'm on the lookout for Number Three. I'm hoping for someone who is more of a prize this time."

Crystal had been listening. "It sounds pretty cold. Whatever happened to romance and love matches?" Then she laughed at herself. "A lot of good that did me. I was crazy about my ex." She gave the rundown on Rixx and his new woman.

Lauren was staring at Vanessa with her brows furrowed. "Why don't you tell them what you do?"

I sensed tensions rising, as if Lauren was somehow upset with Vanessa. I wanted to step in and change the subject, but Vanessa continued before I could manage to interrupt.

"I'm an executive at Peyton Legace in Hillston," she said proudly. "I'm working on something now that should be the icing on the cake of proving myself to my father." There was a wave of impressive sounds from everyone but Lauren. Legace cars were the hottest thing around.

"Well, at least Legace makes an electric car," Lauren said before nudging Courtney and telling her she was next.

Courtney had given herself over to her knitting completely and kept looking at the stitches and adjusting them so they were perfectly even. She waited until she'd reached the end of the row to speak. "I'm Courtney Arlington." She held on to the knitting but didn't start the next row and gave all of her attention to introducing herself. "I'm an attorney and in the middle of an important case and the outcome could affect my whole career. I never would have come if it had been made clear what *unplugged* meant." Her eyes flashed with upset. "I don't know how I'm going to manage using a phone booth." Out of habit she'd put her cell phone on the table and she made a *grrrr* sound as she looked at it.

Lauren nudged her. "What about your personal life?" It took a moment for what Lauren had said to register. "I met Phil in law school. He went into criminal law and I'm a litigator. We have two boys," Courtney said.

"You have a big legal career, kids and a husband who loves you. Wow, you really have it all," Elizabeth said.

"You could say that," Courtney said with a self-effacing shrug.

Zak was up next. He managed to keep his needles moving as he talked. "Zak Stevens reporting," he said with a mock bow of his head. "I'm a field reporter for WNN. I get to be in the middle of what's happening. I'm like a transplant surgeon on call twenty-four-seven. They call and I go."

Courtney tapped him on the shoulder. "Maybe you haven't noticed yet, but your cell phone doesn't work." He shook his head with regret. "I have to get one of those satellite phones. It's happened before that I've had to go the old-fashioned way with a landline. I'll manage. I always do." He turned to Lucinda and Madeleine and explained his mystery invitation to the retreat. "I'm not sure why I'm here. An anonymous source promised me a hot story." He looked over the group. "I'm guessing it has to do with one of you, so I'll be looking around trying to find that dirty laundry in your life." He said it as a joke but it didn't go over that way and they all looked worried.

There was a moment of quiet and it seemed the introductions were over, but then Lauren turned to me. "What about you, Casey?"

They were all looking at me now, waiting for me to say something. I didn't like talking about myself, and considering that Lucinda, my friend and boss, and Madeleine, who had some control over my business, were there, I wondered how much to say. I finally decided just to give the bare basics. "I'm unattached except for Julius, an independent-minded black cat who moved in with me. I inherited the yarn retreat business and a house from my aunt." As I spoke I was thinking how dull I sounded and I was also aware of all I was leaving out, like my nighttime baking, my side job as a magician's assistant, and the men in my life. Or that it had turned out that my aunt had been murdered and I'd found the killer.

"So that's how you ended up here," Vanessa said in a dismissive tone.

Courtney had laid down her needles but kept fidgeting with the few rows of stitches. She glanced at the surroundings. "Whatever works for you, but I'd die in a place like this."

Lauren scowled at the comment. "That's kind of harsh. At least Casey is doing something positive. Knitting is a peaceful pursuit."

"So then you've never been married?" Elizabeth asked and I rolled my eyes.

Crystal stepped in, getting me off the hook. "The plan was to talk *and* knit," she said, noting that they had all put down their needles. "But unfortunately we've run out of time." She showed them how to pack up their work and stow it in their tote bags. Since the tote bags were identical, she passed around a marker to the group and they each put their name on their bag.

"Until tomorrow, knitters," Crystal said, pulling her black wrap around her. It was the only dark spot on her bright outfit.

"And it's ball time for us," Elizabeth said and everyone groaned.

"Ball time?" Zak said with surprise.

Chapter Seven

Crystal left to go home. Madeleine left as well, explaining that she'd just be with us part-time. "I have a number of ceremonial duties this weekend," she said. "This evening we're cutting the ribbon on the sculpture garden we donated outside the natural history museum. It's an installation of giant glass monarch butterflies on milkweed leaves." She faced my group. "You probably don't know this but Cadbury is known for our monarchs. They come every fall like clockwork."

She pulled on her long sweater and then bid them all a good evening.

"You're not serious about that ball nonsense," Vanessa said as she got up from the table, and Elizabeth nodded her head.

"You don't think I lugged them here for nothing. They're what brought us together."

I was barely listening, still thinking about the so-called introductions. First and foremost, I was glad that I hadn't said more. It they were all that judgy about what little I'd said, I could just imagine what their comments would be if I'd told them the rest of it.

I was surprised by the amount of tension among them all. Somehow I'd always thought they were such good buds and I was the outsider. When I thought about it, though, the seeds of who they'd become had been evident in the past. I'd suspected that Vanessa was smarter than she got credit for. Courtney had seemed single-minded and persistent. Lauren thought she was right and somehow purer of heart than the rest of us. And I kind of remembered Elizabeth as having set ideas of when things were supposed to happen in her life. It was no wonder that she seemed to be freaking out about still being single. And Zak had said nothing about any attachments, which made me suspect he was as illusive as ever.

Lucinda nudged me and gestured toward Elizabeth. "I think you better do something." Her comment brought me back to the present and the fuss going on between Elizabeth and Vanessa. Elizabeth appeared almost in tears. "Can't we just do it once for old times' sake?"

Lauren stepped in and tried to plead Elizabeth's case. It *was* the thing that had brought us together, she said. "And there'll be no peace until we do it," Lauren added.

Vanessa finally agreed, but Courtney tried to back out until Elizabeth stood in front of her looking a little crazed, saying that no was not an option. Courtney tried to dismiss Zak, but Elizabeth objected. "I want him there," she snapped. Nobody wanted to mess with Elizabeth now that she seemed a little unhinged and Courtney gave in.

"But no photos or videos," Courtney said. "I'm serious. I can't afford to have a video going viral of our routine. It would be devastating to my image."

I saw Zak roll his eyes and shake his head.

" Lucinda agreed to take Blair's part and quickly took her bag to her room, saying she'd change into something more appropriate.

"We need an indoor spot with no people and enough room," Elizabeth said, staring at me. Luckily I knew the perfect place. We stopped at the Sand and Sea building to pick up the balls and Lucinda, who was now wearing classic white Keds.

Then I led them across the grounds past the Lodge and the Sea Foam dining hall and up a small slope to Hummingbird Hall.

I didn't think they were up for a lecture on architecture so I didn't bother mentioning that the looming dark wood building was the same Arts and Crafts style as the Lodge and dining hall. I just explained that it was used for different kinds of gatherings.

I was glad to see that it was empty, as I expected since it was a Thursday night and there were no other group events going on at Vista Del Mar. It was quite grand inside. The center was open with a stage at the front. The sides and back all had alcoves formed by a series of supports I assumed were holding up the roof. The idea that the structure was part of the design was a main point in the Arts and Crafts style. Rows of windows on the sides and back filled the space with natural light. It was a nice plan and might have brought in enough light in the desert where the sun was unrelenting, but here on the Monterey Peninsula there were just too many clouds. I flipped on the interior lighting and the group filed in. Elizabeth dropped the bag of balls in the center of the open area.

"You thought of everything," I said, noticing she had a small speaker attached to her smart phone.

"We couldn't do it without our music." She had set it out of the way. She fidgeted with the phone and "Cool" from *Westside Story* blared out. She quickly shut it off. "Well, at least *that* works on my phone. Then she turned to the group.

"It's ball time," Elizabeth said. Zak started to go off to the side, but Courtney stepped forward. "Sorry to have to do this, but I really won't be comfortable until I know there's no chance anyone takes photos or videos." She found a basket sitting on the side and went around collecting everyone's phone. Then she put it at the back of the room.

"Is she that important?" Lucinda said, leaning close to me and dropping her voice to a whisper.

"In her own head, for sure," I said.

"Now what?" Lauren asked.

Elizabeth started unloading balls and throwing one to each of us. "We do the routine."

Elizabeth took her ball and did a demonstration without the music. "I'd thought the choreography was lame when we did it and it didn't look any better now. She walked in bouncing the ball with an attitude that was a combination of menacing and slinky and stopped abruptly. "This is where we have the standoff. Like we're two gangs." She told Courtney to stand across from her. Elizabeth started moving from side to side, bouncing the ball with a vengeance, and finally made a move toward Courtney. "You were supposed to come toward me and bounce yours to me." Courtney reluctantly followed her directions. "We repeat this with some free dance thrown in like it's a girl gang knife fight. And then—" Elizabeth threw her ball up and fell to the floor. She waved for Courtney to do the same, but she resisted and Elizabeth shrugged. "We end up on the floor like we've all killed each other."

"Yeah, and the point was that violence doesn't end well," Lauren said.

"That was your idea," Elizabeth said.

"I can't believe you remember all the moves," Lauren said. "I sure don't." She looked to the rest of us and we all nodded in agreement.

Elizabeth was undaunted. "You just think you don't remember. Your head might not, but your hands and feet do." She told Lucinda just to follow along and do the best she could as she arranged us in two lines on opposite sides of the center. "Okay, Sharks and Jets. Hit it." She leaned down and hit something on her phone and rushed to join the shorter line.

I hated to admit it, but Elizabeth was right. At least, sort of. As soon as the music started to play, I instinctively began to snap the fingers on my free hand and my group began to bounce our balls and prance toward the center. We got to the face-off and that's when everything fell apart. I looked at the people facing me and froze with no idea who I was supposed to throw the ball to. It seems as if it was the same for everyone and balls just went flying.

Elizabeth shut the music off and glared at us with consternation. She turned to me first. "I don't remember the order of who threw to who back in the day. So you throw yours to Courtney." She assigned the rest of the ball partners and had us do it again. When we got to the rumble, Courtney and I tossed our balls with no problem. Not so for the rest of them, and all the balls just went flying. I stole a look at Zak, thinking he'd probably fallen asleep from boredom, but he seemed to be enjoying the show.

"That's it," Vanessa said when Elizabeth wanted them to do it a third time. She dropped her ball in the canvas bag and retrieved her phone before going out the door. The rest of them followed suit, and I waited until Elizabeth had packed up the balls and gone to the door. Zak did a mock bow and offered to carry them for her. Elizabeth agreed and then took his arm.

"It looks like she's expanding her net," I said to Lucinda, who'd hung back with me.

"Thanks for being such a good sport and taking Blair's place. There would have been no peace until we did that stupid routine," I said.

"It was fun," Lucinda said. "If only I'd been able to keep it straight who to throw to," she said.

The sun had decided to make an appearance just in time to go down. I always marveled how everything changed when the sky cleared. From the top of the slope we had a view of the ocean. The sun glinted off the water and the trees around us threw shadows on the walkway. Even the dark buildings appeared a little less moody.

"It's easy," I said. "Forget looking at faces. You just find something distinctive about the person's hands." It was simple to pick out Courtney's. She's the only one wearing blood-red nail polish.

"What a good idea," Lucinda said.

"Not that it matters. Our ball performance is done."

But of course that turned out not to be true.

Chapter Eight

We made it through dinner. As expected, Vanessa was horrified at the cafeteria setting but somehow worked it out and got them to make her something special. Lauren's pitch was to be grateful for the food. Courtney came in at the end, having spent who knows how long in one of the phone booths. Elizabeth was still on a high from us doing the ball routine and could have been eating straw. Zak said any day when he didn't have to survive on vending machine food was a good one.

Lucinda worked the table, making sure everyone's ice tea glass was full. No matter what I said about it being her time off, she insisted on helping with the hosting.

Everyone went their own way after the meal. I'd announced we were to meet back in the Lodge for the evening's activities. I took a quick detour to my place and made sure Julius got his dab of stink fish. When I returned, I collected the tote bags in the meeting room and brought them all to the Lodge. Just before the appointed time, I commandeered the seating area around the fireplace. The two leather couches sat in an L shape facing the massive fireplace. They were separated by a shared square table and each couch had its own table on the other end. Two mission-style chairs sat across from the couches with a small table between them. The way the furniture was arranged made it seem like a separate area from the rest of the large room. I had set the red tote bags on the large coffee table that sat in the middle between the couches and chairs to further stake the space out as our own.

Lucinda was the first one there and the only one who knew about my plan to slip away later and go to the Blue Door to bake.

"Are you sure they'll show up," my friend said, glancing around the social hall.

The large room was already abuzz with activity and there was a hum of conversations. Someone cheered a good shot in a game of table tennis. A middle-aged man bent over the pool table and eyed the balls. A young family hovered over a jigsaw puzzle on one of the smaller tables spread around the room. Four women were playing cards. All of the phone booths were in use and several people were checking in at the registration counter.

People streamed in and out of the café. The gift shop at the other end of the building had customers as well. The people were all a blur to me except for the two guests I'd actually talked to. The woman with the name that reminded me of pasta was reading a book in another of the mission-style chairs under the window on the deck side of the room. I recognized the other woman by her loose clothes, though I couldn't recall her name. She was sitting at one of the small game tables and appeared to be playing solitaire.

"They'll come for the same reason the rest of these guests are here. There's nothing else to do in their rooms," I said. Along with all the people, there was an assortment of jackets and different kinds of tote bags scattered around the room. "This is going to be a long, long weekend. I was so glad that I'd stuck to starting it on Thursday instead of Wednesday. It will be over faster," I said with a grin.

"You'll work it out," Lucinda said in a reassuring voice. "By the end they'll be claiming the weekend changed their lives. But I have to admit, it's going to be a challenge. Except for Zak. He's sure a cutie. What's the story between you two? I saw how you looked at him."

"There is no story. I knew him in college."

"And," she said.

"And Zak was the crusading reporter and went after the story no matter the consequences to anyone," I said, thinking back to some of the uproar he'd caused on the Clayton television station when he'd done an exposé of the school bookstore."

"C'mon, I know there's more."

I caved and told her about our romantic encounter in the rain.

"And that was it," I said. "I was disappointed it didn't go anywhere at the time. But I wonder what I would have done if he'd followed through and wanted a relationship. I probably would have taken off."

"Poor Dane," Lucinda said. "He finally gets you to go out with him and now Zak shows up."

"I'm not interested in him anymore. It was just a one-time kiss in the rain. And Dane doesn't own me. We're just going out occasionally with no idea of it heading anywhere."

"Says you. I think he has a definite goal in mind." Lucinda smiled and I rolled my eyes.

"Here they come," Lucinda said. "Except Zak." I followed her gaze and saw the four different-looking women come in and I waved them over.

"We're here," Vanessa said with pursed lips. "What exactly do you have planned?" She seemed out of place in her designer jacket carrying a Prada purse. The rest of the guests were all in cargo pants and jeans with tote bags and recycled grocery bags to carry their things.

"Something called social knitting," Lauren said, showing off her copy of the schedule. She was the only one who thought to take hers out of her tote bag before she left it in the meeting room. "Then there's something called a roast and toast."

"If that's toast as in wine, I can certainly get behind that," Vanessa said.

"Not exactly." I explained the roast involved marshmallows on a metal stick over a campfire and the toast was hot chocolate. It all would take place later in the area called the fire circle.

Vanessa made a face. "This place really is like a glorified camp, isn't it?" She brightened when I told her the café had wine. "That's more like it. Wine for everyone, my treat," she said, glancing back at the others.

"You don't have to always be the one to treat," Lauren said.

"But it's nothing to me," Vanessa said. "And I know the rest of you are struggling." I noticed that Lauren didn't seem happy with the comment and muttered something about Lauren's good heart was only a ruse.

"Where's Zak?" I asked and got shrugs in answer as the four of them spread out on the couches. I'd already put my purse and jacket down on one of the two chairs and Lucinda had taken the other one. I grabbed one of the totes and checked for the owner's name. "We might as well get started." Courtney excused herself and rushed toward a phone booth that had just emptied. Vanessa's gaze was stuck on the café.

"Let's get some wine first," Vanessa said and turned to me. "How do we get someone to take our order?"

"That's not how it works here," I said.

"That's right. We're not at a luxurious hotel," she said in a sarcastic tone. "Let's see what I can do." She sounded all business as she got up. She swished past the coffee table, almost catching her fancy yellow and orange jacket. I thanked my lucky stars when she didn't. There would have been hell to pay, probably for me, if she tore it.

Lauren looked at the red tote bags with concern. "I think I already forgot everything Crystal taught us." I was going to ask Lucinda to help her when Vanessa returned looking stormy-faced and sat down on the couch.

"What's wrong?" I asked. Before she could answer, Kevin St. John was standing next to my chair.

"Did I hear there was a problem?" he said with a solicitous smile.

"We were going to get some wine," Elizabeth said, giving him such an obvious flirty look I wanted to throw up.

"Maybe you can get the woman in the café to give us some service. She was quite unpleasant when I asked her to bring us the wine. It's my treat and I'd be happy to throw in a generous tip." Vanessa was already opening her wallet.

"Anything to please our guests," Kevin said, giving me a sideways glance. "No tip is necessary. What would you like?"

"White zin for me," Vanessa said, as I expected. She turned to the others. Lauren and Courtney wanted white wine spritzers, Elizabeth asked for merlot and Lucinda asked for chardonnay. It was lucky that I had decided to pass on the wine since I was working, because Kevin St. John left without even a glance my way.

"Let me help," Elizabeth said, rushing after him.

"Is she always so obviously on the prowl?" Lucinda asked.

"I think she's feeling a little desperate. As I remember, she had a timetable for her life. There was something about meeting her future husband in school and then marrying him within the year after graduation. By now I'm sure she'd expected to have kids in middle school instead of still being single."

"But Kevin St. John," Lucinda said with a wince. "That's really desperate."

By the time the manager and my schoolmate returned with trays of wineglasses, I'd gotten everyone situated and suggested they grab their tote bags and take out their work. Everyone complied but Vanessa. The wine was handed out and Vanessa proposed a toast. "To us ballers," she said with a mischievous chuckle.

After a few sips, I suggested they keep the wine away from the yarn, and they used the lamp tables at either end of the couches. There was some concern about not mixing up the glasses, but it was easily solved when Courtney and Lauren put their white wine spritzers on tables at the opposite side of the couch. Lucinda put hers on a separate table. Vanessa's white zin was actually pink and she set hers next to Elizabeth's deep red merlot.

"Shall we begin," I said, pointing to the projects on the table. Only Lucinda grabbed her needles and began to knit. The others just stared and I realized Lauren wasn't the only one who'd already forgotten what they'd learned. I regretted not having Crystal make an appearance, but it was too late to get her to come over.

"It looks like it's you and me," I said to Lucinda.

"Just tell me what to do." She put down her work and smiled.

Neither of us were skilled knitters, but then this was so basic, we could handle it. I did a brief demo and then Lucinda and I circulated through the group, helping them individually. Vanessa seemed uninterested and her needles and few rows of knitting were sitting on the table next to her tote bag.

"Thank heavens for the wine," Vanessa said, grabbing her glass of pink wine and taking a generous sip. "The offer's still good about forgetting this yarn stuff and letting me buy you all scarves."

Lauren gave our wealthy Baller-rina a disparaging shake of her head. "You just don't get it. Whatever you would buy wouldn't be the same. These scarves truly will be souvenirs of our time together. And there's something special about a handmade piece."

"Oh, save us your preaching," Vanessa said in an annoyed tone. "You don't really think we'll finish these scarves. Then the souvenir of the weekend will be a bunch of tangled yarn."

"You're sure cross," Elizabeth said. "Maybe this place isn't the Ritz, but the point was for us to get together

"Well, at least this wine is good and has quite a kick," she said, beginning to slur her words. She reached for her glass of wine. I mentioned that it was probably local and that one of the things I'd planned was a wine tasting at a local winery, which of course she would have known if she'd looked at the schedule.

"Now that's something I can get behind," Vanessa said, replacing her glass. "I hope they ship. You all have no idea how much stress I'm under."

I was thinking about how I could slip away unnoticed to go do my baking. I decided to wait until they left for the roast and toast. It would be easy for me to just go out the other door by the driveway and get my car and baking stuff. In the meantime, I sought a moment of respite in the ladies' room. I wondered if the weekend would bring the group closer together. And it was stupid of me to think that they'd just take to knitting. Courtney was too upset that she was cut off from her work. Elizabeth seemed intent on putting the moves on Kevin. Vanessa was right—Lauren was a little preachy and she did seem to see herself as the light in a dark world. And who had invited Zak and why?

I had the ladies' room to myself and took my time washing my hands and finger combing my hair. Finally accepting I couldn't stall anymore, I went back into the main room.

Kevin St. John was working the room, playing the host and talking to the guests. In no time he would work his way back to my group. Then Vanessa would start complaining and Elizabeth would throw herself at him again. Courtney would probably chime in about how busy the phone booths were. I was trying to think of a way to divert him when I noticed the tall skinny desk clerk sliding over the wooden counter. He rushed toward the manager, frantically waving the cordless. Kevin St. John's lips were in an annoyed slash as he went toward the clerk.

The clerk seemed very upset as he pushed the phone on Kevin, and as the manager held the phone to his ear I watched his usually impassive face explode as he looked around the room. I saw his gaze stop under the window on the driveway side of the room not far from where I was standing. A colorful recycled grocery bag was sitting alone with smoke billowing out of the top and the distinct sound of a timer clicking off the seconds.

Kevin banged the phone on the wood counter. "Everybody out," he yelled. "Use the door that leads to the deck and head to the beach."

"We're in the middle of a hand," a man said from one of the tables.

"Get out now and keep going," Kevin bellowed. I made a move to get back to my group, but the rush of people heading to the door carried me with them and I had no choice but to go along. When we got outside, Kevin yelled to keep going and to get as far away as possible. "There's a bomb," he screamed. "It's going to blow."

In the dark it was hard to see who was who and we all rumbled over the boardwalk through the dunes, crossed the street and stepped on to the sand. I tried to find my group but all I could see were silhouettes as everyone surged to the water's edge. I heard sirens in the distance growing louder. I finally bumped into Lucinda and we threw ourselves into each other's arms.

She said she'd heard the bomb squad was on the way. "Cadbury has a bomb squad?" I said, surprised.

"No, I'm sure they borrowed them from somewhere."

"Who'd want to bomb Vista Del Mar?" I said, incredulous.

"I was standing near the clerk who took the phone call and I heard him tell Kevin St. John somebody was upset because the place was unplugged and they claimed it ruined their life."

"What's the world come to when people can't survive without staring at a screen. But blow up the place?" I heard a woman say, who'd overheard our conversation. I looked back toward Vista Del Mar, wondering what was going on, but from here all I could see were the sand dunes and the silhouettes of some cypress trees.

I kept bracing for an explosion as we stood there for what seemed like eternity.

Finally, I saw a light bobbing as someone crossed the street and walked onto the beach. "That looks like Kevin St. John," I said as the light momentarily illuminated his dark suit. When he reached the beach, he began to call out. "Everything's okay. You can all come back now, but please go directly to your rooms. The roast and toast has been canceled and the Lodge is off limits for now." He turned to retrace his steps and used his flashlight to direct everyone to follow him.

Lucinda and I moved with the crowd as they made their way back to the grounds. When we reached the end of the boardwalk, Kevin St. John was using his flashlight to direct everyone to the path that led to the guest room buildings and reminding them that the Lodge was off limits.

"Go on and do your baking. Don't worry about your friends," Lucinda said. "I'll play mother hen if anyone seems upset." I reluctantly took her up on her offer and watched as she continued on toward the Sand and Sea building. I waited until the crowd thinned and looked at the Lodge. It seemed peaceful enough, and I was sure that when Kevin St. John told everyone to stay out, that didn't include me. I wanted to gather up all the knitting stuff and put it back in the meeting room for the morning workshop before I left.

I pulled open the door and went inside. Two men were standing by the window taking off their padded suits. They seemed awfully calm and almost seemed to be joking.

"So everything is really okay?" I said as I approached them.

The taller man nodded. "It was a stupid prank. Just some dry ice in water and a recording of a ticking sound."

The shopping bag I'd seen before had been ripped apart and I saw a round metal container with the top open. The effects of the dry ice were fading and there was just of hint of smoke coming off the water. I asked for the details and the other bomb guy explained.

"There's nothing to worry about—it's just carbon dioxide," the other man said at the end. They went back to packing up their gear and I moved on to the seating area.

In the rush to get out of there, my people had thrown their knitting on the coffee table and the stitches had slipped off the needles. All the balls of yarn had gotten thrown together and it was a terrible tangled mess. I was trying to think of how to transport it all back to the meeting room, and was so wrapped up in trying to figure how I was going to undo the disaster that I almost tripped as I stepped on something soft. When I looked down, I saw it was an arm encased in yellow and orange silk. I rushed to move the coffee table and saw Vanessa was sprawled on the ground.

Chapter Nine

"I think you missed something," I yelled to the two men. By now the bomb squad guys had stripped down to their uniforms and they double-timed it over to where I was standing.

"Geez Louise," the tall cop said. "What happened to her? We thought everyone evacuated."

"Maybe she drank too much wine or she tripped and hit her head when everybody ran out," I said. I started explaining about the retreat and that she was an old friend and that I'd been pushed out the door before I could get to my group. They pretty much ignored me as one of them checked her pulse while the other one used his radio to call the paramedics.

The good news was she still was breathing and the paramedics had just left, so it didn't take long for them to return.

I kept hoping she would suddenly sit up and wonder what had happened. But she didn't, and after some checking, the paramedics loaded her on a gurney and took her back to their rig. I couldn't let her go alone, so I grabbed my retreat tote bag and got in the back of the ambulance. One of the paramedics drove, while the other sat next to her monitoring her vitals. I sat on a bench on the other side of the back area. My stomach roiled and I felt nauseous as the rig rolled down the road. Not only was I worried about Vanessa, but the ride was amazingly rough. You'd think they'd put extra shock absorbers in something that was ferrying sick people.

They took Vanessa in through the ER door and I went into the small lobby. I'd had the forethought to grab my folders of information and was able to give the clerk Vanessa's emergency contact information. Then the waiting began. The hospital was small and the waiting room empty. There was a row of chairs and a stack of out-of-date magazines. A TV was turned to WNN with no sound and it was too small to read the captions.

After what seemed like eternity, the doctor came out. He was wearing a white coat over mint green scrubs. He looked like somebody who spent a lot of time outdoors, and despite the late hour seemed wide awake.

"I'm Casey Feldstein," I said, holding out my hand.

"Dr. Mark Gendel," he said, holding out his as he looked at my face rather intently.

His face broke into a smile. "I know who you are—Muffins by Casey, right?" he said. "They're the best. I always try to snag one when I get off of work." He continued to study my face. "And I know you from something else." He furrowed his brow and then his eyes widened. "You were in that magic show. The medical seminar at the Cypress Inn," he said. I felt myself blushing. Sammy had done a show for a medical meeting at the posh resort and I'd been his assistant. "Very clever how you made it into a comedy routine. Nobody cared that the illusions were all pretty passé." I was hoping that his upbeat manner meant that it was nothing serious with Vanessa.

"So, will she be able to leave with me?" I asked. His pleasant expression faded into somber and he shook his head.

"I'm afraid it's very serious. It looks like a heart attack," he said.

"What? But she's only in her thirties," I protested.

"Heart attacks can be caused by different things. In her case—" He stopped and let out his breath. "Someone else might not have noticed, but I do a lot of diving in Monterey Bay and I have dealt with a lot of divers. When I was listening to her heart, I heard something. We did some tests and it confirmed what I thought. This is going to sound strange to you, but it seems to have been caused by an air bubble. The technical title is an air embolism." He explained that an air bubble acted like a blood clot and cut off the blood supply to her heart.

"How did air get in her?" I asked.

He shook his head. "It doesn't happen on its own. But I noticed there was a needle mark on her arm."

He let it hang there until I got what he was saying. "So you mean that was where the air could have come from?"

He nodded. "It had to be a fairly large amount of air." He looked at me with a question in his eyes. "It seems doubtful that she did it to herself." He explained that even if she was injecting herself with drugs and made a mistake it would have been just a small air bubble, but this was something much larger.

"I don't know. We were all sitting around knitting—well, we were supposed to be knitting, but Vanessa wasn't that interested. She was more interested in her wine." Then I shrugged and explained the bomb threat and that we'd all run out in a panic.

"Except for Vanessa?" he said and I nodded. "She's hanging on for the moment. We've called her family." He looked at me directly. "I'm going to have to notify the police about the air bubble. They're going to want to talk to her—if she recovers." His voice dropped on the last part and he put his hand on my upper arm for reassurance.

After he left, I stood there still processing the information, trying to make some sense of it. Someone has pumped Vanessa full of air? Why? How? The doctor's last comment stuck in my mind. *If she recovered.* She had to recover, I thought, looking skyward. It was only when I glanced around at my surroundings that I remembered I'd ridden there in the ambulance and realized that I was stranded. I called Sammy and asked for a ride home. It didn't seem to matter that it was close to midnight by now. Without even asking for an explanation, he said he'd be there in a few minutes. I wanted to meet him outside so he wouldn't have to go through the hassle of parking, but he insisted he'd come in.

It seemed like I'd barely hung up when he came in through the door. His brows were knit with worry as he glanced over me and I realized he'd thought I'd gone there for treatment.

"I heard about the bomb scare at Vista Del Mar," he said, taking a last look to make sure I was okay.

"It was a prank," I said. "I was here with one of my retreat people." I explained about finding Vanessa and what the doctor had said about the air bubble, since besides being a comedy magician he was actually a doctor.

"It's not something I usually deal with as a urologist." He asked me about the needle mark. "Did she use drugs?"

I shrugged and said I didn't think so. "Well, the needle mark got there somehow," he said.

"Somebody must have done it to her," I said with a shudder. "But it doesn't make sense. Vanessa was so fussy about everything, I can't believe she'd let somebody give her a shot."

He pulled into my driveway. "Case, try to get some sleep. I need you rested and in tip-top form for the show on Sunday."

I thanked him for the ride as I got out.

"Any time," he said with a soft smile.

I looked down as I walked to my door. If only I felt the same way about him that Sammy felt about me. I cared about him, I really did, but there just wasn't any chemistry.

Julius was watching from the window. He'd become my greeter and it was nice to have someone happy to see me when I got home, even if I sometimes thought it was only because I handed out stink fish.

I had my hand on the handle and was about to unlock the door, when I remembered the mess of yarn. No matter what, I still had the retreat to run. I stopped in the guest house and grabbed the handle of a rolling plastic bin, figuring I could load it all in there and went across the street. The big silence of night had fallen over Vista Del Mar and the clatter of the wheels echoed as I went up the driveway. Most of the lights were out in the buildings with the guest rooms, but as always the lights were on in the Lodge. And after what Dr. Gendel had said about the air in Vanessa's heart, I thought it wouldn't hurt to have a look around.

Despite what Kevin had said about the Lodge being off limits, the door was unlocked and there was a clerk behind the desk. Well, sitting there with his head down. I cleared my throat a few times loudly and he snapped to attention, looking a little bewildered and maybe a little freaked out.

"You don't have a bomb or anything?" he asked nervously, looking at the bin I'd brought for the yarn.

"Of course not," I said. "We've never met, but I'm sure you've seen me around. I live across the street and I put on yarn retreats here." I pointed to the bin. "That's why I'm here. My people left their yarn and needles. I want to collect them for our morning workshop." I glanced around the large room. Everything was as it had been before we left for the hospital, except all evidence of the fake bomb was gone.

"I don't know," he said. "Mr. St. John said I was only supposed to let people in if they had to use the phone booths or if they needed something."

"Well, that covers me. I need to get this yarn out of here." I pointed at the mess on the coffee table. "Where's Kevin?" I said, looking around as if I was implying he'd say it was okay. The clerk blanched at hearing the manager referred to by his first name. I never called him Kevin to his face. He insisted on being called by his last name, as he thought befitted his position.

"He went home just when I got here. He was all upset about the fake bomb and then some woman hit her head or something. I heard him trying to get the details and nobody seemed to know her name. I think he's worried she'll sue."

The clerk looked at the bin and shrugged. "I guess it's all right to let you get your stuff," he said finally. "Since you sort of work here." He looked around at the mess in the gathering place. Board games were still set up and playing cards were scattered around. "I suppose I should straighten up," he said half-heartedly.

I offered to help him, which wasn't exactly altruistic. It gave me an excuse to have a look around. While he picked up the Monopoly board and gathered all the fake money and pieces, I went to the area my group had been in. The wineglasses were still on the end tables and the yarn and knitting needles were spread over the coffee table.

I kept thinking of what Sammy had said. That if Vanessa hadn't injected herself, someone else had. How could that have happened? I couldn't picture her being a willing participant. She had to have been passed out. I remembered how she'd said something about the wine having a kick and she'd gotten kind of slurry when she'd barely drunk half a glass of the wine. It hadn't registered then, but for someone who so obviously drank a lot of wine, feeling something after so little alcohol seemed odd. I looked over the four glasses on the end table. It was easy to pick out hers. She was the only one who'd ordered the pink-colored white zinfandel. I picked it up and smelled it. It just smelled like wine to me. I was beginning to feel very guilty for not making sure all my people had left when Kevin announced the bomb scare. There was only one way to see if there was anything wrong with the wine. I sucked in a deep breath and took a generous sip. It seemed okay at first and then the wooziness hit me. I went to put the glass down and then everything went black.

Chapter Ten

I felt something cool wiping my face. I wanted to open my eyes but they didn't seem to want to budge, and then with what felt like herculean effort I finally got them open. Dane was leaning over me with a towel in his hand. The smell hit me all at once—boozy throw-up was the best way to describe it.

"What's going on?" I said, sitting up and looking around the empty interior of the Lodge.

"You had kind of an accident," he said, pointing down at my shirt, and I realized it was the source of the smell. "Lucky for you I stopped by to check over the fake bomb scene again." He looked at the small table at the end of the couch. "What happened? Did you decide to finish off everybody's wine?"

I was still feeling pretty foggy in the head and it took me a while before I remembered everything that had happened. I tried sitting up straighter and wished there was a way to distance myself from my smelly shirt. I told him the whole story about Vanessa and what the doctor said.

"I figured she couldn't have been conscious when someone pumped air into her veins. I thought there might have been some-thing with the wine," I said.

"So you figured you'd find out for sure." Dane shook his head and gave me a stern look. "Not the wisest move to let yourself be a guinea pig." He leaned close and looked over my face. "You look a lot better. It's probably lucky that you threw up and got whatever it was out of your system. If there was anything. I hate to knock the wind out of your sails, but you have no tolerance for wine, and between all the craziness here tonight and that it is very late, it could have just been the wine that knocked you out."

"Sorry. It can't be very pleasant for you."

He used the cloth to wipe my face again. "I've dealt with

79

worse," he said. And then it struck me, he probably had. His mother was an alcoholic.

The foggy feeling was completely gone now and I stood up. Maybe a little too soon. Dane laughed as he caught me as I listed to the side. "Take it easy," he said. "I'll get her home," he said to the clerk, who had gone back behind the counter.

"I've got to get out of these clothes and tell Lucinda what happened. And the retreat group." I looked around frantically. My mind had gone back to the wine. "You should take the wine as evidence," I said.

"That might be a problem," he said. I saw what he meant when I looked at the end table. Apparently when I tried putting the glass down, I'd managed to knock over most of the glasses on the table, including Vanessa's, and their contents had spilled together.

"I guess that's not going to happen." I called out an apology for the mess to the clerk.

I kept looking at the small table and thinking back. "It would have been easy for someone walking by the back of the couch to drop something unnoticed into Vanessa's glass. You can't tell now, but she was the only one drinking pink wine."

"Why don't you table it until tomorrow. Hopefully, she'll be up and around and be able to tell you all about everything," he said. "I'll help you get across the street." I was waiting for him to make some joke about helping me out of my clothes, but he was all serious now. He was acting as Dane the cop, not Dane the sort of boyfriend.

"No," I said. "I want to have a look at her room. Maybe there's a clue to what happened."

"You can do that tomorrow when you don't have to break and enter," Dane said, shaking his head. But I persisted and he shook his head again. "Lieutenant Borgnine better never find out that I helped you. What's the plan, we go in through the window?"

"No breaking and entering. I have a better idea," I said with a smile. "But even so, I wouldn't want to get you in trouble with your superior, so you can leave and I'll take it from here."

"No way," he said, dropping his voice to a whisper. He pointed outside and said he'd be waiting. He gave a salute to the clerk and went out the door. I gave it a few moments before going up to the registration counter.

The clerk took one look at me and took a big step back, and judging by the sound of his voice when he asked what I wanted, he was holding his nose. I held up the black sweater I'd just noticed under the coffee table. "It belongs to the woman who went to the hospital and I need to put it in her room." I went on how it was a designer sweater and very expensive. I'm not sure how much it made sense to the clerk and how much he just wanted to get rid of me, but after hearing her room number, he offered me the second key.

I showed off the key to Dane when I went outside. "Being stinky came in handy," I said, telling him what I'd done. "He didn't want to get close and threw the key to me."

"Good work. I'm impressed," Dane said, and we started up the path toward the Sand and Sea building. "You certainly seem to have recovered."

"Except for the stinkiness," I said, making a face. "It might have come in handy, but now I can't stand being near myself." We stopped and I handed Dane my cream-colored fleece jacket, which miraculously was free of throw-up. I heard Dane suck in his breath as I started to rip off the turtleneck that was the source of the smell. He did a double take and then laughed when he saw that I had a very presentable camisole on underneath. I took the jacket back and was good to go.

The lights streamed out of the lobby area of the Sand and Sea building, but all the guest rooms were dark. We slipped in the entrance and across the empty lobby area to the dark hall. I used the key to unlock the door to Vanessa's room. Dane shut the door soundlessly and I flipped on the light. The windows were all closed and the curtains drawn now, which made the small room feel even smaller and a little stuffy.

"This is exciting," Dane whispered. "Better than ticketing jaywalkers and people who forget to pick up after their dogs." He glanced around the room. "What are we looking for?"

I shrugged my shoulders as I took a moment to check out the room. The two slender beds were still made. One of them had her fancy suitcase on it. I stepped closer to look inside and was surprised to see the contents appeared to be all mixed around. I noticed a single no-show sock on the bed next to it. "Aha," I said in a true Sherlock Holmes moment. "Somebody emptied it and then shoved everything back in." I pointed out the sock as my proof.

"Impressive," Dane said. "My girlfriend the sleuth." I glared at him and he chuckled. "Sorry, I mean the *neighbor that I really like and who if she ever is honest with herself really likes me* sleuth." I gave him a good-natured nudge and rolled my eyes.

"There's something else," I said, walking around the small room. Dane followed me as I checked the closet and the bathroom, and when I stopped he bumped into me. He moved back with an apology and a smile.

"I wouldn't want you to think I'm taking advantage of the situation," he teased. "So, what's the something else?"

"It seems odd that there's nothing hanging in the closet or any toiletries by the sink."

"Maybe she packed everything up in a hurry," Dane offered, "and that's why the stuff in the suitcase is such a mess."

I considered what he said and thought he might have a point, but then I saw something that changed my mind. "No," I said. "Somebody else was in here."

"Okay, hot shot, how can you be so sure?" Dane asked. I pointed to the room key on the floor next to the Prada purse. "She had that purse with her when she came to the Lodge. While everybody was on the beach during the bomb scare, someone picked up her purse, came here and went through her stuff. Though it still doesn't explain why it was all in her suitcase."

There was a sharp rap on the door and we both jumped. Dane mumbled something about how he was a cop and not supposed to get startled, while I went to the door and opened it a crack. The clerk was standing outside looking nervous. He glanced up and down the silent hall.

"My shift is ending and I need that key back." He tried to peer around me. "How long does it take to drop off a sweater, anyway?"

I gave him the key and he waited until I came outside and shut the door behind me. I must have still been a little odorous because the clerk walked on ahead quickly and exited the building before I'd even reached the lobby area.

I went outside and had barely cleared the building when Dane came up behind me and I jumped.

"Sorry," he said, before explaining he'd gone out the window. We both heard something rustling in the undergrowth and froze. A deer came out and walked in front of us.

Dane insisted on escorting me home and I didn't fight him since I was feeling a little wobbly again.

"I wonder how Vanessa is doing," I said. "Maybe I should check on her."

"The hospital is small, but the care is top-notch," Dane said. "I'm sure they're doing everything they can." He caught me as I started to teeter. "You need to call it a night." He looked at his watch. "More like call it a morning."

As we crossed the street I looked back at the Lodge. "I didn't pick up the yarn and tote bags. I should go back."

He turned me so I was facing the street and ordered me to keep going forward. When we got to my house, he came in. He picked up the ends of my hair. "There isn't a nice way to say this, but you need a shower and to wash your hair."

"I guess my hair wasn't as lucky as my jacket," I said. "I'll take care of that right now." I told him he could leave, but he insisted on waiting. I returned with my hair wrapped in a towel, wearing a comfortable gray sweatshirt and pants.

"You look like you might have plans to go somewhere," he said, eyeing my outfit. "I'm not leaving until I see you in bed." He realized what he'd just said and got momentarily flustered. "You know what I mean." He had a no-nonsense tone, which I imagined he'd used on his mother and sister when he was growing up and was the one who got all the dirty work.

I mentioned the yarn and needles again. "I'll go back over there and collect your stuff. And help the clerk clean up the mess." He pointed toward the bedroom. "Now you get some sleep."

Chapter Eleven

Julius was my alarm clock. I awoke to his tongue giving my forehead a sandpaper lick. It was all a plot to get me up so I could dish up some stink fish. I usually tried to ignore his maneuvers as long as possible, but this morning I was already sitting up as he went back for a second lick. I'd fallen asleep before my head even hit the pillow, but it had been a troubled sleep as I fretted about Vanessa. If only I'd made sure all my people got out when the Lodge was evacuated maybe I could have prevented what happened.

It was impossible to gauge the time by the light coming through my window. This morning the sky was a bright white, but there was no way to tell where the sun was. The floor felt cold as I put my feet down and once again I vowed to get a nice little rug for the spot. I was glad to slip on a pair of fuzzy slippers. The black cat hopped off the bed and followed me down the hall to the kitchen. In his self-absorbed cat world, I'm sure he thought I was going there to get him some breakfast. Actually, it was more about getting me some coffee. I needed something to cut through the groggy feeling I had and get my mind going.

I didn't bother brewing a pot, but just took one of the tubes with Starbucks version of instant coffee and put the kettle on to boil. Julius was stationed by the refrigerator and perked up when I opened the door. The can was wrapped in layers of plastic and two plastic bags on top of that and still the smell managed to slip out.

"It's only because I love you," I said as I began unwrapping the open can. I held my nose as I finally got to it and took a spoonful and dropped it in his bowl. The kettle had started to whistle and I hurriedly rewrapped and bagged the can and put it back in the fridge. I washed my hands with lemon soap and got rid of any lingering odor. Oblivious to it all, Julius licked the bowl clean.

I poured the steaming water over the dark crystals and the inviting fragrance of coffee wafted my way. The smell alone started to sharpen my brain, and when I got to drinking it I began to feel present in the moment.

Across the street, my group was still lolling in dreamland with no idea that anything had happened to Vanessa. I would tell them about it at breakfast, hopefully with a positive update. I tried calling the hospital to find out Vanessa's condition. No surprise, they refused to tell me anything. They also refused to put me through to Dr. Gendel, offering only to take a message.

The only answer was to go there. I drank the coffee in a few gulps and dressed in a hurry before rushing to my yellow Mini Cooper. My stomach felt uneasy both from my episode with the wine and my unease about Vanessa. Normally I would have enjoyed the early morning ride along the curving road flanked by towering pines, but this morning the twists and turns were only making my stomach feel worse.

A hospital volunteer was acting as gatekeeper at the reception desk just inside the automatic door. I had already figured my best bet to find out anything was to ask to see Dr. Gendel instead of inquiring about Vanessa. It would have been a good plan if it had worked, but the volunteer took his job a little too seriously and seemed to have decided that I was trouble and wanted to know why I wanted to see the doctor. I mentioned being there the previous night with a patient. I watched the older man's face harden and then changed it to say that Dr. Gendel was a friend.

"First you say it's about a patient, now you claim he's your friend," the older man said, eyeing me warily. "I'll take down your name and phone number and give it to him."

"Could you do it right now," I said. "So he can call me while I'm standing here." I was getting more and more frustrated. "I won't have cell signal later," I said, trying to explain my rush.

"Are you some kind of stalker, a spurned lover, perhaps?" the volunteer asked.

"Don't be ridiculous." I tried to keep my calm and think of the strategies I'd used to get people to talk when I worked for Frank. There didn't seem to be anything in my bag of tricks that would work with this guy. I was relieved when I heard someone call my name. But my heart sank when I recognized the voice.

"I'll handle this," Lieutenant Borgnine said to the volunteer as he stopped next to me. He was dressed in his usual rumpled herringbone jacket, and the way his round head almost sat directly on his shoulders with no neck reminded me of a bulldog. Maybe it was his gruff personality as well.

I wanted to think he was there about something else, but he knocked that down right away when he said, "I assume you're here about Vanessa Peyton-Wilson-Ryerson." He never seemed to have that benign expression referred to as a cop face. This morning he definitely had a perturbed appearance. I wasn't sure if it was the situation or my presence.

We had an uneasy relationship, to put it mildly. He'd been a cop in Los Angeles and moved to Cadbury thinking working in their police department would be like retirement since most of the crime involved things like jaywalking or tourists who drove through town too fast. He hadn't expected so many murders, or interference from me.

Probably the hardest part for him to deal with was that I'd been the one to uncover the killer too many times. But on a positive note, he did like my muffins.

"Is she dead?" I blurted out, being a little more direct than I intended. He answered with a somber nod.

"The doctor said you came in with her. He said she was at Vista Del Mar for some kind of event. I'm assuming she was one of your retreat people."

"Yes," I said, noting that the volunteer receptionist was taking in our conversation with interest.

"Do you want to tell me about her?" Lieutenant Borgnine said, eyeing me intently. I wanted to say no, but he'd never go for that.

Now the older man behind the reception counter was staring at me, no doubt waiting for my answer. And whatever I said would probably be all over town. That was why I wanted to keep Dane's and my relationship on the down low. Life in a small town.

"Why don't we move over there," I said, noting there was a small lobby with chairs arranged in a C shape.

"I was just going to say that," he said quickly, and I got the impression that he was annoyed that I had taken charge. To make up for it, he took charge of where we sat and led the way to some chairs in the far corner.

"Have you talked to her family?" I asked when we were seated. He responded with a sharp jerk of his head.

"Ms. Feldstein, I don't need you to tell me how to do my job."

"I was just trying to see if I needed to call them," I said, hoping to smooth things over, and besides. it was what I'd really meant. He seemed satisfied with what I said and the set of his mouth softened a little.

"Her husband was already on his way here. Dr. Gendel contacted him when she came in. I got him on his cell phone in the car on the way to the airport in Chicago."

I imagined that Vanessa's husband must have taken the first flight from O'Hare in the morning. There were no direct flights from Chicago to Cadbury by the Sea, so either he would fly to Los Angeles and change to a small plane or he'd land in San Jose and drive from there.

Lieutenant Borgnine had taken out a pad and pen. "You were going to tell me about the deceased," he said.

"Did you talk to Dr. Gendel?" I asked. "What did they list as her cause of death?" He glared at me and then relented.

"It was a heart attack, but there seem to be some extenuating circumstances," he said. "Now, if you could tell me what you know about Vanessa Peyton-Wilson-Ryerson." He paused as he wrote something down. "Beyond that she has too many names."

"The extenuating circumstances are like what caused the heart attack, right?" He let out a tired breath and nodded. "I know about the air bubbles," I said.

"I believe the technical term is air embolism," he said.

"And that makes it look like homicide." I watched his shoulders drop in frustration.

"Right now we're just calling it suspicious. Now that we've got all of that out of the way, I'm ready for you to tell me what you know."

I took a deep breath and began. As soon as he heard that this group of retreaters were people I knew from college, his expression changed to deep interest. "So what was the connection between all of you?"

I tried to be vague and say we'd met in a gym class and been teammates.

"Teammates, huh? What was your sport?" He didn't have his pen poised to write anything and I got the feeling the question was more out of personal curiosity than anything about Vanessa's death.

"If you have to know, we were called the Baller-rinas and we did a rhythm ball routine."

He actually chuckled. "Rhythm balls? Here I was thinking a real sport like basketball or badminton." He scribbled something down. "And you've all stayed close since you graduated?"

"I can't speak for the others, but I just reconnected with them." It was just beginning to register that Vanessa was dead and all that it meant.

"I'm going to have to talk to all of them," he said. "It would help if you wouldn't make me out to be the enemy." He gave me a pointed look. "And don't think you can solve it on your own. Don't even try. You can't be objective since they're all your friends."

While he'd been talking, the obvious had sunk in. If it was homicide, Vanessa had been killed by someone in the group. Someone who was expecting the cause of death to be listed as a heart attack and therefore considered natural. I had a proposition for him I thought would help both of us. "What about if we left it that she died of a heart attack with no mention of it being suspicious? The killer would think they were home free and let down their guard."

"We," he yelped. "There's no *we* in this." I could practically see his blood pressure rising and I put my hand up to stop him.

"What I meant was that we both have something to gain. They'll be much more open to you if they don't think they're suspects in a possible homicide. And I still have a retreat to run, and it would certainly go a lot better for me if they didn't think that one of them was a murderer." I left out that they'd be more likely to be open to me as well. No matter what I said to him, I planned on getting to the bottom of what happened.

He seemed a little dubious but was clearly thinking over what I'd said as I watched his eyes flit back and forth. When his eyes finally stopped, he let out his breath like he'd come to a decision. "You make a good point about them clamming up. It's not official anyway until the medical examiner finishes investigating. I suppose I could leave it that she succumbed to a heart attack." He peered at me directly. "But I'll still need to talk to everyone in your group."

"But it can't seem like you're interrogating them. It needs to seem like you're just shooting the breeze. You could join us for knitting. It's a known fact that when people get together to knit they talk a lot, and their guards would certainly be down," I said, and he looked like he was going to choke. "Okay, maybe that won't work." I took a moment to consider other possibilities. "How about this: everybody knows that cops are under a lot of stress—you could say that you're trying to counteract it by meditating and that part of your practice is teaching others how to do it. I can tell my group that I've added it as an activity."

His eyes looked like they were going to pop out of his head. "Meditating, me? Have you been talking to Mrs. Borgnine? She's been on me to try relaxing that way instead of a few beers." He shook his head. "No way would that work. How can I claim to teach anybody how to do it when I don't even know how to do it myself?"

I put on a friendly smile. "All you really have to do is go sit at the beach and stare at the ocean. I've listened to enough meditators at Vista Del Mar as they go through their preparations. I can tell you what to say. Nobody knows what you're really thinking about while you're sitting in the sand. And the walk to and from the beach would give you a chance to get to know your *students*."

I was surprised when he didn't immediately try to dismiss the idea. "Do you really think your friends would buy it?" He looked down at himself.

"You might want to change your wardrobe," I offered.

"To what? I'm not wearing some kind of caftan or anything."

"What about track pants and a T-shirt?" I said, and he brightened.

"Now we're talking. And when Mrs. Borgnine objects, I'll just tell her I'm going undercover." We agreed on a time and place. "Say, what happened?" he said as I got up to leave. "There were no muffins this morning."

I cringed, realizing I'd never done my baking.

Chapter Twelve

The hospital volunteer gave me a steely look as I left. I'm sure he was disappointed that he didn't get to hear our whole conversation. I was glad that Lieutenant Borgnine was being so reasonable this time. He said he would ask Dr. Gendel to keep the air bubble story to himself for now. I supposed it was understandable that I'd forgotten about the Blue Door's desserts and the muffins for the town's coffee spots, but it still upset me. It had never happened before.

I sat in my car and made a bunch of apologetic phone calls to the coffee places who'd been expecting muffins, and my final call was to Tag about the Blue Door desserts. I was worried how he would take it since anything out of order seemed to push him close to the edge. It turned out not to be a problem. Word of the bomb scare had already spread around Cadbury and he was in a panic about Lucinda.

"I don't know what I would do if something happened to her," he said in a frantic voice. I had to reassure him that his wife was fine and there was no need to go to Vista Del Mar to make sure. Thank heavens word about Vanessa hadn't reached him or he really would have been upset. I promised him I'd tell Lucinda to call him. We worked out the dessert situation. He'd get ice cream from a local place that made their own so he could legitimately call the dessert handmade.

I spent the whole drive back to Vista Del Mar practicing what I would say to the group about Vanessa and how I would try to save the weekend. Lieutenant Borgnine had admonished me not to try to solve the mystery of who had injected Vanessa with the air and I hadn't argued, so he probably thought I was agreeing. But of course, I wasn't. Let him talk to them one by one, but I'd have them for the rest of the weekend.

I detoured home before going to Vista Del Mar. Julius did some figure eights around my ankles while I picked up the cordless and called Frank. Since I couldn't tell my group about what really happened to Vanessa, he would be my sounding board and he might have some interesting thoughts.

Now that there was caller ID there was always the chance that he wouldn't pick up when he saw it was me. But he got it on the third ring. He'd barely gotten out a hello when I said one of my retreaters had died.

"We're talking about those girls with the balls? One of your college friends?" I heard his chair squawk and I knew I'd gotten his interest and he was sitting up straight. I was glad he was sitting up this time. I had watched him trying to lean further back in the chair as it let out squeaks of complaint and I had this mental image that one day the chair would not be able to take it anymore and would somehow catapult him out of it.

"Feldstein, I can't believe it. Tell me what happened. Was it something with one of those balls? Did she get hit in the head or something? You never exactly described what they were like. Hard or soft?" he said.

"It had nothing to do with the balls. And for your information, they're like smaller basketballs."

"Oh," he said. I heard the squeak of his chair and I figured he'd gotten tired of sitting up straight and had leaned back again. "I'm all ears."

When I'd finished telling him the events of the evening, I heard him chortle. "Feldstein, I don't how you do it, but you get involved in the most twisted situations. A fake bomb, tainted wine and a syringe full of air as a murder weapon."

"Now that I hear it coming from someone else it does sound pretty strange."

"You do realize the bomb thing was a diversion," he said. Of course he was right. I hadn't had time to put the pieces together and hadn't really thought about it. I wasn't going to admit that to him, though.

"Yeah, right. I figured that right away," I said, trying to sound like it was true.

"And all of your ball team are suspects," he added.

"There's someone else, too," I said. "He didn't register on his own. Someone anonymously invited him. He said they promised him a big story." I realized what I'd said made no sense and backtracked, explaining he was a reporter. "He didn't exactly say it, but I think he'd like to move up the food chain and could use a juicy scoop."

"Hmm, a guy in the midst of all you gals," he said.

"It's not like that," I said. "We all just knew him." There was no way I was going to mention my crush or that kiss in the rain. But Frank being the crack detective he was picked up something in my tone.

"You're leaving something out, Feldstein. That cop who lives down the street has some competition, doesn't he?"

I finally told Frank about the romantic moment with Zak. My old boss chuckled. "I knew there was something more." He let out his breath and his manner changed. "So, what's the plan? Did you call me for advice or just to tell me about your latest adventure?" The chair made more noise and I could tell he was shifting position.

"I'm not sure," I said. "I guess I want your advice. But first I should explain that for now, we're going to leave it that Vanessa died of a heart attack with no mention of how it happened."

"When you say *we're*, who exactly do you mean?" Frank asked.

"I've told you about Lieutenant Borgnine before, right?"

"That's who the *we're* is? You always made him sound like the enemy. Well, cops usually are where PIs are concerned. They don't like us messing in their business." Julius had jumped in my lap and was playing cuddle cat. I told Frank about the guise Lieutenant Borgnine was going to use to talk to my group.

Frank responded with a belly laugh. "I wish I could be there to see that." There was a change in Frank's tone and I knew he was getting impatient and an abrupt goodbye was coming soon.

"So any thoughts?" I said quickly.

"If it was me, I'd want to know who invited your kiss-in-the-rain guy. It was an odd way to kill someone and the killer would have to have some specialized knowledge."

"Like a reporter might have," I said. "Hmm. You think that maybe Zak concocted the anonymous story and invited himself?"

"Why would he do that?"

"I don't know." I thought of something else. "He didn't show up for our group activity last night," I said. "Or at least not that I saw."

"Sounds like you're on the right road. Keep it up and keep me posted." I heard background noises like he was straightening up his desk. "Got to go. A new client is coming in. Ka-ching."

Chapter Thirteen

The breakfast bell had already rung when I crossed over to Vista Del Mar. As I reached the end of the driveway and turned toward the Sea Foam Dining Hall, the smell of coffee mixed with pancakes and bacon came wafting my way. Breakfast was my favorite meal at Vista Del Mar, though at the moment eating was hardly uppermost on my mind.

I had no trouble finding my group. They were at the same table they'd been at for dinner the night before. There were no assigned tables and it just seemed that once a group had picked out a spot, they stuck to it all weekend.

I took a deep breath to steady myself as I looked over the group. Lucinda was acting as host, circling the table with the coffeepot. She was perfectly put together, as usual. She'd let her hair go back to its natural dark brown and was wearing it short in sort of a pixie style. Courtney's glossy dark hair had fallen forward as she hovered over some documents. Elizabeth was cutting her pancakes into neat little pieces while her eyes kept searching the room. Was she on the lookout for Kevin St. John, I thought with a shudder. Lauren was the only one who seemed to be intent on eating. Even from a distance I could see her overflowing plate and the way she seemed to be savoring every bite. Zak was leaning back in his chair with his arm over the back of it, drinking coffee and checking out his surroundings.

They all looked so normal, and I was going to share news that was going to shake them all up—well, all but one of them.

"Hey, Casey," Lucinda said, grabbing a coffee cup and filling it for me. She even pulled out an empty chair. I saw her looking at me a little too long and there was a question in her eyes. She knew me so well, she'd already figured out that something was wrong.

"I guess Princess Vanessa is sleeping in," Elizabeth said, looking toward an empty chair.

I could have grabbed the moment and broken the news then, but I decided that instead of just blurting it out, it was better to ease into it. It's what I called *the cat is on the roof* approach. Besides, the cup of coffee I'd had earlier had worn off and I needed another jolt of caffeine. I wanted to be completely alert and watch how they all reacted to the news. Would any of them have a tell, like maybe the news wasn't such a surprise? Or the opposite and overreact.

"You should eat something," Lucinda said. "Shall I get you a plate of food?"

The food was served cafeteria style and one of the pleasures for me was creating my own little buffet, getting tastes of all the breakfast treats they offered. "Thanks, but I'll get it myself," I said. My stomach still felt uneasy from the night before and I thought getting some food in it would help. And it gave me a little more time to stall. I looked back at the table and they were all doing their thing like it was a regular morning. My news was going to change all that, even the edited version. A difficult weekend was just about to get even worse.

When I got to the food line, I saw that Cloris was working as server. I knew most of the staff at Vista Del Mar, though some more than others. Cloris was one I knew better. She was working there while she went to a community college studying hospitality. I could vouch for her natural ability in that field. She knew I loved their breakfast, and without me saying a word she'd already started making a plate up for me with perfectly scrambled eggs, silver-dollar pancakes oozing with melted butter, cheese blintzes with a dab of strawberry jam and sour cream, and a fruit cup with sliced strawberries, cantaloupe and pineapple.

I thanked her, and as she always did, she said, "It's my pleasure," as she handed me the plate to put on my tray. For a brief moment I lost myself in the delicious smells and forgot about the task ahead. But only for a moment.

My heart rate had already picked up as I turned to walk back to the table mulling how best to break the news. Should I say that Vanessa wasn't sleeping in unless they were talking about the big sleep? I dismissed that as too abrupt. I was deep in thought and temporarily lost track of my surroundings. But suddenly everything came back in focus as I saw Kevin St. John had come into the dining hall and gone directly to our table. In a flash, the mood changed and I saw all of them freeze with their eyes open extra wide. Lucinda looked in my direction and put her hands to her head in concern.

I rushed to join them. "I wanted to offer my condolences to your group. I had no idea that you hadn't shared the sad news with them," the manager said in a tone full of reproach. He looked at my plate of food. "I guess you were too busy thinking about your breakfast."

He issued another "sorry for your loss" and patted Elizabeth on the shoulder before walking away. I noticed he dropped the somber expression as he went to a nearby table and greeted the guests. I put my plate on the table but didn't sit. I felt what I had to say came better if I was standing.

"What happened?" Elizabeth said. "He didn't give any details even though I asked."

I was still intent on the cat-on-the-roof approach and I started with my finding her on the ground in the Lodge after the bomb scare. "Was she drunk?" Elizabeth demanded. "Maybe that wasn't her first glass of wine."

"Vanessa might have been into wine *and*—as in wine with something added like a tranquilizer. She said she was under a lot of stress," Courtney said.

"I don't think it was the wine," I said, choosing my words carefully. "The paramedics came and took her to the hospital." I mentioned riding along and then talking to the doctor. "It was a heart attack and I hoped she would pull through."

"A heart attack?" Zak said. "Not what you'd expect from someone her age. But obviously it happens."

"But she seemed fine, though a little frustrated with the knitting. It seems so sudden." Lauren looked at her plate of food and sighed as she pushed it away. "She looked okay when she was making that fuss about getting the wine. I just can't believe it."

"I don't get it. How could she be fine and then dead?" Elizabeth said. "Something must have caused the heart attack. Maybe it was connected to the bomb scare. It's a known fact that people can get scared to death."

"Bomb scare?" Zak repeated. "Is that what all the fuss was about?"

"Then you weren't there?" I said.

He blew out his breath. "Sorry, friends, but an evening of knitting and watching people play Monopoly was a little too slow for me. I caught an Uber and went to check out some of the local color." He glanced around at the group. "So tell me about this bomb thing."

Elizabeth was only too happy to fill him in based on what she knew, which wasn't much. I stepped in and assured them there was absolutely no danger involved with it.

"But Vanessa didn't know that," Elizabeth protested. "She still could have gotten so scared that she had a heart attack."

"Instead of thinking about her death, I think we should think about Vanessa's life and what she meant to all of us," I said, amazed that I'd come up with something that sounded so saccharine. But it worked and they all started saying nice stuff about our teammate. In the discomfort of telling them about Vanessa, I'd forgotten all about checking their faces for a tell. And now it was too late.

Courtney was dressed in the same classic casual as the day before. She had started gathering up her papers and pushed away her plate of half-eaten food. "I'm so sorry about Vanessa, and I guess that ends our reunion. I'm going to go to the Lodge and call about getting a flight." She glanced around at the group and they all seemed to agree.

I froze. I hadn't considered that they would want to leave. I had to keep them there until we, well, I figured out which of them was . . . responsible—it was hard for me to even mentally say that one of them was a killer. If Lieutenant Borgnine heard the group was scattering, he'd be forced to show his hand and insist they stay. They'd all clam up then. Courtney wasn't a criminal attorney, but I was sure she knew enough legal stuff to tell none of them to talk.

"You know that Vanessa wouldn't want that," I said, looking over all of their faces, hoping they wouldn't pick up that I was doing a total bluff. Vanessa had seemed like she had one foot out the door from the moment she saw the inside of the Lodge. If the situation was reversed and one of the others had died, there would have been no keeping her even though she was the one who suggested the retreat in the first place.

Courtney put her papers back down and let out a sigh. "When you put it that way, I see your point. It's important to value what you have when you have it." Her voice had lost its usual sharpness and she sounded almost wistful.

"And to help us at this difficult time, I've added a new activity. Maybe *activity* is the wrong word. A local policeman I know has a new mission. He's wants to teach the world to meditate and he's offered to give each of you a private session." It seemed a little odd to call him Lieutenant Borgnine to them, but it felt weird to me to call him anything else. Finally, I just left off his title. His name is Theodore Borgnine," I said, trying to let the name roll off my tongue.

My gaze went toward Lucinda, who was fighting to keep in a laugh. I couldn't look at her or I would have lost it. I focused on the rest of them. "He'll be coming by and taking you one at a time for a private session on the beach."

I sensed someone had come up next to me and turned to see Dane had joined us. How did he manage it? He'd had less sleep than I had, and yet he appeared all bright-eyed, decked out in his midnight blue uniform. He managed to combine hot and cute in his own unique way.

"I'll go first," Elizabeth said, raising her hand. She was already starting to get up.

I realized that with what I'd just said and then Dane showing up, she thought he was the meditation guru. "This isn't Theodore," I said. Lucinda had put her hand over her mouth to shield her expression, but I could see by her eyes that she was having a hard time keeping the laugh in. Dane heard the name and gave me a quizzical look.

"I was just telling them about Lieutenant Theodore Borgnine's new mission in life. To teach people to meditate." I was trying to signal Dane with my eyes that something was up, but he mistook it for an effort to flirt on my part and rolled his eyes in response.

"Then what's he doing here?" Courtney said.

I was struck silent but Dane wasn't. "I'm Casey's neighbor," he said. "I wanted to make sure everything was okay after last night." Only I knew what he really meant and I offered him a grateful smile. Elizabeth was still giving him the once-over. Zak seemed to be checking him out, too, but Courtney and Lauren just nodded and smiled.

Lucinda circulated around the table offering refills of coffee, and I pulled Dane off to the side. As soon as we were out of earshot, his eyes got a teasing glint. "Lieutenant Borgnine is giving meditation lessons?"

I explained the situation and Dane's expression changed to admiration. "You have amazing powers if you got him to do that, which makes up for your lack in the flirting department. That was what you were doing back there, right?"

"No," I whispered. "I was trying to signal you to go along with what I said."

He shrugged. "Really, that was what that was? We need to work on our signals." My back was to the group and his eyes narrowed as he looked over my shoulder at the table of my friends. "So you think one of them did it?" I nodded in answer. "Maybe you need a bodyguard then," he said, looking hopeful. "Better than my current assignment." I saw a roll of plastic bags coming out of his pocket. "I'm on doggie detail. Making sure everyone picks up after theirs."

"But you do it with such finesse," I teased. Dane was like the old-fashioned beat cop who helped work things out rather than slapping on cuffs and hauling someone into a cruiser. "I don't want to keep you from your work," I said, trying not to laugh.

Chapter Fourteen

The dining hall had emptied by the time my group finally vacated their table. They all needed time to let the news about Vanessa sink in. Lucinda had to get the coffeepot refilled, but their plates of food had been abandoned once I shared my news. As we all finally headed to the dining hall door, Elizabeth caught up with me.

"Someone should call Blair and tell her what happened," she said. I got the message that the someone she meant was me. Elizabeth had her own sense of what was proper and who was supposed to do what. I bet she was the one in her class who told the substitute teacher that they were supposed to get homework. I added it to the things I had to take care of during the free time until the morning workshop.

It was so different putting on a workshop for a group who didn't knit. Instead of hearing that they'd be gathering during the morning free time to work on projects they'd brought with them, this group had other plans.

Elizabeth wanted to send off some postcards. Zak didn't say what he was going to do and took off alone. Lauren went back to her room and said something about a nap. I assumed Courtney was going to continue what she'd been working on at breakfast. Lucinda and I finally got a moment alone. I began by profusely apologizing about not baking the desserts and explained I'd already talked to Tag.

"If you worked things out with him, you'll get no problem from me. And after all that went on last night, it's not a surprise you forgot to bake," she said. I debated telling her the whole story about Vanessa, but decided that it was best to have just one version of what happened out there for now. I told her that Tag needed to hear from her and she nodded. "I was already planning to call." She offered to help me after that, but I told her this was supposed to be her time off. "Well, then, I'll be in one of those chairs in the Sand and Sea lobby with my feet up and a good book."

My plan had been to go straight to our meeting room and try to fix the mess the yarn and needles were in. Dane had been nice to retrieve them for me and I was sure that meant just scooping everything up, which would have tangled everything even more. But now that Elizabeth had brought up calling Blair, I wanted to get the difficult call out of the way first. Rather than take the time to go across the street, I decided to stop in the Lodge and use one of the phone booths.

The last time I'd been inside the Lodge, it had been in disarray from the bomb scare evacuation, and I wasn't sure what to expect as I went up the stairs to the deck and pulled open the door. I was surprised to see how regular it appeared. I noticed a couple at the registration desk. I heard the noise of a table tennis game in progress. Some teens were busy with the pool table. The seating area looked normal and several people were on the couches and chairs arranged around the large stone fireplace. There was no hint now that anything had happened. I stood staring at the seating area, thinking over what I knew about the previous night, and the order of things clicked in my mind and I understood exactly how the bomb scare worked as a diversion. Someone had dropped something in Vanessa's drink to knock her out. Once the bomb scare emptied the Lodge, the person pumped her with the air.

The phone booths were all occupied, so I wandered further into the large room to where the fake bomb had been. There was nothing to mark the spot and the only reason I found it was that I remembered the bag had been right below the window that looked out on the driveway.

If only I'd known it was really a diversion and not a prank, I thought with regret, I would have looked at that shopping bag more closely. As I glanced around I realized how easily someone could have dropped off the bag unnoticed. There were no chairs or tables close by and the way the seating area was arranged, we had our backs to the spot.

There had to be clues attached to the shopping bag. I wondered what had happened to it, since the whole episode had been written off as a prank. Though I imagined by now Lieutenant Borgnine had connected the dots between the bomb scare and Vanessa's death.

I started back toward the front and saw that the phone booths were still all occupied. As I got near the couches and chairs by the fireplace where we had sat, I recognized one of the women I had checked in. It was easy to remember her name since I'd associated it with pasta. Her last name was Noodleman. It gave me a shiver to realize she was sitting just where Vanessa had been sitting the night before. Her coffee was on the end table in the vicinity of where Vanessa's wine had been. I was going to call out a greeting but then had another idea. I went up to the end table and touched her coffee cup, curious to see if she noticed. She never looked up from her book and I realized how easy it was for someone to have dropped something into Vanessa's wine.

I looked toward the front and saw that someone was just exiting one of the phone booths and I rushed to claim it before someone else grabbed it. The booth might have been vintage, but the pay phone was brand new and took credit cards. I punched in the number and waited for an answer without a clear idea of what I was going to say. It turned out not to be an issue, as it went to voice mail. There was no way I was going to leave a message saying that Vanessa was dead. I finally just identified myself and said I had something important to tell her and that I would try again later.

When I came out of the booth I saw Kevin St. John coming out of the door that led to the back area. Cora and Madeleine Delacorte and a man I didn't recognize were with him. The man was dressed in business attire and headed directly to the door on the driveway side. Kevin spent a moment talking to the Delacorte sisters before they parted company, and my detective radar said something was up.

Cora was overdressed as usual in one of her Chanel suits and low heels. Her bubble of brownish hair seemed recently done and I could see the green eye shadow from where I was standing. She looked perturbed, and after saying a few words to her sister, she also headed to the door. Madeleine saw me and offered me a weak smile.

Whenever I saw the two sisters together I was struck by how different they seemed now. Cora was actually the younger of the two, but with her stiff hairstyle and formal clothes she looked so much older and less fun than Madeleine did in her skinny dark-wash jeans and black turtleneck. It wasn't just the clothes—Madeleine's attitude seemed more youthful, too, as she tried to make up for all the years of living a sheltered proper existence. All was not peaceful between the sisters since Cora had always been the one in charge and completely disapproved of what Madeleine was doing. It bothered the younger sister no end that there was nothing she could do to stop her.

It was obvious they'd had some kind of powwow and the timing made it seem likely it had been about the events of the night before. Madeleine's smile had faded by the time she crossed the space between us and she appeared upset.

"It's such a shock about Vanessa," she said. "You don't think that Kevin is right, that her family might sue us?"

I led her off to the side and asked her why Kevin thought they might sue. "He told us and the attorney said that they might claim we were negligent for not making sure she'd gotten out of the Lodge." Madeleine shook her head sadly. "And that it had something to do with why she had a heart attack." She seemed uncomfortable as she looked at me. "Kevin tried to tell him it was your responsibility to look after your retreaters." She went from uncomfortable to annoyed as she continued. "Kevin said we were only there as a formality and that we shouldn't worry our pretty little heads over it because he'd handle everything." Some people passed close to us and I stepped even closer to keep our conversation private. "Cora and I have always let him run things, but are we really doing the right thing? It's all a little over-whelming."

It figured that Kevin St. John would try to blame me. I wanted to assure her that it wasn't my fault or Vista Del Mar's, but that would have required me telling her that it didn't appear that Vanessa's heart attack was natural. I felt bad that she and Cora had to put up with Kevin's demeaning comments, and I had to bite my tongue to keep from spilling the beans that there was help available in the form of family she didn't know she had. But I couldn't be the one to tell her that Gwen Selwyn was really her niece and that my helper Crystal was her great-niece. Too bad because I could just imagine how Gwen and Crystal would take that *pretty little heads* comment.

"When everything settles, I don't think there will be a problem," I said, trying to be reassuring without giving out any information. Her expression lightened.

"I told Cora that you would figure everything out." She reached out, seeming to want to make some kind of physical contact, but she seemed at a loss to know what to do. "Mother always insisted that we behave in a proper and reserved manner. I see people hugging and doing arm squeezes when they want to show their connection to someone. How do you choose what to do?" She looked to me for an answer. Madeleine was trying so hard to do catch-up and she somehow had taken me as her guide.

I figured a hug would be too much of a stretch for her and suggested that a squeeze of my forearm with her hand would be a nice gesture. She followed my directions and it was apparent that she felt awkward, but she managed to do it. She let out her breath. "Mother would be turning in her grave if she saw me do that." She let out a little chuckle. "Cora wouldn't like it either." To punctuate her comment, Madeleine gave my arm another little squeeze. I reminded her of the workshop and told her she was welcome to come.

"It's always nice to see Crystal," Madeleine said. "She's so colorful."

And a whole lot more.

She went out the door to the driveway and was no doubt headed for the golf cart she used as transportation. I went out the door on the other side of the building. There were a few people sitting out on the deck as I went to the stairs. The clouds were like a thin veil and a hint of blue sky showed through, giving the hope of some sun. I followed the roadway to the Cypress building. As before the door to the other meeting room was closed and only ours was open.

A fire had been laid in the fireplace but not lit. The coffee and tea service hadn't been brought in and the counter was empty except for the tin I'd brought over the day before. I checked the contents and saw that there were cookies left.

Dane had left the bin on wheels next to the table and I dreaded opening the lid. The yarn and needles had been a mess on the table in the Lodge and I imagined it could only be worse now.

I ordered myself to be brave and popped open the top. It was like looking at a sea of black yarn with some silver highlights mixed with the giant red needles. I lifted it out as one mass and put it on the table. The needles slipped out and fell on the table with a loud clack. Some of them rolled off and hit the floor. It was going to be start-all-over-again time once I got all the yarn separated.

I felt through the mess and pulled out a skein of the black worsted and began to rewind it.

"I thought you might need some help," Lucinda said, coming into the room. She saw the mess of yarn on the table. "Wow, it looks like I'm right."

"You're supposed to be off enjoying some time to yourself," I said.

"I had enough reading. You know me, I'm more of an action

person." She glanced around the empty room furtively. "And I thought you could tell me what's really going on. A bomb scare, one of your friends has a heart attack, and Lieutenant Borgnine is giving meditation lessons?"

I hated having to juggle the truth. Lucinda still had no idea that Gwen was really a Delacorte. When I had first found the evidence that Gwen was Edmund Delacorte's love child I had kept the information to myself—unless you counted telling Frank. Against his advice I'd finally passed the information on to Gwen. From then on I'd stayed out of it, figuring it was up to her if she wanted to make it public.

But I realized I could tell Lucinda the whole story about Vanessa. The reason for keeping the cause of her heart attack quiet was to help with the investigation, and since I was one hundred percent sure that Lucinda wasn't a suspect, there was no reason not to tell her.

I made sure no one was coming up the path and shut the door to outside. "How about we work on the yarn while I talk." I pulled out a chair and she did the same. I took the skein I'd been working on and continued rewinding it. She pulled out a skein of the silver yarn and began to follow the trail of the strand.

"The three things you mentioned are connected," I began. Lucinda was fascinated as I described the fake bomb with more details that I surmised from what I'd seen. "They used an automated pet food dish. The top of it was set with a timer, and when it slid open, the dry ice fell into the water and began to 'smoke.' And the ticking sound," I said with a laugh. "There's a setup so the pet owner can record a message and it plays when the top opens. Instead of 'come and get your dinner' someone recorded loud ticking of a clock. It was all very theatrical."

"It sure worked. Everybody ran out without a look back." Lucinda had already finished with her first ball of yarn and reached for another. She listened with rapt attention as I described finding

Vanessa in the Lodge and our trip to the hospital. "What happened? Did you think the bomb thing scared her into a heart attack?"

I shook my head and told her what Dr. Gendel had said about the air embolism. And then I added my experience tasting Vanessa's wine. Lucinda winced. "Maybe that wasn't the smartest thing to do."

"It was the quickest way to find out what was up with the wine," I said. "What do you think those bomb squad boys would have said if I suggested they check out the wine?"

Lucinda nodded in agreement. "None of those officers appreciate help from a nonpro sleuth. Well, except for Dane. But then I think he likes everything you do."

"Funny you should say that." I recounted the effect the tainted wine had on me and who had done the cleanup job.

"Like I said, he's enamored with everything you do, including throwing up." She punctuated it with a laugh. "But getting back to when Vanessa was doing the drinking. So you think the plan was that she'd be immobilized and wouldn't be able to evacuate with the rest of us when the bomb threat came in."

"Exactly. And whoever it was could take their time injecting her with the air. Apparently, it takes quite a bit to do the job." Lucinda was a whiz at rewinding the balls. She kept finishing one and taking another, while I struggled along. "There was a certain amount of choreography needed to pull it off," I said. Someone had to drop the drug in Vanessa's wine, place the bomb and then make the call. And they did it right in front of our eyes," I said, shaking my head with regret. "I was so busy trying to smooth over the whole knitting business and everything else, I wasn't paying much attention to who was where. You were right in the middle of the group. Did you see anything?"

A look of understanding came over Lucinda's angular face. "It didn't register until just now what you were saying. You mean, one of your group is the one who pumped her with air? Geez, that's sure not having team spirit."

"It has to be. I don't think there is some random murderer running around Vista Del Mar who just happened to focus on Vanessa." I let out a sigh of regret. "I feel responsible. I should have ignored Kevin St. John and not left until I saw that everyone got out. Now I have her blood on my hands."

"Nonsense," Lucinda said. "You weren't dealing with a bunch of kids. There was no reason for you to think they all wouldn't leave on their own. And Vanessa hardly seemed the type to be knocked out by one glass of wine. Whose idea was it to have the retreat here?"

"I see where you're going. The only problem is that it was Vanessa who wanted me to set up a retreat for them."

"If whoever had killed Vanessa somewhere else, they might have gotten away with it. But with you on the case, they're as good as caught," my friend said.

"Thanks for the vote of confidence. Maybe I should have you talk to my mother. She's still hung up on me getting a certificate from somewhere to prove I'm a professional." Lucinda knew all about my mother's standing offer to send me to cooking school in Paris or a detective academy in Los Angeles.

"Anytime. You're a professional at lots of things. Does she realize how popular your desserts are at the Blue Door? It used to be that people just ordered their dessert before their entrée because they were afraid we'd run out. Now they've even started ordering their dessert when they make a reservation. They don't even ask what it is anymore, just that it was made by you."

"Spoken like a true best friend. Thank you," I said, taking a mock bow. It was particularly interesting that Lucinda and I had become such good friends despite the fact that she was closer to my mother's age than mine

"And when it comes to sleuthing, isn't the proof really in who's been the one to find the guilty party? All I'm saying is that there's a better chance the killer will be found out because you're on the case."

I found myself blushing at all the praise and was a little bit uncomfortable. I ended the line of conversation by bringing up Zak. "We have to consider him, too."

"But he wasn't even sitting with us. I don't even remember seeing him," Lucinda said.

"That's kind of the point." I told her about my stop in the Lodge before coming there. "I saw this woman I knew. Maybe *knew* is the wrong word. There was no one behind the registration counter yesterday morning and she and another woman were trying to check in and Madeleine asked me to help out. I can't believe she actually got me to climb over that big counter." I rocked my head remembering how Kevin had blown up when he saw me there. "But I've gotten off what I was trying to say. She was sitting right about where Vanessa sat last night and she had a coffee drink on the end table just like Vanessa had her wine. When I touched the coffee cup, the woman didn't even look up from her book." I looked at Lucinda directly to see if she understood what I was getting at.

"So, technically someone not even with us could have come up from behind and slipped something in the wine." Lucinda appeared stricken. "I better not tell Tag. He'll freak out and worry that someone could spike my drink or that something like that could happen at the Blue Door."

There was a knock at the door before it opened and Cloris pushed in a cart with the coffee and tea service for the workshop. It was hard to miss her choppy-looking multicolored hair.

"Sorry this wasn't set up before. Everything is a little off after last night."

"Then you were here for the excitement," I said, surprised because she usually worked in the kitchen

"They were shorthanded in the café last night and I'm always looking for extra hours," the young woman said. "It was crazy. It's so much easier when we have mostly groups. Last night it was all individuals wanting drinks and food." She turned to me. "I'm sorry to say it but that woman from your group was very rude. She got very snippy when I said I couldn't start a tab for her and bring the wine to her." Cloris shook her head at the memory. "It's hard enough for me to make it out into the main room to pick up glasses and dishes." She digressed and started complaining that the pool players were the worst and there were dishes and glasses all over the floor next to the pool table.

"Then you were out in the main room?" I asked.

"Several times." She moved the tin of cookies and put the coffee and hot water urns on the counter.

"Then you must have had a chance to look around," I said. "Did you happen to notice somebody with a colorful recycled grocery bag?"

"There were so many bags of all sorts," she said. "I got my foot caught at least twice in the handles of one kind of bag or another. To be honest, I didn't really pay much attention to what kind of bags they were." She stopped and her eyes widened. "Oh, you mean the so-called bomb was in one of them?" I nodded and she let out an exasperated sigh. "Of all the stupid things to do—a prank bomb so Vista Del Mar will get plugged in again." She threw up her hands.

"You probably get familiar with the guests," I said. "There's a guy in my group," I began, and was about to describe Zak when she nodded.

"Zak Stevens," she said. "He introduced himself when I gave him his breakfast even though I kind of recognized him from WNN."

"Did you happen to see him in the Lodge last night?" I asked.

She stopped to consider for a moment. "I don't think so, but there were a couple of guys wearing baseball caps—I don't know about you, but I think hats really disguise people. They throw shadows on their faces and cover their hair." She shrugged. "Sorry for the long answer. All I'm saying is one of those guys could have been him." She put out cups and the accessories for the drinks.

"You're right about hats," I said and recounted how I'd checked in the women the day before who'd been wearing hats and explained seeing the Noodleman woman in the Lodge. "I only recognized her by her cargo pants and rope sandals."

Cloris was close to being finished and I realized she didn't know about Vanessa. I told her, leaving it just that she'd had a heart attack, and Cloris looked stricken.

"I'm so sorry. I had no idea. I didn't mean to speak ill of her." She opened the cookie tin and saw that it was getting low. "Your group must be so upset. I'm going back to the kitchen right now and find some treats to add to your drinks."

Chapter Fifteen

"I know your friends aren't exactly enthused about knitting, but what did they do—have a yarn fight after I left?" Crystal said, walking into the meeting room. Lucinda and I had made a lot of progress getting the yarn wound up, but there was still a tangle in the middle of the table. My helper was already taking off her black fleece jacket, revealing her colorful outfit. With the orange shirt layered over a yellow one it was as if the sun had just come out in the dim room.

"No yarn fight," I said with a chuckle, imagining what that would look like, "but something did happen— "

"You mean the prank bomb threat?" Crystal said, pulling out one of the chairs. "I stopped for coffee at Maggie's and heard someone talking about it."

"Life in a small town," I said. "So much for Kevin St. John's desire to make it seem like it never happened." Crystal went to pull a ball of yarn out of the mess and I explained I'd been having an impromptu knitting event in the Lodge when we were ordered to evacuate.

"Now I understand." She began working with the yarn she'd pulled out and was like a speed demon when it came to untangling the skein from the mess.

"Did whoever happen to mention anything else happening?" I said.

"You mean there's more?" She'd finished with the first ball and grabbed another. I told her the edited version of what happened to Vanessa and Crystal was stunned. "That's scary. Someone our age has a heart attack and dies. That's it, I'm becoming a vegan." Crystal picked right up on the woes Vanessa's death could cause Vista Del Mar, and I so wanted to tell her Madeleine seemed flummoxed by it all and might be very glad to hear there were some more Delacortes to offer support. But with Lucinda there, I couldn't.

Once Crystal started working on the yarn mess we really made progress, and I was just finishing with the last ball of yarn, when Lauren stuck her head in. "Am I too early?" she asked, seeing the mostly empty room. By now the large red needles were all in a row and the yarn was neatly wound and arranged in piles of plain black, black eyelash and silver. "We're still having the workshop, aren't we?" Her usually peppy voice sounded a little weak, and she seemed a little all in.

"Come in, come in," I said, doing my best to sound upbeat. "Of course we're having the workshop." I gestured to the empty chairs and suggested she have a seat. She pulled out the same chair she'd sat in the day before and hung her black wrap on the back of it. She had on a gray T-shirt over a long-sleeved black one and it seemed as somber as her expression. She poked at the needles and yarn. "Are we starting over?" she asked, and I explained the condition of everybody's work.

She took a pair of needles and a ball of each of the yarns and began to cast on her stitches. She held up the needle when she finished getting on the ten stitches. "I wasn't sure I remembered," she said with a smile, then her shoulders slumped. "I'm just in shock about Vanessa," Lauren said. "Being a social worker, I've had to deal with all kinds of bad situations, but it's different when it's someone you know." There wasn't a trace of brightness on her cute features. "Vanessa had all the advantages, a big job, a family, probably a lot of spa days, too." Lauren let out a heavy sigh. "She could have done so much good, but that doesn't matter now." She reflected for a moment. "I feel bad that I didn't make sure she left with me. I'm embarrassed to admit that when I heard there might be a bomb, I just ran without thinking about anyone else."

Courtney came in next. If there was one word to describe her appearance it was *sleek*. Her mink-colored hair hung about her shoulders in shiny perfection without the hint of a split end. She undid her fleece jacket and uncoiled the scarf around her neck. It was always cool there, but she seemed extra bundled up and I figured she'd tried going out into the street outside Vista Del Mar to get a cell signal. By her expression, I guess it had been unsuccessful. She had a zippered folder with her and quickly put it on the floor under the table. She greeted us and then looked at the yarn and needles. "What happened to the scarves we started?"

Before any of us could say anything, Elizabeth came in. She nodded a greeting at all of us and took off her jacket and very properly hung it on the back of the chair.

Zak arrived a moment later. He did a mock salute as a greeting and looked at the table. "So we're going to have to start all over?" He really had the on-the-go reporter look down. He wore a khaki jacket with a multitude of pockets over jeans and a black merino wool sweater. The brown leather ankle boots were scuffed with wear. He still hadn't shaved and the stubble gave him the look of someone who was too caught up in an adventure to be concerned with a razor. The whole package was very appealing, but I also thought it might be contrived. He was, after all, a TV reporter and image was a factor.

"That's all you have to say?" Elizabeth's expression sagged and became what I'd call a funeral face.

"Sorry if that seemed cold," he said. "I'm a field reporter and I get sent into all kinds of situations. There are usually problems and often disasters. My job is to report on things, not get involved." He took his seat. "But I did do a little research, and heart attacks in people in their thirties aren't common, but aren't unheard of either."

"You did research," Courtney said with interest. "How did you get on the Internet?"

Zak chuckled. "No Internet. I did it the old-fashioned way. I made some phone calls to people I know."

Courtney seemed disgruntled. "That won't work for me."

Cloris came in just as he was finishing and dropped off a tray of oatmeal cookies. Her gaze stopped on Zak and I figured by the way she kept looking at him from different angles that she was trying to picture him in a baseball cap. Finally she put up her hands and shrugged.

I went to the head of the table now that everyone was there. "I'm afraid everything got messed up last night and we had to undo all your work."

"How many times do we have to start over?" Courtney said. "It's not as if any of us really care about knitting anyway. And please don't say we're doing it for the Gipper, or in this case Vanessa. She cared even less about knitting than I do."

Crystal had joined me at the head of the table. "I can understand your point. You're frustrated by all the false starts and you don't see the point of it." Crystal's gaze moved over the whole group. "You may not understand this now, but knitting is a good thing to do when things go bad. Once you cast on again and get through a few rows, you'll see that the rhythm and repetition will relax you. And you'll be watching a scarf grow right before your eyes, which will give you a feeling of accomplishment."

She focused on Courtney. "You seem the tensest in the group, which means you'll probably get the most benefit." Courtney rolled her eyes in disbelief.

"I'm telling you it works. It's what helped me get through it when my rock god husband dumped me for a newer model, and my kids and I ended up at my mother's house."

"Rock god, huh?" Zak said. "Could we have a name please?"

"Why not," Crystal said, putting her hands up in capitulation. "Rixx Smith, and by the way, the rock god is in his eyes only. To me he's just a skunk with a guitar."

She'd won them over, and when I suggested we begin, no one objected. Lauren already had her supplies, and since she'd already cast on, started her first row of stitches. The rest of them reached for a set of needles and three skeins of yarn. Crystal did a demo of casting on and it jogged their memories. Lucinda waited to make sure they were all doing okay and then she quickly started her own scarf and caught up with them. Working with the three strands of yarn was still a little awkward, but they all seemed to manage. Crystal shot me a glance and I grabbed a set of needles, and it gave me a little shiver to realize they were meant for Vanessa.

For a few minutes the room was quiet except for the clicking of needles as everyone worked on the first couple of rows. Once they got a few rows done and could actually see the beginning of the scarf hanging off the needle, everything smoothed out.

The conversation began to flow. Everyone helped themselves to the hot drinks and cookies. I was relieved to see that the mood they'd come in with had lifted.

And then Lieutenant Borgnine showed up. Or should I say Theodore. Gone were the rumpled jacket and slacks, replaced by blue track pants with a white stripe going down the side and a plain navy blue T-shirt with a zippered sweatshirt jacket on top. You know the saying that clothes make the man. Maybe for someone else, but not for him. The casual attire didn't soften his look at all or make it seem like his head wasn't sitting right on his shoulders.

"Remember I mentioned the meditation lessons?" I saw them looking at him with confusion. I almost choked as I introduced him as Theodore Borgnine with no reminder that he was a cop.

He did his best to put on a friendly smile, which actually looked more like a snarl. "You can call me Theo." He let his gaze move over the group as he put his hands together in a prayer posture and then bowed his head. "Namaste." It was a common yoga greeting and something I never expected to come from his mouth. They all mumbled "Namaste" back to him, including Lucinda, who was back to biting her lip to keep from cracking up.

"Meditation is helpful in all sorts of circumstances. I'm sure you'll find this lesson very useful in this difficult time," he continued. He sounded a little stiff, as if it was something he'd lifted from a book. My eyes were flitting back and forth between him and my friends, trying to read their reactions. None of them seemed enthused and Zak appeared downright wary.

"So who wants to be first?" he said, moving his gaze over the group. I noticed that Elizabeth didn't rush to raise her hand this time. Actually, nobody made a move. "I'll pick then." He pointed to Courtney. "How about you?"

She looked to me for approval and I urged her to go.

"She's coming back, right?" Elizabeth said. "I mean, who would have figured that something would happen to Vanessa." We were all watching through the window as the lieutenant and Courtney walked down the path toward the dunes.

"Of course," I said. Everyone but Zak went back to their knitting. He kept his eyes on the window for a long time, as if he was thinking about something.

Courtney returned just as our workshop time was ending. Elizabeth seemed relieved to see her come back and everyone wanted to know how it had gone.

"Okay, I guess. We sat on the beach and he told me to close my eyes and keep saying *om* to myself. He's pretty nosy, though. All the way to the beach and back he kept asking me questions about myself and how I knew Vanessa."

She took her seat and went to pick up her knitting, but Crystal told her to leave it for now.

"It's always better not to leave your knitting in the middle of a row." She suggested the rest of them finish a row and then pack up their work.

Zak held up his knitting to show it off. "It's not something I would wear," he joked. "But it's still pretty impressive if I say so myself. I can add knitter to my résumé now." He was right about the impressive part. It was amazing to see how the three yarns worked together and became something new entirely. The big needles made for an interesting pattern of airy stitches that glittered with the silver and were filled with the fibers of the faux fur. Just as I was feeling relieved that Zak was back to being playful, he said something that made me uneasy.

"Interesting about the cop," he said to Courtney. "You make it sound almost like he was investigating."

It figured that Zak might see through the scam lessons. I had hoped not to make a point that Theodore was a cop, but now that Zak had brought it up, I had to do something quickly. "I think it's really simple. He's just so used to finding out about people, he can't help himself. You can't take the cop out of the meditator," I said in a light tone. "Besides, there's nothing to investigate," I said. I looked around at them and wondered which of them knew that it wasn't true.

We had worked so long that it was already almost time for lunch. Crystal left and said she'd be back for our afternoon session. The group scattered and we agreed to meet in the dining hall. I went down the path toward the main part of Vista Del Mar, or the area I called the heart. The sky had a tinge of apricot as the sun tried to find a way through the clouds. The constant breeze off the ocean kept the air cool.

I decided to make another attempt to reach Blair, and rather than go home I'd try the phone booths again. I had to squeeze past a big silver Legace SUV parked in the driveway near the door despite a prominent sign that said *Loading and Unloading Only.*

As soon as I got inside I realized it was going to be a no-go on the phone call. All the phone booths were full and there was a line of people waiting to use them. A nature walk was just ending and the leader had brought the group back to where they'd first gathered. The seating area was full of people talking or reading. The game tables were occupied and several card games were going at the various tables around the large open room.

It took a moment before I noticed Kevin St. John standing near the massive counter talking to a man. The manager saw me and waved me over. "Here she is," the manager said as I got within earshot. I'd barely had time to give the guy the once-over, but it was long enough to realize he looked like no guest I'd ever seen at Vista Del Mar. He was wearing a blue sport jacket over white jeans, had longish blond streaked hair and wore tan suede driving shoes with no socks. When I got a look at his face, he looked vaguely familiar.

"Casey Feldstein," I said, holding out my hand. "What can I do for you?"

"This is one of your people's husband," Kevin St. John said, dropping his voice to a whisper. "The one who tragically died."

"I'm so sorry—" I began before he interrupted me.

"I don't understand. Vanessa was fine when she left for your weekend." He glanced around with distaste. "People her age don't just die of heart attacks. Somebody was negligent."

Kevin swooped back in. "I can understand how you feel, but your wife was rushed to the hospital as soon as Casey discovered there was a problem. Casey can give you all the details since she's the responsible party for the retreat."

I knew exactly what Kevin St. John was doing. He was trying to shift the problem off of Vista Del Mar onto me. I didn't want to stand there and discuss it and looked for a place to take him. Some space had opened up in the seating area, and though there was no hint there now of what had happened, I knew I would feel too uncomfortable telling him about Vanessa in the very spot where it had all gone down.

I suggested the café and he followed me, looking around the interior of the Lodge and making disparaging sounds just the way Vanessa had. The place was quite busy but I found a table in the corner, where I thought we'd have a little privacy. He touched the cane-back chair with distaste before he sat down.

I offered to get us drinks, thinking along the lines of a couple of cups of coffee. Instead he asked for a ridiculously customized drink. *Really?* Two shots of espresso with three tablespoons of steamed one percent milk and sprinkled with a teaspoon of cocoa powder and cinnamon blended together? The only good part of his ridiculous order was that it gave me some time to think while Stan made it.

The first thought that came to mind was that he should probably be added to the suspect list. It was common knowledge that spouses were number one in that area, and even though it appeared that he'd only recently arrived, I knew that the contact number Vanessa had left was his cell phone. Lieutenant Borgnine had mentioned reaching him in his car as he was on his way to the airport. But who knew if that was true or where he'd really been when he'd gotten the call from the hospital.

I kept referring to him as *him* in my mind and realized he'd never given me his name. Vanessa had still been going by her maiden name for obvious reasons since all the car dealerships were Peyton something or other. I tried to remember the mouthful of last names Lieutenant Borgnine had used for Vanessa since the last one was his, but I came up empty. And Vanessa had never referred to him by name, just number.

As I moved up in the line, I glanced back at Vanessa's husband. He'd taken out his cell phone and was looking at the screen with a confused expression. I was sure he'd just discovered that there was no signal. I tried to remember what Vanessa had said about him.

I thought she'd made him sound like a house-husband and said that he took care of her daughter. So, she was the money, but looking at his clothes and manner, it was obvious he enjoyed the perks. Then my mind flitted to what he could gain if she died. There was probably a prenup, so he wouldn't inherit the works, but he could have a nice insurance policy. Maybe he was tired of being Mr. Vanessa.

One thing I knew from the past and what I'd seen recently, Vanessa had to be in charge. Even with the Baller-rinas. She'd insisted on all the extra practices at her house and even been the one to come up with our lame *Westside Story* routine.

The order for his lah-di-dah espresso drink and my black coffee was finally ready. When I turned to go back to the table, I saw someone sitting in my seat. As I got closer, I saw that it was Elizabeth and she appeared stunned.

"*You're* Vanessa's husband," she shrieked.

Seeing them together jogged my memory and the pieces fell into place. I had to change his look to scruffy jeans and long dark hair, along with knocking off a few years before I recognized him as the guy Elizabeth had so proudly introduced as her boyfriend back in college. It was in our senior year and she had confided to us that all the signs were there and she expected to be engaged before graduation. Typical Elizabeth had everything already planned out. They'd have a small wedding, but we'd all be her bridesmaids.

The *everything* went way beyond the wedding. She'd picked out the perfect place for them to live. It had reasonable rent, a view of Lake Michigan and a good address. He was a business major and she was already planning how she'd help him set up job interviews. She never said it, but I'm sure she had come up with a timeline of when they'd buy a house and have kids.

I had to search my mind to remember why that hadn't all happened. And then I got a mental picture of a rainy night at a downtown restaurant that had become our hangout. Elizabeth was in tears telling us that they'd broken up and that after graduation he was going off to travel—alone.

Now I knew his name was Michael Ryerson and could stop mentally referring to him as *him*. I reached the table and put the drinks down. I didn't know what to say and finally came up with the lamest of statements: "Small world, isn't it?"

Michael narrowed his eyes and reached for his drink. For the first time I got a good look at his face and noted that his had the same glossy, polished appearance that Vanessa's had, which I assumed came from getting a lot of facials.

Elizabeth pushed the chair back and got up. "I can't believe that she bought you." She sounded angry, hurt and rather theatrical.

I reclaimed my seat and Elizabeth left. "I thought she knew. I thought Vanessa told all of you we were married," Michael said, watching her go.

I tested my coffee to make sure it wasn't too hot and then took a sip. "I didn't know, though I can't speak for the others."

"Well, Blair certainly knew," he said. "She must be crushed about Vanessa."

"I'm sure she will be when she hears." I explained about not being able to talk to her yet.

"I thought she was here," he said, instinctively looking around, as if she'd pop from behind a table.

"She was a last-minute no-show." Then I had an idea. "It sounds like she was a lot closer to Vanessa and you than to me. Maybe it would be better if you called her."

"I'm sure she'd take it better coming from you." He looked across the café to the path Elizabeth had taken to leave. "What's her problem?" he said. "It was years ago that we hung out." He took a sip of his custom drink. "I don't know what went on in her head, but frankly, I never thought of anything long-term with her."

I couldn't tell if he was upset that Elizabeth seemed angry or if it was what she said about him being bought. But either way I wanted to hear more. It was partly to see what information I could find out about Vanessa and partly that I was just plain nosy.

When I worked for Frank, my job was getting people to give me information they didn't necessarily want to give. I was good at getting people to talk and they often revealed things they probably had no intention of letting out. I wanted to work my magic on Michael and get him to spill everything. I apologized for not recognizing him immediately. "You've changed a bit," I said, making it seem like it was all for the better. I reached over and offered him an understanding touch on his hand. "You know Elizabeth. She's always planning everything out and she has all these expectations of how things should be. I'm sure you must know she had created a whole script for your future together."

His expression relaxed as he realized he had a sympathetic ear and I knew that I was in. "I would have thought she'd be over all that by now."

I nodded as if I was totally in agreement with him. "How did you end up with Vanessa?"

Any wall that he'd had around himself had melted and he looked at me directly and began to talk. "A couple of years ago I ran into Vanessa at an alumni event. She was getting an award because the Legace dealership had donated money to rehab the student lounge and of course name it after them." He made a face. "That's Vanessa, everything comes with a price." For a moment he seemed upset with what he'd said and he rushed to soften it.

"I just meant that she always had a win-win attitude. The school got the updated area and the dealership and her family got to advertise their name and their philanthropy."

"That's certainly a nice spin to put on it," I said. He seemed relieved at my comment and I saw him let his breath out.

"I'm glad you understand." He picked up the paper cup and drank from it. "Elizabeth was there, too. I ran into her when we were both hitting the refreshment table. She really laid it on thick on how great her life was. She claimed she had some big job at a nonprofit doing fund-raising. Suddenly she got all uptight and then pointed to some guy in a suit and said he was her boyfriend and that he got jealous if he saw her talking to another guy. She said something about me calling her and pushed her business card on me."

He shrugged his shoulders and made sure I understood that Elizabeth had probably made up the story about the guy. I sensed he was doing whatever he could to discredit her because of what she'd said. And I also suspected it was the truth

"I went up to congratulate Vanessa after she got the award and we got talking. We ended up going out for a drink and we hit it off right away. She was recently divorced and looking for some company. I was between jobs and had some time." He stopped himself. "She didn't buy me. We came to an arrangement. You probably know she wasn't one of those people to give it all up for love. Everything for her was about that car dealership and proving herself to her father. He's real old-school and had a hard time accepting that a woman could run a dealership. Even after everything she's done, he still held back on making her president. She was so sure she'd figured out how to finally make him see her worth."

I was listening to what he said, but maybe even more to how he said it. He seemed awfully controlled for someone whose wife had suddenly died. And then his conversation made an abrupt turn and I wondered if somehow he'd been able to read what I was thinking.

"I don't know why I'm going on about Elizabeth and the car dealership. I want to know what happened to Vanessa. I keep getting double-talk. I was told she died from a heart attack, but the cause of death hadn't been determined yet."

"When they say cause of death, they mean was it natural, homicide, or accidental. Sometimes it ends up inconclusive," I explained.

"But she died from a heart attack. How could it be anything but natural?" He sounded a little frantic, which I took as a mark against his innocence. It seemed likely that whoever had killed Vanessa had counted on it being considered natural. It was only because of Dr. Gendel's experience as a diver that he'd caught the signs that made him think it was an air bubble.

"I'm sure you're right," I said, trying to sound understanding. I'd found that appearing understanding had worked like a charm when I was trying to find out information during my time as an assistant detective. Well, detective's assistant, according to Frank. Once people thought I was on their side they would tell me all kinds of stuff, usually much more than I needed to know.

I was preparing to see what else I could find out from Michael about Vanessa when I noticed that Lieutenant Borgnine had just come into the café, and he'd obviously seen me. He crossed the room and stopped next to our table.

I had no choice but to introduce the two men to each other. Lieutenant Borgnine's eyes lit up when he realized who Michael was and I was sure he was thinking the same thing I had about spouses being the number-one suspects. But I absolutely didn't want him to start giving Michael the third degree and give away that Vanessa's death was suspicious.

I quickly jumped in and explained to Michael about Borgnine's new mission to teach the world to meditate. "I'm sure he'd be happy to give you a lesson." I locked eyes with the cop, who was back to wearing the rumpled herringbone sport jacket that was his regular attire. I winked a few times, hoping he'd pick up to keep it cool.

For just a second his mouth registered annoyance and then he winked back at me. "I know about your loss and I'm sure some time on the beach meditating would help you deal with things." The lieutenant actually put his arm through Michael's and helped him up and the two men went toward the door. I heard Michael muttering something about not wanting to ruin his shoes.

I drained my coffee cup and was taking a moment to think over what had just happened. Dane came up to the table, startling me as he leaned down to get into my line of sight. His brows were furrowed and he seemed distressed. "Geez Louise, you and the lieutenant now?" When I didn't get what he was talking about, he elaborated. "The winking back and forth. I saw you two. So you're trying to use the flirting thing on him now and he fell for it?" He rocked his head with dismay.

Before I could say anything, he continued. "Neither one of you are any good at it either. You two couldn't have been more obvious."

I looked to see if Dane was teasing, but he seemed genuinely upset. "You need to let me explain," I said. "But not here." I didn't feel comfortable talking in the café. Even though there was no one around from my group, someone could show up without me realizing it. I stood up and grabbed the two cups off the table and suggested we go for a walk. And maybe I had an ulterior motive.

"Sounds good to me," Dane said. His face had softened into a smile. It was lucky that Dane was a small-town cop. He'd never mastered the bland cop face any more than Lieutenant Borgnine had.

"Where should we walk?" he said when we got outside. I pointed at the boardwalk that led through the sand dunes and Dane was agreeable. I would have thought that Dane was just a happy-go-lucky sort of guy if I didn't know his history. He had character to spare.

When he was in high school, I gathered he'd been pretty convincing at being a badass while going home and doing everything from cooking to helping his sister get her first bra. Most of the time his mother wasn't there or was passed out from her latest binge. His father was totally out of the picture.

And now Dane had turned his garage into a karate studio where the local teens could train and hang out, basically to keep them out of trouble. He cooked copious amounts of pasta with homemade sauce so good you wanted to lick the plate. I knew about his cooking skills firsthand, as he always left me a plate of something.

As we started down the walkway our footsteps echoed on the woodlike surface. The truth was I'd heard the slats were made of out recycled plastic bottles. For the moment we had it to ourselves, and he reached over and took my hand.

"Hey, this isn't a date," I joked. "You're on duty." I gestured toward his midnight blue uniform and all the stuff hanging from his belt and the holstered gun.

"Nobody can see us," he said, shaking his head at how hopeless

I was. "What are you worried about? Afraid Lieutenant Borgnine will get jealous."

I laughed. "You really think I was flirting with Lieutenant Borgnine?" My eyes went skyward. "I'm the first to admit that I'm completely lame in the flirting department, but even if I wasn't I would never try to use flirting on him."

"I figured you must have done something to get him to agree to the meditation lesson cover."

"Actually, he realized it was a really good idea," I said.

"Then what was going on with the winking?" he said. We'd reached a fork in the pathway. Going straight ahead, we'd reach the end of the grounds and the street with the beach beyond. The other way trailed through the dunes. The boardwalk was meant to keep feet from trampling the native plants that dotted the sand. I pointed straight ahead.

"I was trying to signal the Lieutenant." I explained to Dane who Michael was. "I was afraid he'd jump in and try to interrogate him and I was trying to remind him of our plan. And when he winked back I knew he understood. See, no flirting going on at all."

Dane was back to his teasing self. "That's good news. Because I don't think Mrs. Borgnine would take it well that someone was flirting with old Rumpled Jacket." He chuckled. "I was just picturing her knocking on your door, challenging you to a duel or something."

I nudged his arm affectionately at the absurd image. We passed through the gateway that marked the end of the grounds and waited for a car to go by before we crossed the street. Dane started to go onto the sand, but I held him back and pointed to two figures up ahead.

"So that's what this was about," he said, recognizing the rumpled jacket.

I nodded and smiled. "I wanted to see firsthand what his meditation lessons looked like." We stood watching as they walked awkwardly through the silky white sand.

"I'm not officially a detective, but I do know the thing about spouses being prime suspects. Do you think he did it?"

"I don't know. But he could have. All I know is that the killer had it all planned out. It just occurred to me now that the call for the bomb threat must have come from one of the pay phones in the Lodge. The bomb was a distraction, just like in one of Sammy's magic tricks."

Dane was shaking his head again. "You and magic. How long are you going to keep on being his assistant? You have to know that Sammy is hoping you'll be more than his partner in magic." Dane seemed momentarily perturbed. "It would be kinder to just cut things off with him."

I checked Dane's expression and I was pretty sure he was thinking more about himself than helping out Sammy. Maybe he was right, but even though it hadn't worked out romantically for us, I still felt a connection to Sammy. But I didn't want to talk about it or think about it, so I went back to talking about Michael as Vanessa's possible killer.

"What I was trying to say was that it could have been Michael. The Lodge was crowded. I wasn't paying attention to who was where or even who was there. Michael kind of stands out now with the designer hairstyle and all, but put him in a pair of jeans and a baseball cap and he could have blended in with the crowd. He certainly would have known Vanessa's habits—that she would have wanted wine and the particular kind she drank."

I continued to watch the action on the beach and the two men never sat in the sand. Michael appeared uncomfortable and started to walk back toward us. Instantly, I grabbed Dane's hand and hustled him back across the street.

Dane glanced down at our joined hands. "I can't believe what it takes to get you to hold my hand. But I'll take it." He gave my hand a squeeze. As soon as we got across the street, I picked up my speed and we rushed along the boardwalk to the spot where it separated into the path through the dunes and a way directly to the grounds.

We took the took winding walkway and continued until it curved and we were out of sight. "They must have gone past by now," I said, leading the way back to the main path. "You have to go." I pulled away. "The less any of them see me with someone in uniform the better. I don't want there to be any chance of my group thinking anybody is investigating or they'll clam up."

"Okay, I get it," he said. "And I won't take it personally." He grabbed a quick kiss and got ready to depart. "See you later." He did an imitation of Lieutenant Borgnine's wink and then turned to go back toward the street. I sighed. He was such a good guy, if only I could give my heart to him. I started to ruminate about my history of not sticking to things. From there I went to my standard thought that I was really thinking of him and not wanting to hurt him when I eventually left.

Even I was getting tired of that story. *Oh shut up,* I told myself as I went in the other direction.

I trailed far enough behind the pair that they didn't notice me. I followed them as they left the boardwalk and went toward the Lodge. Michael appeared to be pulling ahead and Lieutenant Borgnine kept talking. It was easy to camouflage myself when they went through the Lodge. The lunch bell had started to ring and people were passing me on their way to the door I'd just come in.

I was within earshot when they reached the other side of the large room and Michael got to the door on the driveway side.

"The meditation was interesting," Michael said to the cop, clearly preparing to leave.

"Then you're not staying here?" Borgnine said. He caught himself as his tone sounded a little too sharp. "I just assumed that since . . ." He let his voice trail off.

Michael glanced around at the rustic room with disdain. "No. I'm staying at the Inn at Pebble Beach." I knew the place and it was the antithesis of Vista Del Mar. It had a posh lobby, restaurants, a luxurious spa and rooms with every amenity. It was also where Sammy was doing the magic show on Sunday.

Michael pulled open the door and looked out at the empty driveway. "What happened to my SUV?"

"That was yours?" Lieutenant Borgnine said, pointing to the *Loading and Unloading Only* sign. At the bottom in small print it said all others would be towed.

He might be a sometime meditator, but he was always a cop.

Chapter Sixteen

The lunch bell had stopped ringing by the time I headed to the dining hall. I never worried when Lucinda was part of my retreat because it was natural for her to play host. In fact, it seemed like it was uncomfortable for her not to play host.

As expected, my group was at the same table they'd been at before and Lucinda was refilling glasses from a pitcher of ice tea. As I glanced around the table it sunk in once again that they were all suspects. Something was getting to Courtney and she appeared frazzled. Her usually sleek dark brown hair had a little frizzy puff on the top, as if she'd been grasping at her hair in frustration. She had papers on the table in front of her and I wondered about the case she was working on. I also wondered if Lieutenant Borgnine had found out anything interesting in their talk. But I knew he'd never tell me anyway.

Zak was eyeing the room with interest. Was he trying to see if the big story he was promised was somewhere in the dining hall? His presence at the retreat seemed very contrived and I had the thought again that the whole mystery invitation was really just a cover-up and he'd planned it himself.

I thought back to him in college. He had always been adventurous and fun, but also illusive. I recognized that it was part of his charm. It was easy to fill in the blanks about him with my imagination. One quality that was real was that he'd been set on a journalism career and had tunnel vision when it came to getting ahead. I pictured him living out of a suitcase with no ties to bind him. I fast-forwarded to the day before and tried to remember if there had seemed to be any special connection between him and Vanessa. If anything it seemed like she was annoyed about something.

Lauren seemed intent on her food. Being such a do-gooder, I could see where she might have some differences with Vanessa. But would she kill her over them?

Elizabeth was sitting with her head in her hands, which I assumed had more to do with Michael than Vanessa. By the time I reached the table, Elizabeth had lifted her head and was looking at her fellow diners. "Okay, who knew that Vanessa was married to my old boyfriend?"

Lauren put down her forkful of baby lettuces. "Where did that come from?"

Elizabeth told them about running into him in the café and then she looked at me.

"You must have known. You were sitting with him."

I had to explain that I'd just met him for the first time. I turned to the others. "The hospital called him last night and he flew up here." I turned back to Elizabeth. "I didn't realize who he was until I saw you sitting there and then I got the connection."

Lauren shrugged. "Well, I didn't know until this moment, but what's the difference anyway?"

Courtney looked up from her papers and shrugged. "Vanessa didn't keep me in the loop about her husbands. I didn't even know she wasn't still with the first one."

Elizabeth slumped and leaned on her elbow. "You don't understand. How could you?" She was looking at Lauren and Courtney. "You both have it made. You have careers and families. I was supposed to be in the same place, too. I don't understand how it didn't work out that way for me."

"You ought to think about what you have," Lauren said. "You have your freedom. Juggling a husband, kids, foster kids, and a job isn't easy." She seemed about to say more but stopped herself.

"Casey's not married either," Courtney offered. "Or Zak."

"Leave me out of it," he said with that disarming smile of his. "With my lifestyle it would be unfair to have a wife and kids. As a field reporter, I'm always traveling all over the place and at a moment's notice. It's hard to even have a girlfriend when you don't know where you're going to be next week."

Isn't that just what I'd thought about him?

"And you never know what's in your future," Lucinda said to Elizabeth. "Look at me. I never expected to end up with my high school sweetheart living happily ever after." I noticed Lucinda avoided looking at me when she said the last part.

Elizabeth appeared to perk up. "You're right, you never know what's around the corner, do you?"

I was glad that Elizabeth had calmed down, but I still felt uneasy about the whole situation. I was thinking about going and getting some food when I heard someone say, "Hey, Case."

There was only one person who called me that and before I looked up, I knew Sammy was standing there. He was tall with a hulky build and soulful eyes. "So these are your college friends," he said, checking out the table. His gaze stopped on Zak, who smiled and gave him a salute as a greeting.

I didn't know how to introduce Sammy. I really didn't want to tell them that he was my ex-boyfriend from Chicago or that one of my multitude of professions was being part of his magic act. "This is Sammy. He's a friend of mine from Chicago," I said finally. I was afraid he was going to add something, so I quickly got up and pulled him off to the side.

"What's up?" I asked when we were out of earshot.

"I was hoping we could get in a practice today. This show is a big deal. If we do well, there will be more like it."

"You really need to find another assistant," I said. "I can't get away this afternoon."

"Doing a show at a Pebble Beach resort is a lot better than table magic on the weekends here," he said, making a broad gesture toward the dining hall.

"Now you're dissing this place, too." I threw up my hands. "I remember when you were thrilled to get the gig."

"I'm still happy to do close-up shows here, but you have to admit it's nice doing a show at a fancy resort." He put his hand on my arm in a reassuring manner. "About getting a new assistant—I'll try, but we work so well together. Like I always say, you're the only one who gets me."

"Okay," I said finally. How could I not help him out? He'd come to Cadbury because of me. I felt guilty about the whole thing. I cared about Sammy. I really did. "I'll try to figure a time. It's different with this group. They're people I know, and after what happened to Vanessa, they're all upset."

"You're the best, Case," Sammy said, giving my arm a squeeze before he let go.

They were all staring when I got back to the table. "He seems like more than a friend," Lauren said. I smiled weakly. I was worried how Elizabeth would react to the comment, but her mind seemed elsewhere and I detected a slight smile.

By the time I finally got a plate of lunch and brought it to the table, they'd all finished and left. Only Lucinda hung around and made sure I had lots of ice tea. "Tell me everything. Any closer to who killed Vanessa?" she asked.

"As you heard, her husband showed up." I told her the whole spouse as number-one suspect thing and that he'd been reached by cell phone, which she understood immediately.

"He could have been anywhere when they called him," she said.

I nodded and put down my grilled cheese sandwich. "It would be so much easier if it was him," I said and told her how uncomfortable it was that the entire group were all suspects. "I can't help but wonder if Elizabeth's shock at finding out that Michael was Vanessa's Number Two was really an act."

Lucinda's eye widened. "And she knew all along. I would say she certainly had a motive."

Chapter Seventeen

When I left Lucinda, she was on her way to the Lodge. She promised to take a break from playing host and relax with her knitting. She also promised to keep her ears open.

I was looking forward to a little alone time as the morning had been intense, to say the least. Whipping up some cookies to bring back for the afternoon workshop was just the kind of therapy I needed. I was already thinking about what I was going to bake as I headed up the driveway. Since time was an issue, a pan cookie sounded like the best idea.

I thought I heard a noise behind me, but when I turned to look, there was no one there. When I'd gone a little farther up I turned again, and this time I noticed rustling from one of the bushes that grew around the tall Monterey pines. I convinced myself it was probably just an animal. Deer were always wandering through Vista Del Mar, along with squirrels, raccoons and rabbits.

Even so, I picked up my pace as I crossed the street. I had fished out my key before I got to the kitchen door. It was crazy, but I could feel someone's presence. This time I didn't bother to look behind me as I rushed to open the door and get inside. But before I could manage it, I heard a flurry of footsteps and then someone was behind me pushing me inside.

"I know karate," I yelled, putting my elbows up, ready to strike them in their ribs. I didn't really know karate, despite Dane's offer of lessons, but I figured it sounded menacing. And I'd seen the elbow move on a TV news segment about what to do if you were attacked.

"Don't hurt me. All I want is your WiFi."

"Courtney?" I said, letting my arms go down to my sides. To prove her point she held up a trim leather case and opened it to show me her slim laptop.

The adrenalin rush was starting to subside and I leaned against the door frame to recover. "You could have just asked."

"I think I did in so many words, and when you didn't pick up on it I took matters into my own hands. You said you lived nearby, so when I saw you leaving the grounds I followed you."

"As I told the group, I'm in the midst of a remodel," I said, trying to explain why I hadn't offered my place. *Remodel* was a bit of an overstatement. I was doing some painting and changing the slipcovers on the sofa and chairs in the living room. She looked around the kitchen, which other than a coffee mug in the sink looked in perfect order. I quickly added that the kitchen wasn't part of it and vaguely pointed to the rest of the house.

"I don't care if the walls are ripped off. I just need some time on your WiFi."

She was already inside so I gestured toward the kitchen table. "You can set up there and use my WiFi while I bake something for this afternoon." Julius had come into the kitchen to see what was going on. He eyed her for a moment before jumping on the table. His tail went straight up and swished from side to side. As soon as Courtney saw him, she shrieked and put up her hands, as if to fend him off.

"A cat? You have a cat. Get it out of here. I'm allergic." As if to prove it, she sneezed and waved in his direction, as if that would make him leave.

"Sorry, Bud," I said, grabbing the black cat and taking him out of the room. I promised him it wouldn't be for long as I put him in the bathroom with his cat box, just in case.

When I came back in the kitchen Courtney had already set up her computer. "What's your password?" she demanded.

I must have made a face at her abrupt manner because she apologized and also promised she wouldn't tell the others she'd come over.

The smile she'd put on didn't do much to soften her face. Courtney was neither pretty nor even cute. Mostly I'd describe her as distinctive-looking and formidable. Her squarish jaw gave the impression she was determined, and then there was her prominent nose. *Prominent* was a nice way of saying *big*. The only touch of softness were the pearl studs in her ears. I hated to admit it, but I'd always felt a little intimidated by her and had kept my distance.

She was one of those focused people who seemed to always know where she was headed. She'd never dithered about her major or the direction of her life. Now I remembered that from the first day I'd met her in that gym class, she'd said she was going to be an attorney.

I gave her my password and she logged on. "This must be an important case," I said.

"I'm sure you realize I can't really talk about it," she said as she continued to scroll through the screen without looking up. "A big client of the law firm is being sued and the other side suddenly is interested in settling. Some new information came to light." I thought she was going to leave it at that, but she stopped her scrolling and turned to face me. "I might as well level with you. I work for the attorney who is running the case. That means I'm doing all the grunt work. He expects me to be available all the time. If I flop at this, I'll never move up. So you see I have a lot on the line." Even when she explained, her voice never softened. I wondered if that was the way she talked to her kids. I mean, how could you read a bedtime story in that kind of tone?

I left her to her work and went to the counter next to the sink and began taking out the ingredients for the pan cookies. After a few minutes of a frantic exchange of emails, she looked up. "So you like to bake," she said, sounding mystified. "My motto is that bakeries are there for a reason."

I gave her a brief explanation of how baking was creative and it was my way of bringing pleasure to people. But this was the first opportunity I'd had to talk to her alone. I brought up Vanessa.

"I just can't believe she's gone," I said as an opener. "I hope that meditation interlude helped you."

"It was wasted on me. All that stuff about empty your thoughts."
She shook her head with disbelief. "I have too much on my mind."
Something pinged on her computer and she read whatever it was
and nodded as if it was good news. "I'm sure Theo was just trying
to break the ice when he brought up Vanessa, but it made me a little
wary. I just gave him the basics, like how I knew her and that we'd
mostly lost touch after graduation. I certainly wasn't going to give
him any dirt."

"Dirt?" I repeated. "What do you mean?"

"I guess you didn't know, but then you stayed on the fringe of
the group and never needed anything from her."

"Needed anything? Like what?" I asked, trying not to sound as
interested as I was. I was surprised by her comment but realized it
was really correct. I'd hung out with them, but I'd never really gotten immersed in their lives. Now I wanted to find out what I'd missed.

Courtney appeared uncomfortable. "It's probably best if most of
it goes to the grave with her." The way she hesitated at the end
made me believe that she both wanted to talk and thought she
shouldn't at the same time. I decided the best approach was to say
nothing and see what happened. The silence only lasted for a few
moments and then Courtney continued without any prompting.

"It was the way Vanessa operated," Courtney began and then
seemed frustrated. "It's pointless to talk in generalities." She took a
deep breath. "You must remember that Vanessa made the dean's list
her senior year."

"She made a huge deal out of it as I recall. Her parents put on a
fancy party. Didn't her father give some kind of speech?"

"He did, but most of it was about his hopes that she'd find Mr.
Right. He really underestimated women in general and her
specifically. Vanessa was clever if not traditionally book smart."

"If she wasn't book smart how'd she manage to make the dean's
list?" I asked. At the time I hadn't paid much attention, but now I
wanted to know.

Courtney looked down at the screen on her computer and pursed her lips as she read something and then typed in a response before she answered me. "Let's just say she didn't get there on her own."

Trying to appear casual about the conversation, I continued measuring the flour and sugar while I let the butter soften. "What do you mean?" I asked, hoping to draw her out.

Courtney paused for a moment and seemed to be having an inner debate. "It probably doesn't matter anymore anyway, but even so you have to keep it to yourself. You know how Vanessa always lorded her wealth over everyone. I heard that someone didn't have the money for a tuition payment and was up against a wall. They would have had to drop out in the middle of the semester." Courtney's eyes narrowed and she seemed to be having second thoughts about what she was saying. "This can't go any further. Okay?"

I had begun to put the butter into the mixing bowl. "Sure. Consider my lips sealed," I said.

"Vanessa loaned them the money. She came up with it right away and their semester was saved. Vanessa was paid back. But the thing with her was that there was no free lunch. Instead of charging interest on the money, Vanessa had gotten the person to agree to write a bunch of papers for her and take some tests in her place. The security in those days was pretty lax and anybody probably could have walked in and flashed an ID card. And nobody questioned how she'd gone from being a C student to getting a bunch of As." She seemed concerned. "But with social media, old news like that could come out and mess up the person's reputation."

I thought about what she said and realized something she had missed. "But why would either side want to talk about it? It would look bad for both of them."

Courtney brightened. "You're right. Vanessa wouldn't have wanted her father to know the truth."

I was pretty sure that the someone was Courtney. Would she

have killed Vanessa to cover up the fact that she'd done Vanessa's homework? I didn't think so, but something she said stuck in my mind. She'd said something about it being best if most of it went to the grave with Vanessa. What else was there?

But for now there was nothing to do but go back to my baking. Courtney was already lost in her work.

I turned on the mixer to cream the softened butter. When I looked in the cabinet for the chocolate chips, I realized I'd left the bag of groceries with them in my car.

I turned off the mixer and told Courtney I'd be right back. I could hear Julius banging against the bathroom door and I felt bad about keeping him in there. I'd noticed something strange about Courtney. She'd only sneezed the one time when she first saw Julius. If she were truly allergic, even with him out of the room she'd be sneezing her head off. I bet that saying she was allergic was more acceptable than the truth that she was afraid of cats.

The sun had melted the cloud cover and the warm rays lit up everything. I was always astounded by the change when the sun made a rare appearance. Suddenly there were shadows and light glinting off of leaves. I was taking my time retrieving the chocolate chips, enjoying the change of scenery, when I saw a cruiser go by and then stop. Dane popped out of the car and came up my driveway.

"I got a call there was an unusual sight in your driveway," he said with a smile as he looked up at the blue sky and pointed up at the sun. "I have a break coming." He glanced toward my house.

I shook my head and told him about my company. "I'd rather be spending the time with you," I said. "She's kind of prickly." I decided not to tell him what Courtney had said. I didn't know what it meant, and while he occasionally fed me information it was better for his career if he wasn't involved in my investigations. I did tell him about the pan cookies I was making and showed him the chocolate chips. "I could leave some at your door."

A voice began to crackle on his radio and I heard something about jaywalkers clogging traffic on Grant Street. "Duty calls," he said, giving me a quick hug. "How about I collect the cookies later?" He jogged down the driveway to his car with a backward wave.

Courtney looked up when I came in. "Your landline rang and I answered it. It was Blair returning your call."

"I left her a message asking her for a good time to reach her. I didn't want to break the news about Vanessa in a voice mail."

"You don't have to worry about it anymore. I told her." Courtney let out her breath.

"How'd she take it?" I asked.

"She was stunned and shocked like the rest of us. I tried to talk her out of it, but she's insisting on coming here to be with the group."

I realized I'd have to make the arrangements since I'd given Blair's room to Lucinda, and I went back to mixing up the cookie batter.

When the cookie bars were packed in a tin, I broke the news to Courtney that it was time to go. "But you'll get some more WiFi time," I said. I had expected that the group might find Vista Del Mar too confining, so I'd planned an outing to downtown Cadbury with a stop at Cadbury Yarn. It seemed like a fantasy now, but I'd thought they might be so excited about knitting that they'd want to make plans for other projects and buy some yarn. I showed her the schedule and said that Cadbury Yarn had free WiFi, after I put her outside and let Julius out.

"Sorry for being so difficult," Courtney said as we went back across the street. "I was able to get some things straightened out. Some more WiFi time will let me get ahead of things." I reminded her we'd be leaving in a few minutes as I went off to the meeting room to drop off the cookie bars.

When I got back to the Lodge, the whole group was waiting outside. I'd arranged for a small van to take us to downtown

Cadbury. You'd think they were getting out a jail by the way they rushed into it when it arrived a few minutes later. Lucinda got in last and I sat next to the driver.

As soon as we got under way, I told them about Blair.

"It seems kind of wasteful. It's a long way to travel and she'll barely have any time here," Lauren said. Then she turned to Lucinda to explain who Blair was. "She's the mayor of a Chicago suburb for now. She's on the primary ballot for Congress." Lauren squeezed her shoulders with excitement. "And who knows what after that."

"You seem pretty political," Lucinda said. "I suppose you've given her your two cents."

Lauren shook her head. "Hillston's too rich for us. But you better believe that if she becomes our representative, she'll be hearing from me."

Elizabeth made a face. "Just like she heard from you when she was student body president. I'm sure she can't wait." Elizabeth addressed me. "Lauren has always been the agitator."

Lauren gave her dirty look. "It's better than being complacent."

"I could pitch WNN a story that follows Blair on her campaign. Women running for office is very newsworthy," Zak said. He had his phone out. "I better talk to her first." He glanced around at the rest of us. "Don't think I've forgotten about you guys. If any of you have an idea for a story, I'm all ears."

I traded looks with Lucinda. If only he knew there was a story right under his nose. It had all the elements. Female tycoon killed at moody resort. *Tycoon* might be a bit of a stretch, but it sounded more exciting that car dealership executive. The audience would eat up the setup of the fake bomb and how she died from being pumped with air.

I didn't notice at first that the conversation had ended and they were all staring at their phones. Even Lucinda had hers to her ear.

By then the van had pulled onto Grand Street. Whatever traffic jam the jaywalkers had created seemed to be gone and we cruised into one of the angular parking spots.

"We're here," I said loudly when the van was parked and no one had made a move to get out. I had to repeat it a few more times before I got their attention. They all looked around, seeming surprised at their surroundings. Finally, they all piled out and I told the driver when to pick us up. Lucinda stood with me for a moment, but I saw her looking down the street in the direction of the Blue Door.

"Go on," I said. "You know you want to see Tag."

Lucinda smiled. "You don't mind if I leave you alone with all of them?" I shook my head and she seemed relieved. "I just talked to Tag and even though I've assured him I'm fine, I know he'd feel better if he saw me in person." She looked at me with a guilty smile. "I know I complain about him and say how much I want to get a change, but then I'm always glad to see him. Go figure." I wished her well and she went off down the street.

In the meantime, Lauren, Elizabeth and Courtney were glued to their phones again. Only Zak was actually looking around. He took some photos of downtown Cadbury while I gave him the chamber of commerce's pitch on the charm of the town.

I pointed out that there were no *ye olde* stores or cutesy shops. "Cadbury is known for being authentic. If a building looks Victorian, it really is," I said, pointing out the large yellow house on a corner. "It was originally a residence, but now it's a B and B called the Butterfly Inn." He noticed some bland-looking buildings. "Those were probably considered the height of modern design in the 1950s." I offered to show him the post office with its Spanish-style white stucco and terra-cotta roof, but he gave it a pass.

He caught my eye. "I'm surprised to find you in a small town, no matter how authentic, running yarn retreats." He left an opening for me to respond, but I just shrugged it off and kept to the story I'd given them. I knew it made me sound pretty dull, but so what. I wasn't trying to impress him.

"First stop is Cadbury Yarn," I said, waving my hand in front of their screens to get their attention. I got them to follow me, but I still had to look back to make sure I hadn't lost anyone because their attention was all on their phones.

Cadbury Yarn was in a converted bungalow-style house on a side street that sloped down toward the ocean. The rainbow-colored windsock flapping on the front porch, stirred by the constant breeze that came off the water, made it stand out from the other buildings on the block.

Zak helped me corral the three women and get them to go up the stairs onto the porch. I'd had other groups who'd had a hard time giving up their electronics, but nothing compared to this group. I wondered if they realized how addicted they were.

"Why are we going here?" Elizabeth said. The rest of them chimed in with the same question.

"Crystal is meeting us and she's going to show you some other easy projects." When they still had blank expressions, I put up my hands in capitulation. "I'd hoped you would all be more excited about knitting and want to know about yarn and other easy things you could make."

"Well, I am," Lauren said. "I do volunteer work at a shelter and it might be a nice activity for them."

"You volunteer, too? When do you sleep?" Elizabeth said. "You have a job, your kids, foster kids and a husband. When do you even have time to see him?"

Lauren let out a sigh. "There are some challenges, but somebody has to care about the world."

"Here, here," Zak said. "Spoken like a true do-gooder." He looked ahead at the store. "I for one am interested in seeing some more knitting things. Maybe I can find a story in it."

Crystal was waiting by the door when we came in. "Madeleine is already here." She pointed through the main room to an area beyond that I guessed had been a dining room at one time.

Madeleine was sitting at the oval wood table making something on a set of circular needles.

Crystal's mother, Gwen, was behind the counter and she waved a greeting as we went through the main room. She was nothing like her daughter. Her socks always matched and she went for neutrals rather than all the bright colors Crystal favored.

The two of us led the way as Crystal talked to me in a low tone. "It's so weird knowing that Madeleine is really family. My mother is sure the sisters would take the news badly, and if we went public it would upend everything with no benefit."

"Madeleine really seems to like you," I said. "I get the feeling she'd like having some backup with Vista Del Mar." I gave her a hopeful look, but my helper shook her head.

"Once my mother heard we'd have to fight to get them to live up to their brother's will, she wanted to drop the whole thing. The only reason she went as far as she did was because of Cory." Cory was Crystal's teenage son.

Crystal sighed. "My mother always said she didn't like the Delacortes anyway." Her gaze stopped on Madeleine. "Maybe if my mother got to know her better she'd change her opinion. Cora still seems pretty stuck-up, but ever since Madeleine started this whole personal remodel, she's gotten kind of fun."

I urged my group to stand around the table and then I let Crystal take over. Madeleine looked up from the ivory-colored scarf she was making and offered them a greeting as Crystal began her pitch. I was relieved when they finally put their phones down.

"We thought it would be nice if you got a chance to see that not all knitting needles could double for bats." To illustrate, she held up a pair of the giant red needles and showed the sample of the scarf they were making. To contrast them, she picked up a pair of size 8s and a scarf made with the smaller needles. The group all chuckled. "And we have a selection of yarns here that you're welcome to try. I realize you're all beginners so let me know if you need any help."

She moved on to a display of some other easy projects and said they had instructions available.

Zak was the first one to the table. "I did some research and it appears that fishermen invented knitting to make nets. So men were the first knitters." He looked over the things on the table and picked up the sample Razzle Dazzle scarf and poked his fingers through the stitches. "It almost looks like a fancy net." It was hard for him to extricate his fingers when he tried to put it back. Once his hands were free, he went through the container full of needles and took out a pair of wooden ones that looked to be about a size ten, and then he asked Crystal for a suggestion of what kind of yarn to use.

He'd broken the ice and Lauren and Courtney grabbed some needles, apparently for different reasons. Lauren was interested in teaching her shelter people, but Courtney seemed to be just going through the motions to be polite.

"Why don't you try something, too," I said to Elizabeth, who was hanging back. She seemed doubtful.

"It's not the image I'm going for. All I'd need is a shawl and a rocking chair for the perfect image of a spinster. I want to do things that make me look sexy and exciting." Lauren nudged her and pointed out Zak.

"I think he has it figured out," Lauren said. Zak certainly had managed to give a sexy and exciting touch to knitting, and I tried to pinpoint how he'd done it. His attitude was certainly part of it. He had a sense of adventure, and he honestly seemed to be trying to succeed at working with yarn.

"It's not fair," Elizabeth complained. "It's just because he's a guy." Zak laughed and Elizabeth continued to look unhappy.

"It helps that he's not scowling like you," Lauren said, which only made Elizabeth more upset. I noticed that Courtney had ditched the needles she'd picked out and had drifted off to a side room. She had her computer open, and by the way she was talking I figured she was having a video conference.

Crystal tried to take back the floor. "These days yarn craft appeals to people of all ages for different reasons. Stress reduction is a big benefit now."

"It's too bad that Vanessa didn't learn how to knit a while ago. Maybe it would have helped," Zak said. The smile and twinkle in his eye had been replaced by a soulful caring expression that seemed a little studied.

"It's just so sad," Lauren said.

I noticed that Elizabeth didn't nod or give an indication that she agreed. Finally, she pulled farther away and dropped her voice. "After what she did, it seems like maybe she got what she deserved." She seemed to realize what she'd just said and apologized. "I didn't mean that the way it sounded. It is really sad about Vanessa. She was a good friend to all of us."

As I listened, I thought of what Courtney had said about how Vanessa had helped her out of a jam. Did that qualify as being a good friend since Vanessa had demanded her own kind of interest payment? It made me wonder if she'd had an ulterior motive when she was so insistent on me arranging the retreat.

Lauren was standing next to me. "Poor Elizabeth. She tries so hard to be perfect, and when things don't work out, she crumbles. I can't believe she's still standing after finding out that Vanessa had married her old boyfriend. Vanessa could really be a skunk. You know she turned Elizabeth down when she tried to sell her an ad in a program book. The nonprofit she works for was putting on a fund-raiser. Elizabeth was depending on Vanessa to come through with a full-page ad. You know, to make her look good to her bosses." Lauren seemed annoyed. "Vanessa gave her a b.s. answer about if it was her money, she'd buy the ad, but it was the dealership's money and the return on the ad wouldn't justify it."

"Then you've stayed pretty close to Elizabeth," I said. It took a minute for what I said to compute and then Lauren shook her head. "Not really. She told me about the program book when we were waiting for the shuttle. Who has time these days? With all those kids, a husband and a job—" She stopped herself. "I'm not complaining," she said in a resolute tone. "The only person I sort of stayed in touch with was Vanessa. I had a client I was helping to get a job and I went to Vanessa. These dealerships have all kinds of frills in their service departments like coffee drinks and snacks. Vanessa came through and helped her get a job doing cleanup around the service department café."

"It was great she did that," I said. It seemed that Lauren was going to leave it at that, but she then let her breath out and turned toward me.

"It was nice that she came through, but she recently wanted something from me. Some people aren't happy about some plan she had for the dealership to expand and they were planning a protest. She wanted me to talk them out of it. I don't know why she thought I could do something like that. Just because I did my share of protesting in college and I'm a social worker doesn't mean I can control protests everywhere."

"So why didn't you just tell her that?" I asked.

Lauren let out a sigh and looked at the floor. "I did try to tell her that, but she brought something up." Lauren's face had clouded. "We all do things we don't want anybody to know about and they can come back and haunt us."

"And Vanessa threatened to disclose what you did?" I asked.

She nodded solemnly. "So I had to go out there and lie through my teeth to shut it down. It's horrible to say this, but as much as I'm sorry that she died, there's part of me that's relieved she's gone and I won't be put in a position like that again."

By the end of the time at Cadbury Yarn, they had all settled down and actually gotten caught up in knitting. Even Courtney finally put away her computer. They all found yarn, needles and a pattern for their next project. Crystal promised to help each of them get started during the weekend and give them help by email after they went home. Always wanting to be part of the group, Madeleine had found some yarn for a tea cozy. She was shuffling through her bag looking for her credit card when Crystal's son, Cory, came in the door of the shop. He had the same curly black hair as his mother and a tall lanky build. He slipped behind the wooden counter and gave his grandmother a quick hug as a greeting.

He smiled at the lineup of customers, knowing the shop was keeping his family afloat. His eye fell on Madeleine and he smiled hesitantly.

"Ms. Delacorte," he said, bowing his head in deference. "Cory Smith. You might not remember me, but I used to work part-time at Vista Del Mar." He appeared to feel a little awkward but continued anyway. "I really love the place and I'm hoping to work there over the summer."

Gwen seemed concerned, which was no surprise. It was Cory's love of the place that had made her consider going public with the fact that she was Madeleine's brother's daughter—she refused to use the term *love child*.

I watched Madeleine's response with interest. She looked long and hard at Cory and muttered something about him seeming familiar. I had the feeling it might be that the teen reminded her of her brother. Cory jumped in and reminded her that he'd helped her with her golf cart when it had gotten stuck. "That must be it. Cora and I have never been involved with the hiring, but don't worry, I'll tell Kevin St. John to find a spot for you." She looked at Gwen and Crystal. "You come from a good family."

I thought Gwen's eyes would pop out of her head.

Chapter Eighteen

"Don't do it, Feldstein," Frank said. "You think you have good intentions, but I'm telling you that you will be sorry." When we came back from the trip to town, I'd gone home for a few minutes, and one thing led to another and I'd called Frank. I suppose I knew what he was going to say when I told him about Cory talking to Madeleine. That was probably why I called him. I knew he'd stop me before I did something I'd regret.

"You've already done too much. If it was me, I never would have told the love child who she was. There's nothing in it for you but trouble. Speaking of trouble, what's going on with your friends? Any closer to who offed the rich one?"

I was going to react to him referring to Gwen Selwyn as Edmund Delacorte's love child. There was nothing of Gwen that seemed to go with that title. Not only was she in her fifties and long past being considered a child, but she had a very utilitarian vibe. She dressed for comfort, her hair was short in a neat style that required little attention, and other than a little lipstick, she wasn't much into makeup. In other words, she was nothing like her colorful daughter with her mismatched socks and earrings. She'd taken her daughter and her kids in without a second thought and worked hard to keep them all going. *Love child* sounded like someone in a gauze dress and sandals who never seemed to age.

"No one can accuse you of soft-pedaling," I said. "I don't know who did it, but not letting on that it's murder is certainly making it easier to get them to talk. I'm sure Vanessa wouldn't look at it that way, but it seems she wasn't above blackmail to get her way." I mentioned the "interest" I was pretty sure Courtney had paid for the tuition loan. "It certainly wouldn't help her get ahead in the law firm if it came out she had helped someone cheat in college. And Vanessa seemed to have some kind of information on Lauren. Elizabeth just seems beyond anger at Vanessa for stealing her boyfriend. Though it was years later." I brought up Michael and reminded Frank that spouses were always first in line in the suspect department.

"I knew that, Feldstein, in fact, I think I'm the one who told you about spouses being the usual killer."

"Maybe you did," I said. I could hear noise coming from his end. It was rare that Frank wasn't doing something else while he was talking to me. I asked him what was going on.

"It's the new client. She's sure her husband is cheating on her. She wanted me to tail him since she's sure their trysts are when he's working." I heard Frank take a gulp of something. "The guy drives a truck that delivers and picks up portable toilets. Talk about your glamour jobs," he said with a laugh. "Got to go, Feldstein. I need both hands to take photos. Some woman just showed up. Oh, no, tell me they're not going into one of the deluxe portable toilets." There was a click as he hung up.

Frank got the weirdest surveillance jobs.

He hadn't really been much help other than to talk me out of spilling the beans to Madeleine. Of course he was right. I would be putting myself right into the middle of a mess. I had to leave it up to Gwen and Crystal to decide if they wanted to let Madeleine know who they were.

It was only after I talked to Frank that I realized how much information I'd racked up in a short time. Something stuck in my mind. Lauren and Vanessa were at opposite ends of the spectrum and yet it sounded as if they'd maintained a relationship. I wondered what glue kept them together.

Julius jumped up on the table and started rubbing against my shoulder, and I gave him a few pats. I was still learning how to be a cat's human and had begun to pick up on when he was after stink fish and when it was affection he wanted. This was a love time and I stroked his back all the way to the top of his tail and he began to purr loudly. The black cat finished by giving me a feline version of a kiss. He ran his sandpaper tongue on my check and then walked away.

When I went back across the street to Vista Del Mar, I barely noticed the change in scenery. I was too busy thinking about having a whole group of suspects. It was still disconcerting to think that one of them might have killed Vanessa. I really hoped that the thing about the spouse being the killer was true this time. I didn't like Michael. It wasn't so much that he'd dumped Elizabeth. That was really ancient history anyway.

It was the arrangement, as he called it, with Vanessa. He could call it an arrangement, but really he'd been bought by Vanessa. I thought back to how she'd never even referred to him by name but called him Number Two, and she'd made him sound like he was the little man, staying home and taking care of things. It all felt so cold and calculated on both their parts. I remembered that Vanessa had alluded to a Number Three, so maybe Michael had really been leased instead of bought. It wasn't a stretch to think he might react if he'd figured out his days with her were numbered.

I had no memory of walking there, but suddenly I was facing the door to the Lodge. I pulled it open and went inside expecting to find at least some of my people. I surveyed the large open room, which was relatively quiet. No one was in the sitting area and the game tables were quiet. A few people were gathered at a small table playing cards, but that was it.

This was the time of day when people were out doing things. Vista Del Mar was a good jumping-off point for whale watching excursions, trips to a redwood forest, artichoke and garlic tasting tours, and trips to local wineries. I took the opportunity to book the room for Blair. I had given away her original room to Lucinda and I couldn't take it back, so this room was on me. I'd gone from barely making anything to this weekend costing me.

I checked the Sand and Sea building next to see if any of them were in the lobby, but it was empty. I looked in on our meeting room and it was deserted as well. I was walking back to the area around the Lodge when a car came down the driveway and stopped. Lucinda got out, waved to me and then leaned in the driver's window to give Tag a goodbye kiss.

She was all smiles when she joined me. "Sorry for not coming back with the group, but Tag was having a problem with the menu for tonight. The supplier got the order wrong and left chicken breasts instead of pork cutlets." She continued on about Tag's meltdown and how it was just a simple adjustment to the dish they were offering. Much as she liked getting a change, she liked how much he needed her.

"There you two are," Elizabeth said, coming down the path. "We're all meeting in Hummingbird."

"For what? I didn't schedule anything," I said, suddenly concerned.

"I signed us up to be on the talent show, and when you weren't here, I went ahead and got us a time to practice. Blair will be here for the show." She turned to Lucinda. "We still need you to take Vanessa's place." After she'd said it, she must have realized how cold it sounded, all things considered. "I'm sorry, for a moment I forgot why we needed someone to take Vanessa's place." Her voice softened, but only for the one comment. "We have to hurry. They only gave us a half an hour." She was gone before I could comment.

I waited while Lucinda changed into her Keds. I hadn't said anything, but she knew that I wasn't happy with what Elizabeth had done.

"She's a force of nature when it comes to that ball routine," Lucinda said, trying to smooth things over as we approached Hummingbird Hall a few minutes later.

"She sure is," I said.

"I get it," Lucinda said, picking up on my tone. "She's overstepping."

"I shouldn't care, but I do. I'm supposed to be the leader. Of all the stupid things. To have the group in the talent show." I could hear the *thwack* of the balls as we approached the dark wood building. The inside seemed almost barnlike with the high ceiling and open construction. For now the center was empty and Elizabeth and the others were already warming up bouncing the balls. I was surprised to see Zak.

"I got tagged to be one of the Balladeers," he said, waving at me.

"It's Baller-rinas," Elizabeth corrected. "We needed someone to stand in for Blair."

Lucinda and I took our place and Elizabeth played director. Between the limited time we had and the fact that no one but Elizabeth was enthused about doing the ball routine, we barely managed to go through it twice. Zak really vamped at the part where we walked in and at least made it fun. I just focused on looking for Courtney's long red nails when we got to the part when the Sharks and Jets rumbled, since she was who I threw to. The trouble was not everyone else threw to the right person and balls went flying every which way. Elizabeth gave a lecture that no one but her was taking the routine seriously.

"It'll be better when Blair's here," Elizabeth said when we were packing up the balls. A family of jugglers came in to take our place and I reminded my group about our late afternoon workshop.

Lauren caught up with me as we were walking down the path toward the center of Vista Del Mar. "I tried to talk Elizabeth out of doing our routine for the talent show. Even if we get the steps and bounces right, does anybody really want to watch it?

"You haven't seen one of the talent shows here," I said with a laugh. "It's more about fun than anyone being great or even good, for that matter." I looked back at Elizabeth, who was carrying the cloth bag of balls. Her lips were pursed and she seemed in some kind of reverie. Lauren followed my gaze.

"What else has she got up her sleeve?"

• • •

The cookie bars were a big hit at the workshop and the group surprised me with their sudden enthusiasm for their scarves. Apparently, the trip to the yarn shop had inspired them. They all worked diligently and even continued on when Crystal packed up and went home. Madeleine was a no-show again. Lieutenant Borgnine gave Elizabeth one of his "meditation" lessons. She was still talking when he brought her back and he looked worn out. She plopped back in her seat and said she'd been a perfect student. We were all still working on the scarves when the dinner bell rang. After a moment of showing off to each other how much we'd done, everyone packed up their work.

We walked together to the dining hall and snagged the usual table. "Did Blair say when she'd be here?" Elizabeth asked as she got up to get her food. I mentioned that Courtney was the one who'd spoken to her and all eyes went to her.

"Some time late tonight," Courtney said. "She went online when I was talking to her and found a flight to San Jose and said she could get transportation from there."

"Should someone wait around the Lodge for her?" Elizabeth said, looking at me.

I panicked at the thought since my plan was to do a little social knitting with them after dinner, make sure they all went to the Friday night movie in Hummingbird Hall, and then slip away to do my baking. "She probably won't arrive until after midnight. I'm sure she can get herself checked in."

"Casey's right. Blair runs a town. She can certainly find her room," Courtney said. I promised to leave a tote bag for her with a schedule at the front desk.

"I'll put in some cookie bars," I added and they all smiled.

Because of everything that had happened the night before, I'd moved our social knitting to the lobby of the Sand and Sea building and I'd gotten Crystal to stop by. It was the perfect setting with the wing chairs and a nice fire glowing in the fireplace. At least they were more enthusiastic now.

"Let's see if we can work straight through for an hour," I said. Crystal arrived with their tote bags. She handed them out and said she was there to help if anyone needed it.

Elizabeth took out the yarn and needles she'd gotten at the yarn shop. "Could you help me start this," she said, holding up the pattern for some fingerless gloves.

I knew that Crystal had said something about helping them start another project, but it was too soon. They needed to stay focused on the scarf or they'd never finish it over the weekend.

"It would be better if you stuck with the scarf for now. I'll be around on Sunday and then I'll be happy to help any of you start something you got today."

Elizabeth's face clouded slightly, but she put away her supplies and took out the big red needles with her work hanging off of one of them.

"By Sunday, you'll all have your own Razzle Dazzle." Crystal had taken out the complete scarf she'd shown them at the first workshop and modeled it for them. Because of the big needles, the stitches were also very big and it was actually quite striking.

Lucinda and I had the advantage of being more comfortable with knitting than the newbies. She was already way ahead of them and it didn't take me long to catch up.

Working with the needles wasn't having the usual relaxing effect. If anything it was making me feel more antsy. Lucinda knew that I had to leave and why, but the rest of them didn't. It was probably stupid not to let on that I had more than one occupation, but I still wanted them to think I was making it on the retreats alone. They all seemed to have their lives together. Elizabeth might not be married, but her one job was keeping her afloat. Courtney had it all, a family and working her way up at a law firm. Lauren had the life she wanted. Kids, foster kids, a job helping people, and I imagined an understanding husband.

I put down my knitting and got up, thinking I could slip out. "Where are you going?" Elizabeth said in an accusing voice. "I thought the plan was we'd all work for an hour on our scarves."

"Nowhere," I said, sitting back down. "I was just going to stretch."

• • •

When the hour ended, they were all surprised and pleased at how much knitting they had to show for it.

Lucinda knew what I was up to, and as Crystal gathered up the bags to take them back to our meeting room, she stood up. "Don't forget the movie in Hummingbird Hall. They're showing the original *Star Wars*." Lucinda described how the place we'd been practicing our ball routine in would have been changed into a movie theater by now. "They have a cart making fresh popcorn and a candy counter."

"Sounds good to me," Lauren said. "I'm in."

"I'll go get the tote bag set up to leave for Blair," I said. I implied that I would catch up with them later and no one objected when I headed to the door.

I got to the meeting room with Crystal, and as she left the group's bags, I picked up one I'd left as a spare. I dropped it off at the registration counter and then headed up the driveway feeling giddy with my freedom. Putting on a retreat for people I knew was a lot more intense than I'd expected. I rushed across the street and made a quick detour inside to make sure Julius had food and water. The phone was ringing and I saw by the screen it was my mother. I'd avoided several of her calls and knew if I didn't answer this one, she'd call Sammy and stir things up, saying she was worried.

I grabbed the handset and clicked it on. "Hello, Babs," I said.

She hated that I'd taken to calling her by her name rather than her position. I did it in an effort to make it appear we were on equal footing now.

"Do you have to call me that?" she said, making a *tsk* sound.

"It seems more appropriate than Mom or Mommy, now that we're both adults," I said, trying to not sound like a defiant child.

"You never called me Mommy," she said. "You always stuck to the more formal Mother." She was lucky I didn't call her Dr. Mother. Both my parents were doctors. She was a cardiologist and I liked to say she fixed broken hearts. My father was a pediatrician, and as you'd expect, he was the more easygoing of the two. It bothered my mother no end that I was juggling professions and wasn't a professional anything—at least by her standards. To be a true professional in her eyes, I'd need to have a diploma to prove it. She'd been pushing me to go to cooking school in Paris or even to some detective academy—all on her dime.

There'd been times when I considered taking her up on it, but then something always happened to make me want to stay doing what I was doing in Cadbury.

"So, how is the weekend with your friends going?" she asked, getting right to the point. It was two hours later in Chicago and I pictured her in their apartment in the Hancock building with the view of Lake Michigan. Though by this hour it was too dark to see it. She would have changed out of whatever pantsuit she'd worn that day and was probably wearing her sleep clothes. The dangle earrings stayed on.

It had been my aim all along to avoid her calls for the whole weekend. I didn't want to have her ask about them because then I'd have to tell her how accomplished they all were and had husbands, families and professions, and have her bounce it back at me. And I certainly didn't want to tell her that someone had died under my watch and that it was probably one of my friends who had killed her.

But no matter what I called her, she was still in the same position and in no time got the whole story out of me.

"Oh, dear," she said. "Not the story I expected to hear from you."

Now that it was all out there, I asked her about the air embolism. "A pulmonary embolism caused by air. I've heard about it but never encountered it. I do know it takes quite a bit of air. Whoever did it would have to have some knowledge," she said.

"Or know how to do research," I said.

"I take that to mean you're investigating what happened." There was a pause and I knew what was coming next and she didn't disappoint. "Your application for the detective academy in Los Angeles is still open."

"Thanks but no thanks," I said.

"Have it your way," she said, sounding disappointed, then her voice lifted. "What about Sammy?"

"What do you mean, what about him?" I asked. I was just being difficult. I knew what she was trying to find out. She was hoping some miracle had happened and I'd changed my mind and we were back together. She'd begun asking about Sammy on a regular basis. It annoyed me, but it was better than what she used to say. She'd end our calls by reminding me that at my age, she'd been a mother, a doctor and a wife and that I wasn't any of those things.

I heard her making exasperated sounds and I relented. "Sammy's fine and I'm still his assistant, but he's looking for a replacement." My mother laughed.

"I'm sure he's scouring the area," she said facetiously. "I just hope you wise up before it's too late." I started to object and she continued. "I know, I know there's no spark. But that fades over time anyway. Sammy's a good man and that counts for a lot."

It was hard to argue with that. Sammy was definitely a good man, but only as a friend. Thankfully our call was coming to an end. Just before my mother signed off, she surprised me once again. "I shouldn't encourage you, but whoever killed Vanessa probably was familiar with hypodermic needles. Are any of your group diabetic? Or has a drug problem? Just a thought."

Who would have thought my mother would actually offer something useful. I looked out the window laughing to myself to see if pigs were flying. It was an inside joke I had with myself every time she did something that totally surprised me. Not that I could have even seen an airborne porcine if there was one since it was dark.

Julius had been watching the whole thing. When I hung up, he followed me to the door and looked up at me. I wasn't sure if he had mischief in mind and was glad to see me go, or if he longed for my company and was sad that I was leaving. It was hard to read a cat's expression. I filed what my mother had said in the back of my mind and zipped off to downtown Cadbury in my yellow Mini Cooper.

Even though it was Friday night things were beginning to quiet down. All of the stores were closed and the restaurants would soon join them. Cadbury wasn't a late-night town. I pulled my car into one of the angled spots on Grand Street. The Blue Door had been a small residence at one time and was oddly situated so the side of the building actually faced the main street. A long porch ran along the front of the white shingled building and was where the blue-doored entrance was.

The former living room and now main dining area was almost empty. The arrangement of tables could best be described as cozy, making it easy to see what everyone else was eating and overhear conversations. It had turned out to be a good thing for me because it had helped spread the word about my desserts to new diners. More than once I'd heard a regular customer rave about my desserts and suggest that it needed to be ordered early because the cake or pie was likely to run out.

Tag was collecting the check from the last diners at a small table by the window. I felt a tug of regret when I saw the ice cream dishes on their table. But all things considered it was no surprise that I hadn't been able to make the desserts the night before. One of the servers looked up from her job of setting up for the morning and offered me a greeting.

The best I could do was a nod of my head since both my hands were taken up with shopping bags with muffin supplies. The chef was just exiting the kitchen as I walked in. He already had his backpack slung over his shoulder. I knew it contained his knives. That was the point—they were *his* knives. He really could have left them there. I wouldn't have bothered them. He gave me a lift of his chin in acknowledgment as he passed. It bordered on surly. He had this territorial thing going about the kitchen and apparently viewed me as an intruder. I sort of felt the same way about him.

Once I heard the door close and knew that he'd really left, I began to empty the bags and stake out my claim on the room. I'd wait until Tag and the server left to really begin. For now I just arranged things. I always made the desserts for the restaurant first and afterward mixed up the muffins.

Tag came in just as I was finishing measuring the flour for the carrot cakes. His eye went right to the flour that had missed the measuring cup and had scattered on the counter. I could see he was fighting with himself to keep from coming over and wiping up the errant white powder. "The waitstaff have all taken off," he said with his eye still on the flour. "Lucinda's okay?" he asked.

It had only been hours since he'd seen her. I thought it was sweet that he missed her. I assured him that she was fine and didn't mention that she seemed to be enjoying her time away. He was still staring at the flour and finally I couldn't take it anymore and wiped it up. He let out a sigh of relief and left. I finished measuring the ingredients and then I went into the other room to turn on the soft jazz I liked to listen to while I baked. I glanced around the main room and all seemed peaceful, but then I heard a noise. I wasn't sure what it was or where it was coming from, but it instantly made me nervous. It wasn't unusual for someone to show up to visit, though they always announced themselves right away. I looked around and had the uneasy feeling that someone was watching me. The windows that looked out on the street were too high up for any one who wasn't a basketball player to see in. I looked at the front door. The top half was glass, and while I couldn't see anyone, if anyone was watching that seemed most likely where they'd be. My way was to confront things instead of running away from them even if they were scary, so I grabbed a frying pan, just in case, and pulled open the front door.

When I didn't see anyone, I stepped out onto the porch and glanced around. As I did I thought I heard the soft sound of a door closing. I checked behind me and the front door of the restaurant was open as I'd left it. When I turned back around, I remembered the door at the very end of the porch that led directly to the kitchen. It was only used when tables were set out there and was surely locked.

Convinced that I'd just been hearing things, I went back inside. I turned on the soft jazz and returned to the kitchen, replacing the frying pan. I began to pour the ingredients for the cakes in a bowl. There was no need for a mixer as the batter was hand-stirred. I enjoyed the peace of not having to listen to a motor, but I kept getting the feeling that someone was watching me. I knew that was probably hokum about being able to feel eyes on you, and besides there was no one there. Then I heard a rustling followed by something falling in the pantry. I took a moment to consider who might be watching me. Had the killer somehow figured out that I was investigating? It seemed unlikely. I knew I was stalling, nervous about what was behind that door.

I reminded myself that I wasn't one to run away from danger. I rearmed myself with the frying pan and pulled open the door, ready to do damage. At first I saw no one, then there was a rustle and I felt the air stir as someone passed behind me.

I rushed out of the small room after whoever. I caught up with the figure when I entered the main room. I had my frying pan poised as I went to grab the hoodie on the figure in front of me. The hood of the sweatshirt came off.

"Zak!" I said. "What are you doing here?" I demanded. He glanced around the empty restaurant.

"I could ask you the same thing."

"I asked first," I said, holding my ground. He eyed the frying pan in my hand and then reached out and lowered it.

"Maybe the others bought that life you described, but it didn't sound like the person I remembered who was always in the middle of things. The retreat business seemed out of character and a little shaky. I figured you had something else going on. Then tonight it was pretty obvious you had someplace to go, so I arranged for an Uber so I could follow you. I saw you go into the restaurant, but when it closed and you didn't come out, I figured whatever you were running was coming out of here. I found an unlocked door and hid to see what you were up to." He looked at me with a quizzical expression. "What are you up to? Is it something to do with opioids? Gambling? Hookers?"

I urged him to follow me back into the kitchen and hung the frying pan back on its hook. "How about none of the above. Sorry to disappoint you, but my secret business is baking," I said and pointed out the bowl full of batter. "I didn't want everyone to know that my life is really a patchwork quilt of professions. I make desserts for the restaurant and I bake muffins and deliver them to the assorted coffee spots in town. All of you seem to have found your callings and are making a life at it."

Zak leaned against the counter and scratched his head. In that moment he looked just like the boy I'd known in college who I'd shared that kiss in the rain with. "I doubt that the others' lives are as great as you think. As for me, I'm living my dream of being a journalist, but I'm not where I want to be yet." He let out a sigh. "I tried being an anchor in a small market, but sitting behind a desk reading copy somebody else wrote isn't for me. I want to be out there where the news is happening, but with a regular beat." His face lit with a wry smile. "Instead of being on call hoping for a hurricane to get an assignment. So, I'm trying to come up with stories to take to them," he said. "That's why this weekend interested me so much." He looked at me directly. "And of course seeing all of you again."

His mention of the promised story piqued my curiosity. "Do you have any idea who your mystery benefactor for this weekend is?"

He leaned against the counter and let out a sigh. "I'm pretty sure it was Vanessa. And the big story was probably something about the dealership." He looked at the bowl of ingredients and urged me to go on with my work. "She got in touch with me a while ago. She had this idea of making commercials featuring me for the dealership. She thought I'd work for nothing because according to her it would make me a personality." He winced. "And be the end of my news career. Actors can get away with it, but not newspeople. You don't see Anderson Cooper doing an ad for Hank's Tires."

"Was that all she had in mind?" I asked, remembering that she'd mentioned something about looking for Number Three and wanting someone who had something going on their own. In other words, a trophy husband.

"Oh, you mean was she trying to put a ring on my finger?" he joked. "I was definitely not here for that. I thought there might actually be something I could pitch to WNN about her dealership or I'd find something else." He smiled at me. "Like you were running some kind of gambling operation out of a closed restaurant."

"Sorry, I'm not doing anything more exciting," I said, matching his smile. "So then Vanessa never told you for sure that she was your benefactor."

"No. She seemed annoyed about something. But she did say she wanted to talk to me privately." He shrugged. "And I guess that's not going to happen."

I was hoping to see if he had any idea of what she wanted to talk about, but just then I heard a knock at the glass pane on the front door. Dane stopped by regularly and we'd come up with the special knock so I'd know it was him. He'd come by for his cookie bars.

Zak appeared uneasy as he followed me to the door, and when Dane came in dressed in his uniform, Zak seemed even more uncomfortable. It was a bit of a standoff. Both Zak and Dane looked at each other as if they were intruders.

I tried to smooth things over, but it didn't go well. Things got worse when Sammy showed up a few minutes later, saying he thought we could talk about our act while I was baking. He and Dane were used to each other, but they both looked at Zak with daggers in their eyes.

Zak seemed unconcerned with their reaction and was far more interested in finding out about the "act" Sammy was talking about.

Dane rolled his eyes, while Sammy explained. "Case is my assistant. I'm the Amazing Doctor Sammy," he said, holding out his hand. Zak still didn't quite get it and then Sammy made a coin appear from Dane's ear. "Amazing as in an amazing magician." Sammy seemed pleased with himself.

"So you put on retreats, bake and you're a magician's assistant?" Zak said with a smile. "Anything else?" He looked at me expectantly and I shook my head. "Not exactly material for an exposé," he joked, "but as I thought, a lot more interesting than you made it sound."

All this meet-and-greet stuff was taking up my baking time. I tried to nicely show them all the door, but it didn't go smoothly. Sammy said he really needed to talk to me. Dane said he'd act as my sous chef during his break and Zak had to arrange for an Uber. I promised to meet Sammy the next day at the venue and told Dane I could manage on my own. They weren't about to leave Zak there, and at Dane's suggestion, Sammy offered him a ride back to Vista Del Mar.

With them all gone, I finished up mixing the carrot cakes and put them in the oven. I was just setting out the ingredients for the muffins, when I heard someone jiggling the handle on the kitchen door, and too late I realized that with all the company I'd forgotten to lock it.

I grabbed for the frying pan and raised my hand, ready to strike as the door opened and someone came in.

I paused just a moment too long and a hand grabbed mine. "I could arrest you for that," Lieutenant Borgnine said. "Assaulting a police officer."

I was too stunned to speak. Lieutenant Borgnine, dressed in his traditional rumpled sport jacket, was standing in front of me. "You certainly have a lot of company. I don't know how you have time to bake anything." I noticed him sniffing the air and checking out the counter for the muffin ingredients.

I found my voice and asked him what he was doing there. "I thought it would be the best time to catch you alone." He laughed at the thought. "This meditation idea isn't working at all. All I got out of Courtney was that her personal life was in shambles, like I was some kind of advice columnist."

I asked for details and he rocked his head. "I don't remember. Well, actually I stopped listening when I heard the words 'my husband didn't understand.'" He watched as I started measuring baking powder. "And the other one. Elizabeth." His eyes went skyward. "She wouldn't stop talking. Something about waiting for things to come to her, but now she was taking control of her life."

"What about Vanessa's husband?" I asked.

"At least he didn't start complaining about his life," Borgnine said. "But I don't think you'll be happy with what he talked about." I wondered if I was going to have to convince the lieutenant to tell me what the subject of their conversation was, but he spilled it all on his own. "Mr. Ryerson was all about who was negligent and talking to his lawyer."

"I kind of knew that already," I said, thinking back to when I'd first seen Michael with Kevin St. John.

"I'm not sure about this whole plan," he said. "I barely got a chance to look around the victim's room." My ears perked up and I wanted to ask him if he thought it was strange that Vanessa's things were packed in her suitcase or that it was odd that her purse was in the room, but I couldn't admit that I'd been in there.

The lieutenant cleared his throat a few times like he was having trouble with what he was going to say before he finally got it out. "I know I told you no investigating on your own, but you never listen. Have you found out anything I should know?"

What he'd said was an opening and for a moment I considered mentioning what I'd seen in the room, but I quickly decided against it. No matter what he'd just said, I was sure admitting that I'd gone into her room would come back to bite me. As for anything else— these were my friends, well, acquaintances and I felt a certain loyalty to them. I knew that one was undeserving of my protection and that I would gladly turn them over—once I figured out who it was.

Lieutenant Borgnine read my silence correctly and tried to get past my nonanswer by asking questions about Zak. "What's going on between you two? Is he some old boyfriend?"

"No," I said finally. I gave him a quick rundown on Zak's profession.

"There was something between you," he said. "I saw how you looked at him. There's some unfinished business between you two, right?"

"Wrong," I said, trying to remember how I had looked at Zak and what I'd been thinking. "If you have to know there was one romantic walk in the rain and we might have kissed. That's all."

He glanced up and his gruff face softened. "That's a lot. All the thoughts of what might have been, maybe still could be. A reporter, traveling the world in search of a story. He's just the kind that you ladies fall for. Irresponsible charm, resisting any ties and most of all a lot of blanks for you to fill in with your imagination."

I looked at the stocky cop with new appreciation. He had more insight than I'd imagined. "It was never that way with me," I protested. "I always saw him for what he is. A romantic moment, not a future."

"Just as well, you have enough men you're stringing along." He sniffed the air again. "What's in the oven?" I knew he had a weakness for sweets and his wife was on him, trying to get him to eat a healthier diet.

"Carrot cakes for the restaurant," I answered, thinking about how to react to his first comment. Somehow I thought I'd handled things so nobody really noticed my relationships. It was unsettling to realize that he knew what was going on.

I saw him looking at the bowl on the counter. "What kind of muffins are you making?" He was able to bypass the desserts at the Blue Door, but I knew my muffins were a regular temptation when he picked up a coffee at one of the spots in town. I considered what to call them. I had a running problem with the Cadbury powers that be. They were so into being authentic that they reacted to any sort of what they called *cutesy* names. They'd won out and vanilla muffins were called just that, not Plain Janes as I'd named them. I thought of tonight's creation as Kernels of Truth muffins, but if I was going to have to keep the peace, I'd have to call them simply corn muffins.

"What's taking so long? It seems like a pretty straightforward question," he said, peering at me.

"Sorry," I said. "I'm not trying to withhold any information." I smiled, trying to lighten the moment. "They're going to be corn muffins, but that title doesn't do them justice. I include whole corn and a few other touches that make them stand above your regular corn muffins."

"Really? I suppose they could be considered kind of healthy with the corn and all." Then he caught himself. "But that's not what I'm here to say. I think I'm going to have to talk to the rest of your group, the regular way, as a cop wanting to know what they know." I had begun putting the dry ingredients in the large bowl.

I panicked. "You can't do that. When they realize the meditation thing was a ruse, they'll go nuts. Courtney's a lawyer and she might accuse you of trying to set her up. Lauren will organize a protest against some sort of police misbehavior. Elizabeth will throw a fit, saying you weren't playing by the rules. And Zak will figure that's his big story and go pitch small-town police corruption to WNN."

He shook his head with regret. "I should have never listened to you to start with. It seems like we have a lose-lose thing going here. Whatever I do is going to come out wrong."

"Maybe not," I said. I thought of what my mother had said and told him. "You could ask them about health issues and find out if anybody is giving themselves shots." I finished spooning the muffin batter into the paper-lined tins and loaded them all in the oven.

"Too bad we didn't think of that before I started." He hesitated and seemed to be fussing with himself. "Don't take this as free rein to go off on your own, but do you suppose you could find out if Courtney or Elizabeth is doing something that would make them knowledgeable about needles and syringes?" I agreed and he grumbled with himself, wondering if he was making a mistake.

"My wife is the only one thrilled about this meditation nonsense." He glanced at me and his expression lightened. "Though I have to admit I'm pretty good at faking it. This meditation business seems like a big nothing to me. What's the big fuss? You just sit and look at the ocean and keep saying *om* over and over again."

"You're actually doing that? Saying *om* in your head and not thinking about any of your cop stuff?"

He shrugged. "Yeah. Though I gotta say your people don't seem to do as well. There's a lot of squirming around going on next to me." He shook his head regretfully. "Okay, I'll stick with it until I talk to all of them. But after that I go back to old-fashioned interrogation." He sniffed the air. "How long until they're done?"

"Not that long. Do you want to wait?" He nodded and I rolled my eyes.

Chapter Nineteen

I awoke to the sound of someone banging on my kitchen door. Julius went flying off the bed when I ripped back the covers and rushed to the door expecting some kind of disaster. Instead it was a very fit-looking Dane in his jogging shorts and a gray T-shirt.

"I forgot to get the cookie bars last night and I was looking forward to having them for breakfast," he said.

It took a moment for it to compute and then I stumbled toward the counter where I'd left the bag. I didn't for a minute think that was the real reason he was there. Dane was not a cookie-bar-for-breakfast sort. I started to hand him the bag but he was already on his way in the door.

"If ever I saw someone who needed coffee," he said, nodding toward me. "I'll do the honors." As an afterthought he glanced over my attire and smiled. "Nice choice of lingerie."

I'd been so all in when I'd gotten home that I'd fallen asleep in my clothes. I reached up and touched my hair and could feel that it was sticking up. He urged me to sit and joined me a few minutes later with two cups of steaming coffee.

"How about a Kernels of Truth muffin instead of the cookie bars?" I said, offering him one of the runts I'd brought home.

He took a bite and complimented me on another success and then got down to why he really had stopped by and casually brought up my company at the Blue Door. I distracted him by telling him about who'd come after they all left.

"Let me get his straight now," he said, appearing incredulous when I finished. "Lieutenant Borgnine stayed until you were done baking and then he personally escorted you around town to make your deliveries?" I answered with a nod.

"It's not such a big deal," I said. "I gave him his own special supply of muffins and I suppose in gratitude he insisted on giving me the police escort."

Dane shook his head in disbelief. "I can't believe that you've won him over."

"You know what they say about the best way to a man's heart. It wasn't me that won him over—it was all the corn muffins. He's sure his wife won't have a problem with him eating them since they have vegetables in them," I said with a chuckle.

"I'm not so sure I like it," Dane said. "If you're not at odds with him, you won't need me anymore." He made a disappointed face then smiled. "But then, I never liked it that I was just a source of information to you." I knew he was teasing, but I reacted anyway and assured him he was more to me than that.

Then he turned the conversation to what he really wanted to know. "So, who is Zak exactly?" He got up to get the coffeepot and topped off both of our cups. Julius was hanging by the refrigerator, looking hopeful.

I explained that Zak had been in the boys' class who got to see the Baller-rinas in action and afterward had become a friend with the group. I threw in Zak's desire to be a journalist and finished by saying he was a correspondent for WNN.

"That's all good and well, but what's he doing being the rooster in the henhouse?"

"It's sort of a mystery," I said and then gave him the lowdown on Zak's invitation to the retreat. "Though he thinks it was Vanessa who invited him."

"So maybe there was something going on with them." Dane seemed momentarily at ease, but then he appeared wary. "But that doesn't explain why he showed up at the Blue Door."

I simply told him the truth, that Zak couldn't believe I was as dull as I'd made myself out to be and had followed me. There was no reason to mention our moment in the past.

"Or so he said. He's a suspect along with the rest of them. You didn't tell him the truth about Vanessa's death or that you were investigating, did you?" Dane said in a concerned tone.

"No, I didn't tell him anything. Everybody but you, me, Lucinda and Lieutenant Borgnine think her death is being treated as if it was from natural causes."

"I still think you ought to avoid being alone with him." Dane seemed to be speaking as a cop, but I still thought part of him was acting as my sort-of boyfriend. "You really should take me up on my offer of karate lessons." He looked over at Julius still hanging by the refrigerator and took pity on the cat. He took out the stink fish and went through all the unwrapping to give the cat some. Purring loudly, Julius rubbed against his ankle in appreciation.

"Thanks, but no thanks. No way do I want to start hanging out in your garage with a bunch of teenagers."

"I'm sure we could arrange some private lessons," he said. All the seriousness was gone and he was back to being playful.

"I'll keep it in mind," I said, draining my coffee cup. "But for now I still have a retreat to run and a killer to catch." I handed him the package of cookie bars. He put both of our mugs in the sink, stole a kiss and went out the door.

What was wrong with me? He really had it all—surface and substance. He was adorable and had character to spare. But even so I still couldn't commit.

I peeled off the clothes from the day before and quickly showered. I grabbed a pair of black jeans and a taupe turtleneck. It needed a little something, so I added a knitted vest I'd found among my aunt's creations. It was made with a nubby brown wool with specks of white. I always liked to wear something handmade during my retreats and this had the added advantage of adding a little warmth. Julius followed me to the door and I gave him a few strokes and urged him to stay out of trouble.

The brisk morning air refreshed me as it always did as I walked across the street. I was still tired from the late-night baking and all the company that had dropped by, but it was satisfying to know that Cadburians had their muffins and the Blue Door had fresh cake.

I could smell breakfast as I passed the Lodge and my stomach gurgled in response. The bell had already rung and most of the people were already inside. I waved at my group and then went directly to the cafeteria line. Cloris was behind the counter and made a mini buffet up for me and handed me the tray.

I was on the way to the table when I crossed paths with a slender woman with shoulder-length brown hair. I started to walk past her but she stopped. "Casey," she said in an excited voice. "It's me, Blair Hansen." She reached to hug me, trying not to jostle my tray.

"I'm so glad you're here," I said, using my free hand to reciprocate the hug. "The group's over here." I led the way and asked her when she'd arrived.

"I don't even know what time it was other than it was late." I asked her about her trip and she sighed. "It was long, but I'm here now."

"I'm sorry I wasn't there to greet you." She assured me that it was fine. "Then you found your room and everything?" I asked and she shrugged it off.

"It's not the Ritz, but who cares." She glanced down at her outfit of skinny jeans and fitted white turtleneck. "I wasn't sure how to dress."

I pointed out my own outfit. My jeans weren't as fitted as hers, but the idea was the same. "I think you nailed it."

"Tell me all about yourself," she said and then she sighed before I said a word. "It's so tragic about Vanessa. I'm still reeling from the news. Courtney said you saw her after her collapse and went to the hospital with her. What happened?"

I thought about telling Blair the truth about the air bubbles and all, but it seemed like it was best to keep the story the same for everyone. I mentioned the prank bomb threat and then finding Vanessa on the floor and riding with her to the hospital.

"Poor you," she said. "It must have been terrible." She glanced toward the table. "What can I do? Her family's been notified, right? Do we have to make any arrangements for her, uh, body?"

I assured her that Vanessa's husband and family were responsible for that and Blair let out a heavy sigh. "It's situations like this that make you reevaluate your priorities. I just told my staff to put everything on hold, that I had to go and be with my girls. Now I'm sorry I didn't do that to start with instead of letting work keep me in Hillston."

When we got to the table, everyone started to get up, but Blair urged them to sit and instead she worked her way to each of them. If I were to pick a word to describe Blair it would be *vivacious*. With her natural charisma she was perfect for politics. She had just the right mixture of authority and warmth. She'd easily been elected president of our college's student body after a term as treasurer.

"It's great that you're here," Elizabeth said. "We're doing the routine tonight for the talent show. Practice is after breakfast." She pulled the bag of balls from under the table to illustrate. Blair's smile faded and she seemed less than enthused.

"You always were so serious about the balls, weren't you." She gave Elizabeth's shoulder a squeeze and glanced around the table as if she was looking for someone.

"Zak's not here. He told me he was going to sleep in," Courtney said. I must have given Courtney a funny look because after that she explained. "He pushed a note under my door. He said he had a late night and he didn't want the rest of you to worry."

Blair greeted Lauren and then seemed confused when her gaze moved to Lucinda. I quickly stepped in to introduce her, but left out that I'd given her Blair's room. I didn't want Lucinda to feel uncomfortable.

"I'm starved," Blair said when she'd finished greeting everyone. Lucinda pointed her toward the back of the room and she went off to get her food.

"Everything will be better now that Blair's here," Elizabeth said.

I hoped she was right.

Chapter Twenty

Elizabeth was already out of her chair, grabbing the bag of balls as Lucinda went to make the rounds with the coffeepot. "No time for that now," Elizabeth said and waved for the rest of us to follow her.

"I guess there's no stopping her," Blair said, watching as Courtney and Lauren followed our former ballatarian out of the dining hall. Lucinda ditched the coffeepot and joined them. Blair and I took up the rear and went to the door.

When we got outside, Blair pulled her sweater around her and scrutinized my fleece jacket. "I think that's better suited for this weather." She glanced around at the surroundings as we followed the group to Hummingbird Hall. "This place looks a lot different in the daylight." I gave her a brief history of the hotel and conference center and broke the news about Vista Del Mar being unplugged.

"It should be all right," she said with a shrug. "It's only for today and tomorrow." It was a relief to have somebody not go crazy over not being able to stare at their cell phone. "I should really say something to Vanessa's husband," Blair said.

I sparked at her comment, realizing she might have some information about their relationship. "Then you know him?" I asked. "And that he was Elizabeth's ex?"

"He's Elizabeth's ex?" she said, surprised. She thought about it for a moment and then nodded. "I didn't put it together until now. Other than being at their wedding, I never saw much of him. Vanessa just called him Number Two when she spoke about him."

"I don't suppose you know anything about what kind of arrangement they had," I said.

"My impression was that it was more like a business deal. Whenever I saw them, she was in the center of things and he was on the side holding her coat." Blair stopped for a moment to collect her thoughts. "It always used to be the men who had the identity, but in their case it was her. I wonder where that leaves him."

"It sounds like you kept in touch with her. Did you know anything about her looking to replace him with a Number Three?" I asked.

"I wouldn't say I was in touch with her. We just ran into each other at events. She could have been looking to replace him," Blair said with a shrug. "The only man in her life who meant anything was her father. Her reason to be was to prove her worth to him. Apparently, he'd always been disappointed that she wasn't a boy." She let out her breath in a sigh. "I just can't process that she's gone." Her voice cracked and it seemed as if she was swallowing back tears.

We'd reached Hummingbird Hall and I led the way inside. It was still set up like an auditorium with rows of chairs in the center of the barnlike space. The popcorn cart and candy counter were gone and the movie screen folded up.

"We'll have to use the stage," Elizabeth said, leading the way. She urged everyone to hurry because we only had the space for a short time. Once we were all on the stage, Elizabeth became the director. She gave Blair the same speech she'd given the rest of us about her muscles remembering the moves.

Elizabeth did give Lucinda a quick refresher on the moves and then she bounced us all our balls, reminding everyone who they were to throw to in the rumble. I was certainly hoping that it was true that my muscles remembered the dance because my mind was on what Blair had said about Michael. *Where did it leave him?*

"No, no," Elizabeth said as she cut the music. She was glaring at me. "You're supposed to throw to Courtney." I was confused until she pointed out that I'd thrown to Blair.

I apologized, and when we did it again made sure I looked for Courtney's long red nails.

As a family of yodelers came in to take our place, I announced that we'd go directly to our meeting room for our morning workshop.

Zak was sitting in the room talking to Crystal when we got

there. I was glad that everything was in order. The fireplace was giving off a cozy glow and the drinks were set up on the counter.

He'd been slouching in his chair with his feet on another one but snapped to attention when we filed in. He actually stood when he saw Blair was with us. He bowed his head and used his arm to make a flourish.

"At last you're here," he said with a grin. "How do I address you? Your Mayorship? Your Honor?"

"How about the next congressperson," she countered.

"I like your confidence," Zak said.

"So what brought you here? Did you become an honorary Baller-rina?" she asked and he turned to me.

"Then nobody told her about my mysterious benefactor." I shook my head and he explained how he'd happened to come to our reunion. "I'm pretty sure it was Vanessa, and whatever story she had in mind went with her. But I could still use a scoop, so if you know anything . . ." He looked at Blair.

"I'm just beginning my campaign, but any publicity would be helpful. And something national would be phenomenal."

"We'll have to put our heads together and see what we come up with," he said.

Crystal got the group's attention and suggested they get to their knitting. There was the scraping of chairs as everyone but Blair and I sat down. She glanced around the room and seemed at a loss for what to do. I introduced her to Crystal and explained her sudden appearance.

"I'm sorry for the reason you came, but I hope the knitting can help you bond with your friends." Crystal's arm jangled with some silver bangles as she gathered up a pair of needles and the three skeins of yarn and looked for a tote bag.

"I left one for you last night. But it's no problem." I had an empty one in my larger bag and handed it to her, and Crystal said she'd show her how to cast on.

"It seems kind of late to start," Blair said, eyeing the amount of work hanging off the other sets of needles on the table. "Maybe I'll just hang out while the rest of you work."

Crystal assured her that once she got going she'd catch up with the group in no time. Blair appeared as if she'd been cornered and finally agreed to the lesson. I was glad that Crystal had gotten rid of Vanessa's tote bag. It would have been a sad testament to her absence.

I had started the scarf with them, but I was caught in that confusion about whether to be a member of the group or the leader. While I was considering what to do, Lieutenant Borgnine came in the door. I still wasn't used to seeing him in anything but the rumpled herringbone jacket and I did a double take seeing him in the casual outfit. I went to meet him and we stepped outside, out of earshot of the group.

"Back for more meditation lessons," he said, doing his best to sound friendly. Nobody could say that he wasn't observant. In the moment he'd been in the room, he'd picked up on Blair. "I see we have someone new."

"Her name is Blair Hansen. She was a no-show, but when she heard about Vanessa she came last night to be with the group." Not that it mattered, but I told him she was the mayor of a Chicago suburb and was running for Congress.

I started to suggest that he didn't have to give her one of his lessons, but he shook his head and gave me a look. "That's what separates the amateurs from the professionals. It would look suspicious if I treated her different than the rest. In fact, I probably should take her first."

I had to admit he had a point and I went over to Blair with him in tow. "This is Theodore—well, in his other life he's Lieutenant Borgnine of the Cadbury PD—and he's been offering our group meditation lessons to help them cope with the loss of Vanessa. He'd like to give you a turn." It was still hard to say the whole business about meditation lessons with a straight face, but Blair bought it with ease.

She put down the needle and got up. "Sounds good to me."

I watched them go down the path toward the boardwalk. I finally decided to be part of the group and sat down with them. The knitting worked its magic and I relaxed, a little anyway.

When Blair returned, Theodore took Lauren with him. I heard her muttering something about how much she needed the meditation time with all that she had going on.

I was dying to ask him if he'd found out anything useful, but I knew he wouldn't tell me if he had. I was on my own to figure it out.

Zak got a fair amount of teasing about what he'd been up to the night before that he had to sleep in. I hadn't cautioned him to keep my other life to himself, but he'd figured that out on his own and kept quiet.

Having Blair there did make a difference. She was a natural-born leader and entertained the table with stories of the lighter side of being mayor and we heard all about ribbon cutting and riding in the Fourth of July parade. "It's not all fun things like lighting holiday trees," she said. "Sometimes there are tough decisions and the buck stops with moi."

"What about your personal life?" Elizabeth asked. "You didn't say anything about it."

Blair's smile faded. "That's because I barely have one. Nicholas is my significant other. We have talked about getting married and having kids, but it always gets put on hold because of some hurdle. Now it's the upcoming election. One of these days I'm afraid he'll have had enough and I'll find a note on my pillow saying he's gone."

"Are you considering anything after Congress?" Courtney asked.

Blair got a dreamy smile. "I can tell you guys because we're friends. Who knows, maybe sometime in the future you'll be calling me Madame President."

They all got her to promise to invite them to the inaugural ball and were discussing what they'd wear when Lauren returned and plopped in her seat. Whatever Lieutenant Borgnine was doing seemed to have worked with her, she actually looked relaxed.

When the allotted time for the workshop was up, Crystal packed up her things and left, saying she'd be back in the late afternoon. The rest of the group hung around, continuing to work on the scarves. They'd all made a lot of progress and seemed pleased with the results. It turned out that Blair had a natural touch for knitting and she almost caught up with them.

I reminded them of the coffee and tea and cookie bars and mentioned the winery tour and lunch I'd arranged and told them the van would be leaving at noon. They all seemed to want to fortify themselves before the outing and hung in a knot by the counter with the goodies.

Blair pulled me aside. "The knitting is so much better than I'd imagined. I have a lot of stress and it seems like the perfect antidote. And how fun, a winery tour," she said. Her face grew serious for a moment. "Should we feel guilty about enjoying ourselves after what happened to Vanessa?"

Elizabeth had inserted herself in our conversation. "If it had anything to do with wine, she would have been on board."

"Though if they didn't have her pink wine, she'd probably be unhappy," Blair said with a sad smile. "I suppose they'll have a service for her next week in Chicago." She turned to me. "Her family must be making arrangements to ship her home." Blair's voice cracked a little at the end of her statement.

I was thinking about what to say. I certainly didn't want to open the door to any questions about her cause of death by mentioning an autopsy and the medical examiner having to finish his investigation before her body could go anywhere. But Elizabeth came to my rescue and immediately began blabbing about our big performance.

When they all finally left, Lucinda hung back. "Are you going on the winery tour?" she asked.

I shook my head and let out a sigh. "I promised Sammy to go over stuff for his show," I said. "And I need a break. I didn't realize how much harder it is to be both a participant and leader." Lucinda commented that the ball performance only added to the work.

"Don't I know it," I said. "I can't believe that I screwed up and threw to the wrong person."

Lucinda urged me to forgive myself. "You probably just weren't thinking." She pulled on her Ralph Lauren sweater. "Go on and enjoy your afternoon. Don't worry about the group. I'll play host and keep my ears open," she said with a smile before she took off.

Chapter Twenty-one

I didn't plan to hang around to see them off to the winery tour, figuring that it would point out that I wasn't going along. I went down the path and cut through the Lodge. It was quiet inside and I was surprised to see Madeleine and Cora Delacorte coming out from the back area. I laughed inside remembering how the two sisters had looked almost like twins when I'd first gotten to Cadbury—both dressing in formal suits with helmet-like hairstyles. Now they looked barely related.

Cora greeted me and seemed to be leaving. When she saw that Madeleine had stopped next to me, she seemed perturbed. "I'll be waiting in the golf cart," Cora said. "Remember I have to get to the Women's Club of Cadbury for the meeting." The last part of the comment came out in a snippy tone and Cora gave her sister a final disparaging glance.

Madeleine closed her eyes briefly and let out a sigh. "Cora is so used to being in charge—she's having a hard time now that I've started to assert myself." She grabbed my hand. "I'm sorry I missed another workshop, but Kevin had us come in."

"What was it? Another meeting about what happened the other night?" I asked.

She seemed distressed. "Kevin has already heard from her husband threatening to sue for negligence. Our attorney suggested offering him a settlement to end it quickly."

"I wouldn't rush into anything," I said. "Once all the facts come out, her husband might not have a case."

"That was my suggestion, too—to wait," Madeleine said, brimming with pride. Then she shook her head in annoyance. "If I hear that nonsense about not worrying our pretty little heads again I don't know what I'll do." Her expression changed back to positive. "As long as we were here, I tried to put in a good word for Crystal's son, Cory. It seems like someone who wants to work at Vista Del

Mar as much as he does should have a job. Is he planning on college?" There was a honk from the golf cart and she made a face. "Cora can just wait. Cory seems like such a nice young man. And I like his mother so much. I was thinking maybe I could help him."

It was only hearing Frank's voice in my mind's ear that kept me from blurting out the truth about Cory. I took Madeleine's hand and squeezed it. "I'm sure his whole family would appreciate anything you did." There was another honk from the golf cart and Madeleine said she had to go.

I gave them a moment to let them drive away. So, Vanessa's husband was looking for some quick money. I'd have to tell Lieutenant Borgnine.

I went across to my place just long enough to check on Julius and get the sparkly costume Sammy had dropped off. Julius looked up from his favorite spot on one of the living room chairs. He seemed totally unconcerned about my "remodel" as long as he had access to his chair. He'd put his head back down and closed his eyes before I could finish asking him what he'd been up to. "I guess that means you've been a good boy," I said, giving his head a soft stroke.

Sammy had said something about hoping to so some kind of run-through of the illusion and I put on the spangly romper just in case. I avoided looking in the mirror and regretted that I hadn't insisted on picking something out myself. But then if I did that it would have made it seem like I was planning to continue as his assistant instead of just being a placeholder until he found someone else. I dropped on a long cotton dress over the romper, grabbed my stuff and hit the road.

I had to take the 17-Mile Drive to get to the Inn at Pebble Beach. The magic show was going to be the entertainment for a very fancy anniversary party in one of the private rooms at the Inn, as it was usually referred to. The 17-Mile Drive was a private road that was considered one of most scenic rides in the world. Once I passed the guardhouse, the surroundings had some of the same wild feeling of Vista Del Mar, but there was nothing rustic about the mansions and resorts in its confines.

There were numerous photo ops along the winding road, which I ignored, but judging by the cars parked along the road, others hadn't. The busiest was probably the iconic lone cypress that grew on a rock with the restless ocean as a backdrop. The mansions had fanciful names like Wit's End, which I was convinced was owned by a comedian—get it, the place was the end result of his or her wit. I passed through a huge forest of Monterey cypress trees with their horizontal shape from the constant wind. As I rose higher, I actually got above the clouds and had blue sky and sunshine on me as I glanced down at the white blanket covering the area below.

I finally pulled into the resort and the rustic feeling ended as I walked past the perfectly manicured lawn with rows of bright flowers along the edge. I followed a driveway that went to the entrance of the single-story main building. Valets were clustered near the entrance ready to park or retrieve cars. A tall man in a uniform greeted me and opened the main door.

Inside I bypassed the white registration counter and went into the lobby. With its elegant décor, it couldn't have been more different than Vista Del Mar. At the end of the space windows looked out on the patio restaurant filled with well-dressed patrons. Beyond there was more perfect lawn that sloped down to the water.

I'd been there before and knew that the guest rooms were in a separate building and all had views of the water. There were also villas near the golf course.

I sat down in one of the extremely comfortable easy chairs. I'd barely settled before a server came by and offered me a mimosa. The last thing I wanted was a fuzzy brain, so I thanked her but refused and got a coffee from the complimentary station. It wasn't the worst place to have to wait. I had a view of the entrance, which included the concierge desk, and it was a good place for people watching. The vibe was so different than at Vista Del Mar and the people were dressed in pastel resort-wear instead of cargo pants and sensible sandals.

Sammy was usually early, so I began to wonder if I might have simply not seen him. I stood up and looked around the whole area. There was no Sammy, but there was someone else who got my attention. More like two someone elses. I picked up my coffee and moved closer to get a better view. It was kind of like déjà vu from a scene at the Vista Del Mar café, but the vibe seemed different. Elizabeth and Michael were sitting next to each other and they had accepted the mimosas. Elizabeth had changed her clothes from what I'd seen her wearing at breakfast. She was wearing coral-colored pants and a white polo shirt. I tried to get closer so I could eavesdrop, but there was no way without making my presence known. She had her head closer to his and I saw her put her hand on his. He didn't snatch his away either.

"Hey, Case," Sammy said, stopping next to me. He picked up that I was staring at someone and looked to see what it was. "Isn't that one of your people?"

I shushed him, which was ridiculous because they couldn't hear anyway. "I'd really like to hear what they're talking about," I said.

"Why don't you just go over and say hello," he offered. "You can invite them to watch us rehearse."

"No on all of that," I said. "I'd like to hear what they're talking about without them seeing me." Sammy seemed confused and I reminded him that one of my people had died in a weird way that seemed like murder.

"That's right," he said. He apologized for being so self-absorbed. "Let me help you." He instantly stepped in front of me to act as a shield and then turned to face me.

"How about I back toward them, keeping you hidden?" he offered. Sammy was taller than me and with his bigger build it would work. I stepped close to him and he carefully backed toward the next bank of chairs. I stole a glance around him and the pair seem oblivious to us.

Sammy kept glancing over his shoulder to make sure he wasn't going to trip or hit anything. "Case, this is exciting being part of one of your investigations. I'll listen too," he said as we got as close as we could and he stopped. I strained my ears to hear.

"You shouldn't have come," he said.

"I know you said it wouldn't look good for us to be seen together, but if anybody says anything, I'm an old friend just here to comfort you," Elizabeth said. "Nobody knows I'm here anyway."

"That's a good story, but I don't want to take any chances. We really shouldn't be seen together for now."

Elizabeth started to say something about Vanessa, but she'd dropped her voice and I leaned into Sammy, hoping to be able to hear more. Just then I sensed someone had stopped next to us. A very tan man in white pants and a white polo shirt was peering at us.

"Folks, I was just wondering if I could see your room key, or if you haven't registered yet, I can check your reservation for you." His tone was all friendly, but there was an edge of authority to it. He might be dressed casually, but the earpiece and cord gave away that he was security.

Sammy didn't miss a beat. "I'm the Amazing Dr. Sammy and this is my assistant. We're the entertainment for the Bigelson anniversary party. We're here to do a run-through." Sammy turned to me. "Case, show him your costume."

I nudged Sammy and whispered that I had it on under my dress. Meanwhile the security guy had leaned down and picked something up. I recognized the sparkly disk as having come off the romper. Oh, no, I was shedding, too. I snatched it from his hand and apologized. He turned to speak into something on the collar of his shirt and after a moment turned back to us. "Sorry. We can't be too careful. I don't know who said you could rehearse here. I can show you the room the Bigelsons have, but it's in use now."

I was still trying to listen to Elizabeth and Michael. I couldn't very well shush the security guy and was leaning to one side to hear them better. But in the end all I heard was Elizabeth saying something about seizing the moment and changing her life.

The next thing I knew we were being whisked down a corridor with carpet so thick it felt like I was walking on pillows. The man with the earpiece opened a door and let us look inside. A crowd of people were lined up at a long buffet table. Round tables with lavender tablecloths were scattered around the room. "Seen enough?" the man asked. Apparently, he also answered for us as he shut the door, making us pull back.

We were on our own going back down the hall. There was no chance we'd get lost, as I'd left a trail of sparkly disks on the way in. When we got back to the lobby Michael and Elizabeth were gone.

"Sorry you couldn't listen longer," Sammy said. "Did you hear anything incriminating?"

"Maybe not incriminating, but certainly suspicious." I glanced around the lobby. "Talking about looking suspicious—maybe we should get out of here." I looked down at the floor and saw that the sparkly disks had started falling off in droves and were gathering around my feet.

"Your outfit probably has bald spots," Sammy said with a worried look. "We better replace it." But I had a better idea.

Sammy was upset that we hadn't gotten to rehearse, but I reminded him that spontaneity was part of the act's charm.

"Case, you are absolutely the best." He gave me a thank-you bear hug and we both went to our cars. Actually, he followed behind me, picking up the trail of sparkly disks.

I didn't much notice the scenery on the ride back. I was too busy thinking about Michael and Elizabeth. Was she just moving in on him now that Vanessa was dead, or were they working as a team to begin with?

Chapter Twenty-two

I pulled the yellow Mini Cooper into my driveway. Julius was waiting on the back stoop. "I hope you're staying out of trouble," I said as I climbed the two steps. He looked up at me and blinked a few times.

He waited until I opened the door and then followed me in. He did a few figure eights around my ankles and then headed for the refrigerator with a plaintive meow. I didn't have to know cat language to get what he wanted. I dropped my stuff and opened the refrigerator.

"One dab of stink fish coming up," I said, pulling out the plastic bag and automatically holding my nose. It took multiple unwrappings to get to the actual can, which had a plastic lid on it. When I released the lid, the smell hit me despite my holding my nose and I made a face. "Why couldn't your favorite be something like chicken," I said, doling out his spoonful of the fish. He was lapping it up with joy as I left the room.

I changed back into my jeans and turtleneck and threw the romper on the bed. "I'll attend to you later," I said, throwing the handful of discs Sammy had picked up on top of it.

I felt guilty for not going with the group and thought I would assuage it by bringing fresh cookies for the afternoon workshop. I had just turned on the oven to preheat it when the landline started to ring. I grabbed the phone.

"Hey, Feldstein," Frank said. "I had a minute and needed a little entertainment. So how's your weekend going? Found the perp yet?"

I chuckled inside. Frank was always acting like he was doing me a favor to talk to me, but I knew inside he was really interested in what was going on. "No," I said regretfully.

"Tick tock, Feldstein. Not only are most suspects rounded up in the first forty-eight hours, but you've got the added problem that they'll all be leaving."

"Thanks a lot," I said with a groan.

"I'm just trying to be helpful. It's tough this time because the suspects are all people you know, right?" he said.

"Maybe." He was probably right, but I hated to admit it. "But I might be on to something," I added quickly, both for him and for myself. I told him about seeing Elizabeth and Michael and they're history. In an attempt to lighten the moment I said, "I think the whole group would like to murder Elizabeth since she's pushed us into doing the stupid ball routine for the talent show."

I heard Frank laugh. "I don't suppose there will be video available."

"Not if any of us can help it. Particularly Blair," I said. I realized he didn't know who she was and explained her late arrival. "Maybe I should count her as a suspect."

"Feldstein, you're dithering. I get it—you're trying to stay away from the obvious. Mr. Romantic Kiss in the Moonlight."

"It was a kiss in the rain," I corrected.

"Whatever," Frank said dismissively. "He's the oddball in the mix. That story about a mysterious invitation . . ." His voice trailed off and I imagined Frank shaking his head.

"He told me he thought Vanessa had invited him."

"That's convenient since she's not there to confirm or deny."

"I think she could have invited him. He said they had a previous connection and, well, she said she was on the lookout for husband number three and she wanted someone accomplished this time."

Frank made a disbelieving noise. "I'm telling you—*cherchez l'homme.*"

"Since when do you speak French?" I asked. I had sliced the cookie dough as we were talking, put the discs on the baking sheet and had put them in the oven. I looked at the timer and saw they'd be done soon.

"I have a lot of talents you don't know about." Then he grunted. "I see what you're doing. Evading the subject isn't going to change things."

Is that what I was doing? Maybe I did have a soft spot for Zak and was avoiding making him the prime suspect. The timer went off and I took the sheets out of the oven. As I did it, I remembered something. "Aha, I know it wasn't him," I said.

"This ought to be good, Feldstein. I'm all ears."

"I just thought about something that happened the night of. After my trip to the hospital, I had a look around Vanessa's room. It was really weird—her suitcase appeared to have been packed up. But that's not the point. Vanessa's purse was on the floor." I gave him the lowdown on the designer name along with the price tag.

"Are those relevant details?" he asked.

"Not exactly. I was trying to give you a little color. The point is that the purse was with Vanessa when the bomb scare happened. So, the killer must have taken it when they shot her up with the air. And a guy wouldn't have wanted to carry a purse. It might look kind of obvious."

Frank seemed confused. "Why did the killer bring the purse to her room?"

"I'm guessing because her room key was in the bag," I said.

"It's kind of a weak excuse to eliminate Mr. Romance. But there's a bigger point here," he said. "Why did someone want the key in the first place?" Frank was starting to sound impatient. "C'mon, Feldstein. Do I have to spell it out for you?"

Suddenly I got what he meant. How could I have missed something so obvious? I wasn't going to admit to it though. "No," I said with just a touch of attitude. "They wanted the key so they could get in her room and look for something." I used a singsongy tone, as if it was no big revelation.

"Bingo. Now you just have to figure out what it was." I heard the squeak of his chair and I pictured him leaning back in it.

"You're working Saturday afternoon?" I said, and I mentioned hearing his chair, thinking it showed off my detection skills.

"The chair sounds, huh?" he said. "Wrong assumption since I

have the same chair at home." He paused a beat. "But actually you're right. I am at the office about to go on a surveillance. Thank heavens for cheating husbands and wives that want to catch them. You can figure this thing out, Feldstein. Remember, you were trained by the best." Then he hung up.

Really? He didn't train me. When I worked for him, he just gave me a list of people to call and told me what information I should get out of them. I figured out how to do it on my own.

I packed up the cookies and headed across the street. The van that had taken them to the winery tour was going up the driveway, having let everyone off. When I neared the Lodge, I saw Lucinda standing outside with several canvas bags holding wine bottles.

"Let me help," I said, picking up my speed. "It looks like somebody had a good time." I eyed her purchases, taking one of the bags out of her hands.

We started to walk toward the Sand and Sea building. She looked around and saw that we were on the path alone. "Lots of weird stuff went on," she began. "Elizabeth said she had a headache and wasn't going. But something was up, she was wearing mascara."

"I know she didn't go and what she was up to," I said before sharing what I'd seen at the Inn.

"That seems suspicious to me. Maybe all that whining about being single and complaining about him marrying Vanessa was an act," Lucinda said as we walked up the slope toward the Sand and Sea building.

I agreed that it was certainly a possibility and then asked about the others. "As you can figure, they were on their phones as soon as they got a signal. The winery had WiFi and Courtney had her laptop. She seemed particularly frantic and practically came unglued after she got a couple of calls on the way back."

I was almost afraid to ask about Zak, but Lucinda volunteered the information before I had a chance to ask. "He spent the whole ride there typing something into his phone. He had what I'd call a self-satisfied smile. And Lauren," Lucinda said with a disbelieving shake of her head. "She simply disappeared."

"What?" I exclaimed and asked for more details.

"We started out at the tasting room and restaurant. She was there for lunch, but when the wine trolley came to take us to the vineyard and processing area, she was gone. I glanced around the mini mall the restaurant was in, but I didn't see her. But when the trolley brought us back, she was just suddenly there."

"Good work," I said, wishing I knew what any of it meant. We'd reached the building her room was in and I thanked her for acting as host. "This was supposed to be a weekend for you to kick back and all you've done is help me out and play host. Oh, and get hooked into the nonsense with the balls."

"I think I've discovered something about myself," she said with laugh. "I don't like kicking back, really. There is no way I could enjoy just sitting around during the meals. I like to be the one making sure everyone has what they need. And I'm always thinking about the restaurant." She held up the cloth carrier of wine bottles. "Even this is for the Blue Door." The bottles of wine she'd gotten were for Tag and her to try out. If they liked them they'd order cases for the restaurant. "However, coming to the retreats does give me a chance to sort of air out my mind. I always go home less bothered by Tag's fussiness. At least for a little while." She chuckled.

I insisted on carrying the bag all the way to her room. When we got to her door I handed her the bag and was almost ready to leave when I thought of my phone call with Frank. Lucinda's room was right next to Vanessa's. I told her about finding the purse in there and my theory about how it got there. "The killer could have been in there when you came back to your room after the all-clear on the bomb."

Lucinda's eyes darted back and forth as she tried to think back.

"You know, I did hear the door open and close and then some footsteps in the hall."

"I wish you'd peeked out your door," I said. "Then we'd know who killed her."

Chapter Twenty-three

"Hi," I said in surprise. I had expected to find the meeting room empty, but Madeleine was sitting at the table. The huge red knitting needles clacked as she worked with the three strands of yarn. She looked up at my greeting.

"I'm afraid I've missed a lot of knitting time, so I came early." She held up her work and had to untwist it to show me how much she'd done. "Look at how long it is already. These big needles are the best." She went to rearrange the three balls of yarn so they wouldn't get tangled and then straightened the scarf in progress again. In the process, she skewered it on the tip of one of the needles and I had to help her get everything untangled.

I added the tin of cookies to the coffee and tea service. The fire was going in the fireplace and it seemed like a typical workshop, except I was focused on trying to figure out a way to unmask the killer before time ran out.

Lieutenant Borgnine stuck his head in the door, and when he saw Madeleine his expression darkened and he stepped back outside, waving for me to join him. "I'll be right back," I said to Madeleine. She was engrossed in her knitting and I didn't think she'd even noticed the lieutenant's arrival.

Theo, as he asked to be called when he was doing the meditation thing, was pacing. His grim expression was a contrast to his casual clothes, but then his bulldog looks made him always appear like he was in a bad mood. I noticed he was massaging his temple, which made me think he was getting a headache. He'd had that reaction when dealing with me in the past.

"I can't believe I let you talk me into this ridiculous plan," he said. "All this airy-fairy stuff hasn't gotten me anywhere. I still say I should switch to my usual approach. None of this *tell me about yourself* stuff. More like *where did you go during the bomb scare and who can vouch for it?*"

I thought of offering again what my mother had brought up—suggesting that he inquire if his meditation students had anything to do with needles—but I didn't think he would take it well.

"You just have Zak left, and if you have time you could offer someone a second session. Why not stick with the meditation thing for them and then tomorrow, if nothing turns up, you can use the last workshop to grill them. Have you thought about motive?" I asked and he gave me a steely glance.

"Do you know something you haven't told me?" he asked.

I considered telling him about Michael looking for some fast money in a settlement, but after seeing him with Elizabeth I wanted to see if they were working as a team before I said anything to the lieutenant. I wondered if I should tell him I'd figured out that someone had gone into Vanessa's room that night and whatever they were looking for must have had to do with why she was killed. But then he'd want to know how I knew, which would require me to admit that I'd been in her room. It could only lead to trouble for me, so I mentally shook my head and diverted his attention by suggesting he have coffee and some cookies while he waited for everyone to arrive.

There was no question that he would accept.

He was munching on his third cookie and drinking black coffee as my people came in. Lucinda looked over the group and then up at me and I knew what she was thinking—one of them was a killer. I was still having a hard time accepting that fact and I was sure it was slowing down my investigating process. I pulled myself together and put on a bright smile.

I mentioned the fresh cookies and drinks and that Theo was there to give more meditation lessons. He didn't appear very enthused about it but forced himself to sort of smile. He zeroed in on Zak. "You're up," he said, putting down his coffee cup.

Zak's face clouded. "Why not ladies first," he said, indicating Madeleine and Lucinda.

I stepped in and said the point of the lessons was to help the group deal with Vanessa's death. "After Zak, Theo will be offering second sessions to anyone interested."

Zak shook his head. "I don't really need a lesson. I know my way around a mantra. I did a story on a Buddhist monastery and I spent time with the meditators in Iowa." To further prove his point, he bowed to the cop and said, "Namaste."

Zak was all friendly smiles, but something in the way he looked at Lieutenant Borgnine made me think he'd seen through the ruse.

Madeleine had already put down her needles. "I'll gladly take his place. I've heard about meditating." She went on about the new chapter in her life and how she was all about trying new things. She was out of her chair and on her way to the door before I could find an excuse for her not to have a lesson.

As Lieutenant Borgnine left with Madeleine, he threw me a backward look. Whatever good cheer the coffee and cookies had brought was gone. Not only was it a waste of time for him to talk to Madeleine, but he had to watch himself because she and Cora were heads of the Police Benevolent Committee.

Crystal had arrived looking like a rainbow just as they were leaving. On the way out Madeleine reached out and grabbed her hand. "Tell Cory I put in a good word for him."

"What was that about?" Crystal said to me.

"She really likes your son and I think she wants to help him. She always says nice things about you, too," I added. My helper's expression clouded, but then she put on her game face before going to the head of the table. She laid a couple of samples of the scarves on the table and offered help to anyone who needed it.

They'd already taken out their knitting and were working on the scarves. When I saw how much they'd done and how comfortable they'd become with knitting, I believed they would be able to finish by Sunday. I decided to sit down with them and took out the scarf I was working on, thinking it might be easier to pick up information if it seemed like I was one of them.

I pulled out an empty chair next to Zak. He'd really taken to knitting and was surprisingly dexterous with the needles. It wasn't a stretch to think he could handle other kinds of needles, too. I was sure Frank was wrong that I was going soft on him. If Zak was the guilty party, I'd go after him. My concern must have shown in my face because he suddenly leaned close to me and whispered, "Don't worry, I didn't let anything out about last night."

"You two look pretty cozy," Blair said. "Getting together for old times' sake?"

Zak looked at me and seemed a little uncertain. "There is no old times' sake. I think we were always circling each other but we never connected."

It stung that he didn't remember the walk in the rain, but then it probably didn't mean anything to him. Lucinda threw me a sympathetic look. Courtney seemed very tense and dropped one of the big plastic needles a number of times. She struggled through a row of stitches. She glared down at her work and let out a loud *ugh* and threw her work down on the table. "This is a hopeless mess. I thought knitting was supposed to calm your nerves."

Courtney had always seemed so poised and in control, it was strange to see her melt down over some yarn. Crystal leaned over and picked up the needle that had her work on it and examined the stitches. The worst of the problem seemed to be that the eyelash yarn was hanging off in a loose loop. Crystal undid a few stitches and picked up the errant yarn so that all the stitches now had all three strands. Then she straightened the three balls of yarn and handed it all back to Courtney. "There, it should be better now."

Despite having her work straightened out, the lawyer Baller-rina didn't seem any better. "What's wrong?" I asked. "It seems like it's more than twisted yarn."

Courtney was staring straight ahead now. "I'm finished," she said. "Over, done with."

"What do you mean?" Lauren said, putting a hand on her shoulder.

"They've gone ahead and settled the case I was working on," she said.

"That sounds like a good thing," Lauren said.

"You would see it that way. You were always the one to smooth everything over. But it's not good at all. Our side is the loser in the settlement. I'm getting the blame because I was supposed to be available and they couldn't reach me about some documents I had. I would have if I could have, but there was no way with no WiFi or cell reception."

"Maybe if you explain the situation, your boss will understand," Lauren offered, still trying to make everything okay.

Courtney snorted. "Are you kidding? Excuses aren't allowed. You have to do what's expected of you or you're dead."

"At least you've got your family," Elizabeth said.

Courtney seemed surprised by the comment and shook her head with regret. "It's all Vanessa's fault." But then it was as if Courtney suddenly realized what she'd said and her expression changed abruptly as she straightened up. "Forget I said any of that. It was just a momentary lapse. I'm fine. You're right, Lauren, I'll straighten it out and I'm sure I can make them understand." Despite her words, she still looked like a rubber band pulled too tight.

It was then that I noticed that Lieutenant Borgnine had returned. I didn't know how long he'd been standing in the doorway, but he was definitely eyeing Courtney with interest. He was alone and I wondered what had happened to Madeleine. I went over to talk to him.

"Where's Madeleine?" I asked. I had visions of her lost in la-la land still sitting on the sand. "Was there a problem?"

He almost smiled. "No. She was so happy with her lesson she went off to talk to Kevin St. John about adding a meditation class to the Vista Del Mar events. She even asked me if I'd be willing to teach it." He'd kept his voice low and I knew he was choosing his words carefully so as not to let on that his meditation credentials were limited, to say the least.

Courtney was already pushing her chair away. "I'll take a second session." I had a feeling it was more about making an exit after her outburst than any hope the meditation would help.

He ushered her out the door and looked back at me with a hopeful nod. To his thinking Courtney had walked right into his web.

Lauren checked around, and when she seemed satisfied they were gone she turned to the rest of us. "Her career is everything to her. She did it all by herself with no support from her family. She was always jealous of Vanessa and the way everything seemed to fall in her lap." She made another check to make sure they were gone. "I think there's something off with her family, too."

"I'm stunned," Blair said. "If I'd guessed there was one of us who would never crumble, I would have picked Courtney. I used to laugh when I heard her worrying about grades. I don't think she even knew what a C was."

"If she'd ever gotten a C, I think she would have died on the spot," Elizabeth said.

"It gets worse than that," Lauren said. "I ran into her when she was in law school. She was upset about something, and you know me, I asked her what was wrong, hoping I could help somehow. She let down her defenses and told me how worried she was that she wasn't first in her class anymore. I tried to smooth it over and said that second in her class sounded pretty good to me. But she said as far as she was concerned it was number one or you were number none. To her, being second was the same as being at the bottom of her class."

"Poor Courtney," Elizabeth said. There was just the glint of satisfaction in her expression.

"I wonder what she meant about it being Vanessa's fault," Blair said.

There was no chance to ask Courtney about her Vanessa comment. When she came back from the meditation interlude it was as if she'd never had the meltdown. She took her seat and picked up her knitting and went back to work. It was a little spooky how she could go from falling apart to poised and in control.

Lieutenant Borgnine made a half-hearted attempt at offering anyone a second session and seemed relieved when no one said a word.

"Well, then namaste to you all," he said with a rushed bow and headed for the door. I followed him out the door, saying something to the group about wanting to thank him.

"Well?" I said expectantly when I caught up with him. The afternoon was fading and the air felt cold without a jacket.

"Well, nothing. That Courtney is sure tense, but also very controlled about what she says. I couldn't get anything out of her about Vanessa. I tried to act like the understanding older male figure."

"You mean like a father?"

"No," he said quickly. "I was thinking more like an older brother. I am not old enough to be her father," he said indignantly. He shook his head with regret. "I shouldn't have let you talk me into wasting this afternoon. The time with Madeleine was a complete waste. Not for her," he said. "She wanted to know all about meditation and said it would do her sister some good. She's probably right. That sister of hers is sure a sourpuss. Then Madeleine started telling me I ought to try wearing jeans. She said they have stretchy ones that would be perfect for me," he said. I was having a hard time not chuckling picturing the stumpy man in stretchy denim. "I thought I might get something out of your lawyer friend, but every time I tried to get her to talk about what was on her mind she just turned to me and said *om* over and over." I think it's rather suspicious that Zak begged off. But that's all over with. I'm going to tell them the truth that Vanessa was murdered and go to standard procedure and tell them that nobody leaves until I get a chance to talk to them. And no nicey-nice either. It's going to be sit them down and shine a light in their face."

"You can't do that," I said.

He got a half smile. "Oh yes I can."

"It won't work. Just like I told you before. Once they figure out they're suspects they won't talk."

He was back to his usual unhappy self. "They won't talk about themselves, but I bet they'll talk about each other." He turned like he was going to go back in the room and start interrogating. We bartered back and forth and I finally got him to agree to leave everything as is until the morning. There were a lot of muffins promised and a lecture on how he'd never listen to me again.

Only Lucinda looked up when I returned and I gave her a secret thumbs-up. When the allotted time ended, there was a run on the cookies and drinks. I started to remind them they had free time until dinner, but Elizabeth started to shake her head.

"No free time. It's our last chance to rehearse before our performance," she said. There was a lot of head shaking, but she persisted. "I'll go get the balls and meet you all there."

"Are we really doing this?" Courtney said. "Who wants to watch us bounce balls with lame dance moves?"

"It'll be fun," Lauren said. "Nobody cares if we suck."

"Easy for you to say," I said. "Nobody knows any of you. It's a different story for me." Then I thought about it. It would be hardly the first time I'd done something embarrassing in public, or the last, as I thought of the Sunday magic show. "Fine, you're right, who cares?"

"Meet you all there," Elizabeth said, going out the door. I hung back to help clear stuff up. Lucinda left with them, saying she needed to change her ballet flats into sneakers.

"Sorry I'm going to miss the show," Crystal said with a chuckle. I told her she was welcome to observe, but she passed. Just as she was about to go, I reminded her of Madeleine's comments about Cory.

Crystal grabbed her tote bag. "I'll mention it to my mother, but don't expect her to change her mind."

I was about to shut off the lights when I saw that Crystal had forgotten the sample scarves. I put them in my bag and went to catch up with her. But I forgot all about it when I found Zak waiting outside. He seemed to have something on his mind. "About what I said back there." He looked at me intently. "It is true that we always seemed to be circling each other, but we did make contact. I do remember a very special walk on a rainy night. But it seemed like you didn't want them to know."

Chapter Twenty-four

I was thinking over what Zak had said as I went to Humming-bird Hall. So he did remember after all, and I liked the way he said we'd been circling each other. Elizabeth was waiting on the stage bouncing one of the red balls, impatient to start. The rehearsal was short and sweet, maybe not so sweet. We all did the swagger in okay, but when it came to the rumble all hell broke loose. I found myself going on autopilot when it came time to throw my ball and I threw it to the wrong person again. I had to deal with the wrath of Elizabeth, and even my explanation didn't help. "You were the one who said our bodies would remember the moves. I just went back to who I threw to back in the day."

"Forget I said that about your body remembering." Elizabeth glared at me, shaking her head. "This is now and you throw to Courtney." She pushed bandanas on us as costumes. The Sharks got red ones and the Jets got black ones. I think we were all on the same page. *Just get this stupid thing over with.*

There was still a little time before dinner and everyone scattered. I cut through the Lodge thinking of going home for a few minutes. As I passed the registration desk, the clerk called me over.

"They have you doing this now," I said, recognizing Cloris with her choppy multicolored short hair. She reminded me that she was always looking for extra hours and someone had been let go recently and she was filling in until they got a replacement. I was pretty sure I knew who'd been let go, but that was beside the point.

She held up an envelope. "This is for one of your people. I think it's been here for a while. Everything has been a little off since the bomb scare."

I opened it and found an itinerary and boarding pass for a flight to Chicago on Friday for Vanessa. Now I understood why her suitcase had been packed up. She'd been planning to leave. As I looked over the documents I realized that when she'd disappeared during our lunch at the Blue Door she'd gone down the street to Cadbury Travel to make the arrangements. I wondered if it was just because she was so unhappy with the accommodations or if it was something else.

"It's kind of pointless now," I said. "These flights have long gone and Vanessa is the one who had the heart attack." I suggested she put it in the pigeonhole for Vanessa's room and give it to her husband. I noticed something as I looked over the wooden slots. The red tote bag I'd left for Blair was stuck in one of them. When I told Cloris it was supposed to have been given to Blair, she got very apologetic.

"I wasn't on duty then, but like I said, everything has been a little off." She went to hand me the tote bag and mentioned that the keys were still in the slot. "They must have given her a different room."

I stuffed the tote bag inside my larger one and realized I still had Crystal's sample scarves. I'd give them back to her tomorrow. The time to go home had disappeared and the dinner bell had started to ring. Cloris told me she'd be working breakfast. "I heard they're making popovers."

I joined the rest of my group at the table. Elizabeth was already wearing her red bandana and wanted the rest of us to put ours on. She got a couple of cold stares in response. Lucinda shrugged and put on hers, mentioning it added a spot of color to her black Eileen Fisher outfit. She grabbed the ice tea pitcher and made the rounds. Zak had a wicked smile on his face and seemed to be enjoying the group's preperformance jitters. I was sure he was planning on making a video of our moment in the spotlight and would probably torment all of us with it afterward.

They were just worried about looking like fools with red balls, but Frank's *tick tock* was going off in my head. Why couldn't I figure out who had killed Vanessa?

There was no hanging around the table having second cups of

coffee. Kevin St. John went around the dining hall urging everyone to move on to Hummingbird Hall for the talent show. Not that anyone seemed to mind the rush. I was sure that at least Lauren and Courtney were on the same page I was—anxious to be done with it.

Lucky for us, we were second on the roster, so we just stood by the side of the stage right behind the first group.

Kevin St. John was acting as master of ceremonies. I'd never realized how much he liked being in the spotlight until I saw him take the microphone and keep it for too long. Did anyone really care that the Saturday night talent show was left over from the time Vista Del Mar was a camp, like over a hundred years ago?

I glanced over the audience and was surprised to see Lieutenant Borgnine back to his cop clothes sitting in the third row. He'd agreed not to interrogate anyone until tomorrow, but he hadn't said he wouldn't keep an eye on them.

A family of jugglers went on first and they were quite accomplished, though a little repetitive, and their act seemed to go on forever. My nerves were jangling when they finally took their bows.

I listened as Kevin introduced us. Elizabeth must have given him the copy. He gave the rundown that our act had started in a gym class and we'd stayed friends through the years. He didn't mention anything about Vanessa or that Lucinda had taken her place. As we took our positions, I saw Zak, and he was holding his phone up, no doubt already taping. I hoped he didn't have blackmail in mind.

The song from *West Side Story* began and we did out strut in. I tried to just focus on the next few minutes and get it right. We did our bouncing and then turned to our so-called menacing poses before the rumble began. I was determined not to make a mistake, but when our dancing fight began I started to throw to the wrong person again. But I managed to stop myself in time. Even so the balls went all over the place. Not that it really mattered—we still ended by all falling to the ground. Elizabeth had added her own finish and stood up and said, "Violence is never the answer."

As we were leaving the stage I looked over the audience, who were politely clapping, still thinking about how I'd almost screwed up again. When the woman I'd checked in with the name like pasta waved at me and gave me a thumbs-up, it suddenly came to me why I kept messing up. I didn't go with the others when they went to join Zak, who was holding seats for them. Kevin had figured out a way to keep the audience for the whole show by giving out door prizes throughout the evening. And then afterward there was a wrap party.

I didn't care about the prizes or the party. Something was swirling in my mind and I thought I finally knew who had killed Vanessa. With everybody occupied in Hummingbird Hall, it was the perfect time to check things out.

The Lodge was deserted when I went inside and Cloris was still handling the registration counter. I felt bad about lying to her, but it was for the greater good. I told her that Lucinda had misplaced her key and I needed to get some medicine for her. Cloris gave me a master key without a second thought. She didn't hesitate to answer when I asked her a few questions about who was in what room.

The grounds were eerily still and fog had begun to creep in, shrouding everything in a white veil. I went up the slope to the Sand and Sea building. There was no one in the lobby and the fire was dying in the fireplace. I climbed the stairs to the second floor and looked down the dark hall. It was deserted and silent. I found the room and stopped outside, listening to make sure no one was inside. With a hard swallow, I unlocked the door and went in. The cold blast of air surprised me, but when I flipped on the light I saw that the windows had been left wide open. My plan was to look around, and if I found some incriminating evidence, turn it over to Lieutenant Borgnine. The first order of business was to see if my guess was right. It only took a quick glance at a boarding pass sitting on the table next to the bed to see that I was. But it wasn't enough to give to the lieutenant. I needed to find whatever had been taken from Vanessa's room. But talk about looking for a needle in a haystack—I had no idea even what it was.

I didn't think it would be in plain sight so I ignored everything on the sink or table between the narrow twin beds. A suitcase was sitting on a stand and seemed like a good place to start. It was mostly empty except for a pair of jeans, a shirt and a hat that I recognized. I saw a pair of heavy gloves stuck in one of the pockets. I began to fumble through another pocket along the side and saw something white. When I felt it I realized it was an envelope, and I had my hand inside of it when I heard a key scraping in the lock. My heart went into overdrive as I looked for an escape. There was only the one door, and being on the second floor I couldn't go out the window. I frantically came up with my only option. It was an old trick but I'd seen it work before and I hoped it would now. Grateful that these old locks were slow to work, I quickly turned off the lights and slipped next to the entrance. As the door opened and someone came in, I'd slip out before they turned on the light.

I held my breath and waited as the scraping of the key stopped and the door began to open, but my plan was ruined when the light came on before she stepped inside.

"What are you doing here?" Blair demanded when she saw me.

"I could say the same since this room is registered to Barbara Henderson." She was speechless for a moment. "It was a mistake not to check in again, this time as you," I said.

Her lively face had grown grim. "There's no crime in arriving incognito," she said.

"Unless you're planning to plant a fake bomb and use it as a diversion to kill someone."

"I don't know what you're talking about. Vanessa had a heart attack. You said so yourself."

"But I left something out—like an air embolism was the cause of it. And since Vanessa hadn't been doing any diving, it was obvious someone had pumped air into her vein."

"That's all supposition. There's no way to prove anything. Why would I kill Vanessa when she was such a good friend?"

I wanted to kick myself for being such a blabbermouth when what I really needed to focus on was getting out of there. "You know you're right. Of course, you were a good friend of Vanessa's." I'd begun edging to the door.

Blair suddenly looked wary and moved to block the exit. Then I saw the small gun in her hand. It was silver with turquoise stones in the handle. "These days politicians are targets and we have to carry protection." She glanced around the room. "I could say I came back for something and found an intruder in my room, shot first and asked questions later. Everyone is still at the talent show, so nobody would even hear the gunshot."

Now I wanted to stall her. "Vanessa wasn't such a good friend, was she?" I said, hoping to get her talking.

Blair appeared angry. "Vanessa had put me in a corner. The Legace dealership is in Hillston and she was insisting that I get the zoning changed to commercial on some land she bought adjacent to it. The only reasonably priced apartments in Hillston are on the land now. As soon as she got the zoning change she was going to push out all the tenants and level the buildings so she could add onto the dealership, making it the biggest in the world and finally making her the shining star in her father's eyes." Blair shifted her weight. "She wouldn't listen to me when I told her I couldn't do it. She kept telling me I could do it by an executive act."

"And if you didn't do it?" I asked. Blair looked around, seeming uncomfortable.

"You were always an outsider in the group and you didn't need anything. So you didn't know how Vanessa operated. She could seem like your guardian angel, but then you'd find out you had the devil to pay. The deadline was this weekend." She seemed suddenly impatient and mumbled something about where it would be best to shoot me.

Shoot me? That sounded painful and final. I was in trouble now. What could I do? All I had was my tote bag and my imagination.

A gust of damp wind blew in and she shivered. She must have left Hummingbird Hall in a hurry and hadn't grabbed her sweater. And suddenly I had a crazy idea, remembering something Zak had said.

"You know a real scarf would warm you right up. And not that silly cotton bandana Elizabeth gave you," I said. Instinctively Blair looked down at her red bandana and began to tug it off.

"I have the sample scarves Crystal left." I reached into the bag and pulled one of them out. Since she had a gun and I didn't, Blair didn't seem worried about my fumbling with the black and silver neckwear. I reached out with it as if I was about to hand it to her, but instead I tossed the middle of it toward the gun as if it was a net. The big loose stitches caught the silver girly weapon. I gave it a pull and it left her hand before she realized what was happening and could stop it. I didn't have time to think about what to do with it and on sheer impulse sent the scarf-wrapped gun sailing out the open window. I wasn't expecting what happened next. There was a bang as it landed and I realized the gun had gone off.

Blair was stunned, but only for a moment, and she made a run to get away. She'd pulled open the door and was about to go out when in a last-ditch effort to stop her I threw the other scarf around her ankles. She tripped and fell as footsteps came running down the hall.

"What's going on? I heard a gunshot," Lieutenant Borgnine said. He had his gun out and looked at me and then at Blair, who was still sprawled on the ground but was now trying to crawl away.

"When I saw you leave, I figured you were up to something." He shook his head with annoyance. "I thought we were clear you weren't going to investigate on your own."

Chapter Twenty-five

Lieutenant Borgnine hustled us out of there and to his car. He put her in the front seat and me in the back and admonished us to be quiet. I could tell that Blair was fuming and really nervous by the way she was breathing. I was sure it wasn't lost on Lieutenant Borgnine. I was pretty jumpy myself, anxious to tell him what I knew.

I'd never been inside the Cadbury police station and this wasn't the time to consider the décor, other than it seemed rather gloomy. He handed me off to a uniform and told him to put me in "the office."

He took Blair off somewhere else, which I hoped was a locked room with the bright lights he'd talked about.

"The office" turned out to be the break room. It had a white table and a few chairs and a counter with a coffeepot. I could tell by the smell that it was ancient and undrinkable. Not that I needed anything to give me a boost. I still hadn't come down from the adrenalin rush brought on by the whole confrontation.

Lieutenant Borgnine finally came in. He actually poured himself a cup of the old coffee.

"So, what did she have to say?" I asked.

"She said that you were an intruder and might be crazy as well. When I asked her about Vanessa, she said that the rest of you didn't know, but that your friend had been under tremendous stress and started mixing pills and wine and also had a bad heart."

"You didn't buy that story." I looked at him directly. "You know that I'm not crazy."

He moved his head back and forth as if he was considering that point. Finally, he shrugged. "I'm not saying you're crazy, but Blair made a good point. The doctor could have been wrong."

"But that doesn't explain why she checked in early under a different name. And there's the bomb scare."

"She had some excuse why she was traveling incognito and

there's no law saying she couldn't do that. As for the bomb scare, she simply denied having anything to do with it," he said. "Is there any proof she did?"

"You're going to let her go, aren't you, and drop the whole thing?" I must have sounded a little panicky, because he actually patted my hand in a move to calm me. And I noticed that he didn't deny what I'd said. I thought back to being in the room and remembered the gloves I'd seen. They were obviously for handling the dry ice, but there probably wasn't any way to prove it. I shoved my hand in my jacket pocket, feeling frustrated and annoyed, and then I felt something. The envelope I'd found in Blair's suitcase. I'd been looking at it when I heard the key in the lock. I must have gone into automatic pilot and stuffed it in my pocket. I told the lieutenant where I'd found it and laid it on the table.

He used a pen to poke inside, and a moment later a flash drive rolled out.

"I suppose we could have a look at what's on it." He led me to a desk in the reception area that had a computer on it and popped in the drive.

We both looked at the screen expectantly, but it turned out not to be something to read but rather something to be listened to. There was a time and date stamp from years ago when all of us had been students. It became obvious that it was a voice-mail message from Blair to Vanessa. Blair sounded distraught and was saying something about wanting her to call her back as soon as she got the message, no matter how late. Then Vanessa picked up the call but didn't turn off the voice mail, so the rest of the call was recorded.

"Vanessa, I'm in trouble," Blair began in a shaking voice. "The admin wants to look at the books for student government. There's money missing from the treasury. What am I going to do?"

"Blair, you didn't. I thought you were clean. What is it now? Pills?"

"Heroin," Blair said, choking on the word. "I thought I wouldn't get addicted."

"So you took the money from the treasury to pay for it?" Vanessa asked.

"Yes," Blair whispered. "I'll be ruined if the admin finds out. And I'll probably be arrested. There goes my future. Being on drugs is bad enough, but embezzling money to pay for them . . ." Her voice trailed off and it sounded like she was crying.

There was a pause before Vanessa spoke. "How much are we talking about? Hundreds, thousands?"

"Thousands," Blair choked out. "It's five thousand dollars and I need it by tomorrow."

Vanessa made some annoyed sounds and then agreed to give her the money. "But you have to go to rehab," she admonished. There were a lot of profuse thank-yous from Blair and promises to pay it back with interest before she signed off.

"Now I understand," I said. I told the lieutenant about the zoning change Vanessa had demanded. "And I bet the deal was that unless Blair came through, Vanessa was going to go public with the phone message. It would kill Blair's chances of running for Congress and anything beyond. She wouldn't even be able to finish out her term as mayor." And there was something else I now understood. Why Vanessa had invited Zak. Blair had said this weekend was the deadline for her getting the zoning change. If Vanessa had lived, I bet she would have played the recording for Zak and the big story would have had a headline like *Political Rising Star's Hopes Destroyed by Her Past.*

I looked at the lieutenant panic-stricken. "You didn't already let her go, did you?"

"Ms. Feldstein, I am an experienced police officer. No, I didn't let her go." He pushed his chair back and announced that he was going back to have another little talk with her. He grabbed the flash drive and muttered a thank-you to me.

His second conversation was a lot different from the first. Once she saw he had the flash drive she crumpled and asked for a lawyer.

• • •

I was now free to go. Just as I was wondering how I was going to get home, Dane came into the station having just ended his shift. He did a double take seeing me there, and before I could even ask for a ride Lieutenant Borgnine did it for me.

"I bet you have something interesting to tell me," Dane said as he opened the door to his red Ford 150 truck.

"You can say that again," I said, climbing in. I'd managed to give him the bare details by the time he pulled into my driveway a few minutes later.

"I can't believe my mother was right. It was somebody who was familiar with needles because of drugs," I said, unlocking my back door. He followed me inside and I heard him chuckle. When I turned he was gazing out the kitchen window.

"What are you looking for?"

"You just said your mother was right. Something I never expected to hear. I was looking to see if there were any pigs flying by." His face broke into a grin and I gave him a friendly nudge. "But seriously, you seem a little wired. I think some hot chocolate is in order."

I didn't argue when he poked through the cabinets and found some instant hot chocolate, which he made a thousand times better by adding milk instead of water and tossing in some marshmallows.

He asked me to tell him the whole story from start to finish again, and by the end I was beginning to feel more relaxed. I drank the last of the hot chocolate, which by now was lukewarm, and thanked him.

"Hey, it was almost like a date." He ruffled my hair affectionately. "You better get some sleep now. You have a big day ahead of you."

Wasn't that the truth?

Chapter Twenty-six

I was already at the table when everyone came in for breakfast. I waited until they'd all gotten their food and Lucinda had filled their coffee cups. And then I broke the news about Blair. They were shocked and confused.

"I don't understand," Elizabeth said. "I thought Vanessa died of a heart attack."

"About that—I'm afraid I didn't tell you the whole story." And then I explained what had caused it and why I'd left out that detail.

"You mean, you thought we were all suspects?" Lauren said, and I reluctantly nodded.

"I want all the details," Zak said. "How did Blair pull it off and why exactly did she do it?"

I explained that Blair had really arrived before them, but in disguise. "With the baggy clothes and baseball cap along with a subdued manner, I didn't recognize her. She gave her name as Barbara Henderson." I mentioned that people often seemed to use the same initials when they gave a fake name. "She rigged the fake bomb and put it in a recycled plastic shopping bag and had it sitting in the Lodge waiting for her to set it off. She had some sort of remote that would open the lid of the pet food bowl and let the dry ice fall in and begin to smoke.

"She knew that Vanessa would be having wine and she also knew that Vanessa drank white zinfandel, which was easy to pick out because of its pink color. The wineglasses were on the table next to the couch and easily accessible from behind. Blair, dressed as Barbara, just came by and dropped some tranquilizers in Vanessa's glass without any of us noticing. Then she waited until Vanessa was getting woozy. She made the call about the bomb to Vista Del Mar from one of the phone booths, just as she used the remote to have the dry ice drop in the bowl of water. While everyone ran out in a panic, she stayed behind.

"By then Vanessa was out cold. Then Blair pumped a large amount of air into the unconscious Vanessa's arm. She was out of the building by the time the bomb squad arrived.

"That covers the how, but what about the why?" Zak asked.

"I bet Vanessa had something on Blair," Courtney said, finding her voice, and I nodded.

I told them about the taped phone call that showed Blair had been addicted to heroin and embezzled money to pay for it. "And if that came to light it would kill Blair's political aspirations," Lauren said, shaking her head with regret. "And to think I offered to work on her campaign."

I told them what Vanessa wanted from Blair to keep it quiet about her past. They all agreed that even if Blair had gotten the zoning change, Vanessa would have kept making demands.

"And Zak," I said, turning to him. "I'm pretty sure that big story you were promised was either going to be about Vanessa and the expansion of the Legace dealership or about Blair's past. Or at least Vanessa used the threat of telling you about Blair's past. She probably told Blair she was going to play the recording of that incriminating phone call for you if Blair didn't come through."

"I'm sure you're right," Zak said. "But that doesn't explain how you figured out that it was Blair." He turned to the rest of the group. "Casey has a rep around town as a crack amateur sleuth."

He laughed when he saw my surprise and explained that he'd gotten the 411 on my exploits when he'd gone out for a beer on that first night.

I considered explaining that the amateur part wasn't exactly correct and that while I hadn't been paid to do it, I had successfully tracked down a number of killers. But then he had said "crack," so instead I just answered his question. "It was really all because of the Baller-rinas' performance," I began. I went back to Blair/Barbara's early arrival and how I'd barely noticed a mark on her wrist. "It didn't register as familiar when I saw it," I said, and reminded them of how I'd suddenly started throwing to the wrong person during the rumble. "My way of knowing who to throw to was by noticing something distinctive about their hands. Courtney has red nail polish, so when it came time to throw the ball, that's what I looked for. But then I started throwing to the wrong person and I couldn't understand why until I remembered what Elizabeth had said at the beginning—that we might not think we remembered the steps but our bodies did. It turned out that my body remembered who I threw to in the gym class and it came back to me that I'd known who to throw to by a birthmark on her wrist.

"I didn't realize it meant anything until I found out why Blair didn't get the tote bag I left for her. She'd never checked in, at least not as Blair Hansen. And then at our performance I saw a woman who'd checked in at the same time as Barbara Henderson, which pinged my memory. I recalled that the woman had showed off a tattoo of a rose on her wrist and talked to Barbara about getting a tattoo to cover the birthmark on her wrist. That's when it all came together and I suspected that Barbara and Blair were the same person." I went on about getting into Barbara/Blair's room and what I'd found.

I turned to Zak. "By the way, you were right about the scarves you're all making being like nets." And then I told them how I'd gotten the gun away and they all sucked in their breath. Lucinda rolled her eyes and shook her head in amazement.

"I wish I could have seen that," Zak said.

"What will happen to Blair?" Elizabeth asked.

"She'll probably be charged with first-degree murder and something for calling in a bomb threat. Maybe they'll throw in something for threatening me. But any way you look at it, her political career is over and she's probably going to be spending a long time in prison," I said.

"I'll visit her," Lauren offered. "I'm sure she's remorseful for what she did. Maybe I can convince her to use her leadership qualities to help the other prisoners."

They all had seconds on coffee, but their food had been forgotten. We all sat there until the dining hall was empty.

Now that the whole story was out, I didn't have to convince them to come to the workshop. They needed the comfort of the repetitive motion of knitting and we walked as a group to our meeting room. Crystal had gotten there early and was waiting for us.

Before she started with the group, she pulled me aside. "I told my mother about Madeleine wanting to help Cory," she began. "It got to her and she changed her mind about going directly to the sisters with the DNA info that proves she's their niece." Crystal let out a breath. "She wondered if you could put the meeting together and be there as sort of a moderator."

"I started it all, so it's the least I can do." We agreed to talk about it more after the retreat ended. It was then that Crystal noticed that Blair was missing and I told her what had happened. She was stunned.

"What a weekend," she said, shaking her head.

My group were already busy working on finishing up their scarves, which were now long and covering the table.

"What happened this weekend has made me think things over," Courtney said. She stopped knitting and addressed the group. "I wasn't exactly honest with you. The story about me being the woman who has it all was just that, a story. Actually, I'm divorced and he has custody of the kids. I always had a hard time transitioning from attorney to mom. My ex said I talked to the kids like they were on the witness stand." She let out a sigh. "I'm pretty sure I can save my job, but it's more important that I fix my relationship with my kids."

Lauren put her arm around Courtney's shoulder to comfort her and offered to help, reminding her that was the kind of thing social workers did.

Elizabeth seemed to have something on her mind. "What do you think about me starting things up with Michael again?"

"Vanessa's body is barely cold," Courtney said, shaking her head.

"I didn't mean right away exactly. I mean, I did already talk to him about it. He wants to wait and see what his situation is."

Lauren looked skyward. "Don't do it. You're better than that. You have to get past this idea that just being a man is enough for someone to qualify. You need to find the right man." I held my breath wondering if Elizabeth was going to bring up Kevin St. John as another option, but Zak added his opinion.

"Speaking from the other side, desperation is a turnoff. Relax and you'll meet someone. By the way, that thing about waiting to see what his situation is sounds like a brush-off to me."

"You're right. I'm better than that," Elizabeth said, holding her head up proudly. "I wonder what Michael will do now."

My first thought was that he wouldn't be suing Vista Del Mar.

"I bet he gets Vanessa's job and becomes the son Mr. Peyton always wanted," Courtney said.

"I'll check it out," Lauren said. "Maybe I can talk Mr. Peyton into leaving the apartment buildings as they are."

"Why don't you suggest that if they want to expand the dealership that they build up instead of out," Courtney said. "Better yet, I'll go with you and tell him myself. " We all gave her a thumbs-up.

"It's great how you manage to do everything. You're going to try to help those people not lose their apartments and you keep it going with your family. You really have your life together," Courtney said to Lauren. Lauren's cute face broke into a smile and she appeared as if she was going to agree, and then her face clouded.

"I can't lie. I know I talk a big game about saving the world, but sometimes I just want to save me. Back in college I envied Vanessa and all her spa treatments. She took me along for a weekend once.

We had all different kinds of massages, facials and luxury. I'm ashamed to admit that I loved it and longed for more." Lauren stopped and let out a sigh. "It hardly goes with my image—then or now. My family doesn't even know that Vanessa kept treating me to pricey treatments over the years. I've missed work and family things to be wrapped in a fluffy robe and treated like a princess. But Vanessa being Vanessa knew I didn't want it to come out and she used it as leverage. It was nothing compared with what she had on Blair, but she got me to shut down a protest at those buildings she'd bought. I had no idea what her real plan was for that land." She hung her head in shame. "And there's more," she said, kicking off her shoe and showing off the blue polish on her toenails. Her big toe featured a glittery decal.

"While you were looking at grapes and wine vats, I was getting a massage and a pedicure. I used my birthday money that I'd said I was going to put toward a new composter. I'm decadent and terrible."

"How can you feel guilty about that?" Lucinda said. "We all have our secret pleasures. What's wrong with having pretty toenails?" Courtney and Elizabeth stepped in to comfort Lauren.

By now they'd all finished their scarves and Crystal showed them how to bind off and offered help for starting any new projects with the yarn they'd bought at Cadbury Yarn the day before.

Elizabeth pulled out a skein of yarn and a pattern and Crystal showed her how to start it.

"Zak, you've been pretty quiet," Courtney said. "Anything you want to tell us?"

Zak sat up straight. "You mean like confess that I'm unhappy that I don't have a family and a normal life?" He got sort of a far-away look. "I'm not saying it never crossed my mind, but I'm a gypsy at heart and I don't think it would have worked out. I'll talk to WNN about the Blair and Vanessa story, but they may think I'm too close to the story. In the meantime I do have an assignment. I'm going up to San Francisco to cover some muscleman who's going to try to break Jack Lalanne's record of swimming from Alcatraz towing boats." He looked around the table. "And then who knows?" He seemed to want to be out of the spotlight and turned to me. "Don't you think you ought to fess up?"

Lucinda nodded in agreement and I finally told them about my double life, at least most of it. I left out being a magician's assistant since it was more of a favor than a career. Lucinda added how popular the desserts and muffins were.

"Why didn't you tell us?" Elizabeth asked. I shrugged and simply told them the truth—that their lives seemed so together and mine was cobbled together like a crazy quilt.

"Really? After all that we just said?" Courtney asked with a sigh. After that, we promised we'd stay in touch, really in touch, unlike before. They wanted me to put together another retreat.

When the workshop time ended, they packed up their finished scarves and thanked Crystal for all her help. It was their last group activity. There was just lunch and then they'd go to the airport and Lucinda would go back to Tag.

I hugged everyone and said my goodbyes there. I always felt an emotional tug when a retreat ended, but this was different because of everything that had happened and because they were all friends. I didn't want to be there when they got in the shuttle. Honestly, I was afraid I would cry. So as they went to lunch, I went back across the street, considering the retreat over.

The phone was ringing when I went inside. "Frank!" I said in surprise. "You called me on a Sunday. Is something wrong?"

I heard the squawk of his chair. "Naw, Feldstein. I just wondered—did you get things locked up?"

I chuckled to myself. For all his tough guy talk, he really did care about my investigating. I threw him a bone and told him that he was right. By the sudden squeak of the chair, I gathered he must have sat up in surprise.

"I'm right," he repeated. "Tell me more."

He was a little disappointed when I told him what he was right about was that my friends' lives weren't as perfect as I'd imagined. "So, did you find out who pumped the rich girl with air?" he asked.

"Yes," I said with a certain amount of pride and then gave him all the details.

"What about Mr. Kiss in the Moonlight?"

I repeated that it was Mr. Kiss in the Rain and then told him there was nothing to tell. "He's going off to San Francisco to do a story and I'm staying here."

"Probably for the best," he said, then I could tell he was getting ready to end the call.

"You know, if you have any spare cookies lying around, you could send them to me," he said. I laughed and told him a box would be in the mail in a couple of days and he signed off.

Chapter Twenty-seven

I looked at the clock and figured that my friends had finished their lunch and were piling into the shuttle. As for me, it was time to get ready for Sammy's big show. I made a few adjustments to the spangles on the romper before I put it on and put a trench coat on over it. Sammy was bubbling with a combination of preshow jitters and excitement when he came to pick me up. He was wearing his performance tuxedo and viewed the trench coat with concern until I flashed it open. "Case, thanks for being such a good sport," he said when he saw that I was wearing the romper.

We spent the whole ride to the Inn going over what we were going to say. It wasn't a hard-and-fast script and there was plenty of room for improv. The end of the private room had been curtained off, and as the guests enjoyed their buffet, Sammy set everything up and then it was showtime.

The curtain opened and Sammy did a bunch of campy tricks while I added some jokey asides. He did a few more illusions and then it was time for the grand finale—making me levitate.

He had me lie down on a pad on the floor as he explained to the audience that he was going to hypnotize me and that he was so good at it he could get me to rise off the floor.

We played this part straight. He did all his waving a pendulum in front of me and then he commanded me to lift off the floor. And of course, I did. He demonstrated with a metal ring that there was nothing holding me up and then went to take a bow.

"Uh-oh, I'm awake," I said in a panicked voice and suddenly I started dropping to the ground. Sammy whipped out the pendulum and appeared to re-hypnotize me and I rose up again. And so it went until I was lowering when he turned to the audience and rising again when he waved the pendulum. Then I started rising and lowering for no reason. Pretending frustration with the whole act, when I was at the highest spot, I finally rolled off, landing on my feet. I did a shimmy, and as I'd planned the spangles tumbled off the romper in a sparkly shower. My final line was "I think we need to rehearse more" and the audience laughed and applauded.

Sammy was flushed with success and I was flushed with embarrassment as we took our bows and I got a look at the audience. I hadn't noticed before, but the back of the private room had been opened up so that anyone in the hotel could see our act. Elizabeth, Courtney, Lauren, Zak and Lucinda were all in a row, laughing and waving.

They met me outside when Sammy was packing up his stuff.

"I told them about the profession you left out," Zak said, beaming his charming crooked smile. "I hope you don't mind."

"Why didn't you tell us? As soon as we heard we couldn't leave without seeing your show," Courtney said. "You're sure a person of many talents."

"And who knew you were funny, too," Lauren said.

"And not always intentionally," I quipped.

Elizabeth was the only one who seemed a little bummed. "I was really hoping that you were leading a boring life in a small town. Maybe you can give me some hints about how to be more interesting."

Lucinda hugged me and admitted to arranging everything. "Including a special dinner for us all at the Blue Door," she said. She told the others we'd have the place to ourselves since they were usually closed on Sundays. She invited Sammy to join us, but he said something about not wanting to intrude.

I managed to make a pitstop at home and change out of the silly costume. The dinner was a big success. But this time there was no avoiding seeing them off. The airport shuttle was waiting down the street from the Blue Door. There were a lot of hugs and promises, along with a few tears before Elizabeth, Lauren and Courtney climbed in. Zak's rental car was parked down the street. He was heading up north for his story.

"Well, that's a wrap," he said as the shuttle drove away.

"Safe travels," I said to him. He flashed his famous smile and with a wave walked away. I turned and began to walk back to the restaurant.

"That was too cold of an exit," Zak said, catching up with me. He took my hand and we faced each other. "I can see now that it was my loss to leave it at just once. There's no rain, but there's fog," he said, gesturing to the veil of silvery moisture that was settling in. He leaned in and kissed me. "We truly are just two ships passing by," he whispered. "If I was into trying a regular life, you'd be my pick to share it with." And then he pulled away and went down the street. I could still hear his footsteps as he disappeared into the fog.

• • •

An hour later Lucinda and Tag had left and I had the Blue Door to myself. I put on my favorite soft jazz and started to lay out the ingredients for pound cakes. I had everything for more of the Kernels of Truth muffins in the recycled grocery bags. I had just turned on the oven when I heard someone tapping at the glass part of the door.

Dane was standing on the porch in the darkness. When I opened the door I was surprised to see his brows furrowed in worry. He was in uniform, which meant he was still on duty. I invited him in and he glanced around the empty restaurant.

"I wasn't sure you'd be here," he said.

"Where else would I be on a Sunday night?" I said with a shrug.

"I saw you earlier." And suddenly I knew why his brow was furrowed. Before I could explain he continued. "Look, I'm just a small-town cop, not a TV reporter. I can't offer the excitement that he can."

I started to protest, but he shushed me by putting his finger to my lips. "Don't go ruining my romantic moment." He waited to see if I was going to follow his order, and when I stayed quiet he continued. "What I'm trying to say is that what I *can* offer you is my heart, all of it, and forever."

I didn't know what to say. He understood my silence and touched my cheek. "Think about it. You know where to find me." And then he went back out into the night.

Razzle Dazzle Scarf

Easy to make
Finished dimensions approximately 64" x 7"
Gauge not important

Supplies

1 skein Red Heart Super Saver, black, 7 oz (198g), 364 yds (333m), 100% acrylic, medium weight 4
1 skein Lion Brand Vanna's Glamour, platinum-150, 1.75 oz (50g), 202 yds (185m), acrylic, fine weight 2
1 skein Lion Brand Fun Fur, black, 1¼ oz (50g), 60 yds (54m), polyester, eyelash
1 pair U.S. 50 (25mm), 14" (35cm) long knitting needles
U.S. I-9/5.50mm crochet hook (to weave in ends)

Directions

Leaving a long tail, cast on 10 stitches using all three yarns together.

Row 1: Knit across using all three yarns together

Repeat Row 1 until the scarf measures approximately 64". Bind off, leaving a long tail.

Weave in ends using the crochet hook. It works best to weave in the tails along the width of the scarf.

Kernel of Truth Muffins

1 cup unbleached all-purpose flour
1 cup corn meal
2 tablespoons sugar
3 teaspoons baking powder
¾ teaspoon salt
2 eggs, beaten
1 cup milk
⅓ cup melted butter
½ cup canned whole kernel corn, drained

Preheat oven to 400 degrees F. Line 12-cup muffin tin with paper baking cups.

In a medium bowl combine flour, corn meal, sugar, baking powder and salt.

In a separate bowl mix eggs, milk and melted butter.

Make a well in dry ingredients and add the egg mixture all at once. Stir until just moistened.

Stir in corn.

Fill baking cups and bake for approximately 15 minutes until a toothpick comes out clean.

Acknowledgments

I want to thank Bill Harris for all of his patience and editorial help. I am excited about working with Jessica Faust in this new way.

It always amazes me how things from my past end up in my books. I certainly never expected the rhythm ball routine in that long-ago gym class ever to come in handy. The real thing was a little different than Casey and her friends experience. The University of Illinois was in the midst of moving their Chicago campus from Navy Pier to the new Chicago Circle campus. The women's gym wasn't completed and we were bused to a YMCA on skid row for gym.

I honestly don't remember the choreography other than we came in snapping our fingers and bouncing the balls to a song from *West Side Story.* I'm pretty sure we had a hard time keeping a straight face.

It was fun showing off the Razzle Dazzle scarf to my knit and crochet group. They all laughed when they saw the giant needles but were impressed when they saw how the scarf turned out. I'd be lost without: Rene Biederman, Diane Carver, Najime Chawdhry, Terry Cohen, Sonia Flaum, Lily Gillis, Winnie Hinson, Reva Mallon, Elayne Moschin, Charlotte Newman, Diana Shiroyan, Vicki Stotsman, Paul Tesler and Anne Thomeson. Linda Hopkins will always be with us in spirit.

Roberta Martia has been one of my staunchest supporters since the beginning. Burl, Max, Sam and Jakey, as always you guys are the best.

About the Author

Betty Hechtman is the national bestselling author of the Crochet Mysteries and the Yarn Retreat Mysteries. Handicrafts and writing are her passions and she is thrilled to be able to combine them in both of her series.

Betty grew up on the South Side of Chicago and has a degree in Fine Art. Since College, she has studied everything from improve comedy to magic. She has had an assortment of professions, including volunteer farm worker picking fruit on a kibbutz tucked between Lebanon and Syria, nanny at a summer resort, waitress at a coffee house, telephone operator, office worker at the Writer's Guild, public relations assistant at a firm with celebrity clients, and newsletter editor at a Waldorf school. She has written newspaper and magazine pieces, short stories, screenplays, and a middle-grade mystery, *Stolen Treasure*. She lives with her family and stash of yarn in Southern California.

See BettyHechtman.com for more information, excerpts from all her books, and photos of all the projects of the patterns included in her books. She blogs on Fridays at Killerhobbies.blogspot.com, and you can join her on Facebook at BettyHechtmanAuthor and Twitter at @BettyHechtman.

Made in the USA
Las Vegas, NV
23 December 2023

83475167R00142